The Choice
Monica Belle

This book is a work of fiction.
In real life, make sure you practise safe,
sane and consensual sex.

Published by Black Lace 2009

2 4 6 8 10 9 7 5 3 1

First published in Great Britain in 2009 by
Black Lace
Virgin Books
Random House, 20 Vauxhall Bridge Road
London SW1V 2SA

www.black-lace-books.com
www.virginbooks.com
www.rbooks.co.uk

Addresses for companies within The Random House Group Limited can be found at:
www.randomhouse.co.uk/offices.htm

The Random House Group Limited Reg. No. 954009

Distributed in the USA by Macmillan, 175 Fifth Avenue, New York, NY 10010, USA

A CIP catalogue record for this book is available from the British Library

ISBN 9780352345127

The Random House Group Limited supports The Forest Stewardship Council [FSC], the leading
international forest certification organisation. All our titles that are printed on Greenpeace
approved FSC certified paper carry the FSC logo.
Our paper procurement policy can be found at www.rbooks.co.uk/environment

Mixed Sources
Product group from well-managed
forests and other controlled sources
www.fsc.org Cert no. TT-COC-2139
© 1996 Forest Stewardship Council
FSC

Typeset by Palimpsest Book Production Limited, Grangemouth, Stirlingshire
Printed and bound in Great Britain by CPI Bookmarque, Croydon CR0 4TD

1

I was sat astride him, my eyes shut but alert to every tiny sensation; the feel of Ewan's hard thighs beneath my own, his big hands where they gripped my hips, my own hair tickling my back and bottom, the taut, urgent feeling of my nipples and, best of all, what was inside me, seeming to fill not just my sex but my entire body as I rode my orgasm.

It looked as if Ewan had finished at the same time, to judge by his big lopsided grin, and as always I found it impossible not to smile back as I let myself slump forwards, nestling my head against his chest. His arms came around me in a hug, tender enough but very far from the cuddle I would have liked. I could tell he wanted me to get off, and I obliged, feeling the first touch of inevitable regret as our bodies came apart for what would probably be the last time. His voice came behind as I hurried for the bathroom.

'Don't you ever tell the boys I let you go on top, or else, and I mean that.'

He didn't, for all his macho image, and I was hardly likely to be describing the intimate details of our sex life to his friends in any case. Still his words gave me a familiar and delicious thrill, the strong man talking tough to his girlfriend, something I've always liked. I can afford to.

As I began to wash he hauled up his jeans and briefs. In two years I'd only seen him naked a handful of times, while he liked me stripped as soon I got through the door. That was all part of the fun, a game I enjoyed because of the way it made me feel, while he seemed to take his natural dominance absolutely for granted, completely confident in his masculinity, just as he was completely confident of his status as number one among the young men of the town.

My clothes were scattered along the hallway, and he followed me out of the bedroom as I went to retrieve them, applying a slap to my bottom as I bent to pick up my knickers.

'And watch those geeks and ponces at uni. You're my girl, Poppy, remember that.'

Had there been the slightest trace of uncertainty in his voice my nerve would probably have failed me, but his sheer arrogance prompted me to speak out.

'Actually, Ewan, I've been meaning to talk to you about that.'

'About what?'

'About us, and me going to university.'

'What about it?'

'Well, we're going to be a long way apart, I don't want to think of you sitting here waiting for me on your own...'

'Hey, don't worry about me. I'll be fine.'

I was sure he would. There were half-a-dozen other girls queuing up to take my place and he'd almost certainly been to bed with at least two of them while we'd been together. That wasn't the issue, but this was no time for the truth – or, at least, not the whole truth.

'Exactly. I want you to be fine, and if Nikki, or Carrie, or anybody else wants to come around, don't feel bad about me.'

His brow furrowed. I'd broken an unspoken rule, admitting that I'd guessed what had been going on but not instantly going postal. He couldn't handle it at all.

'It's always been you and me, babe.'

I'd been dressing as we spoke, and hurried into my jeans before replying.

'Please, Ewan, we're not teenagers any more ... well, you're not anyway. Let's be adult about this. We're going to be two hundred miles apart, you've got your job and every girl from here to Exeter wants you. I don't want you to feel guilty, and I don't want to either.'

He looked at me as if he couldn't believe what he was hearing, once again sparing me the worst of my ill feeling as I went on. 'It makes sense, Ewan, you know it does, and I'm not saying I want to find somebody else, not at all. Do you really think anyone at Oxford is going to compare with you?'

He didn't. We both knew that. Ever since I'd first said I was applying he'd treated the idea with mingled amusement and contempt, as a flight of fancy from which I'd eventually recover to take my place as his wife and the mother of his children – changing nappies while he enjoyed himself with Nikki or Carrie – both together if he got half a chance. It wasn't going to happen.

'Yeah, but, Pops ...'

'I'm sorry, Ewan. Look, I have to go. I've got a cab booked for eleven.'

There could have been a lot more to say, all of it pointless. I left, not even kissing him goodbye, and there was a sick feeling in my throat as I hurried up the hill. I'd done it, but I didn't feel good about it, even as I told myself that it was the honest thing to do and, more importantly, what needed to be done. I was not going to be pushing a pram by twenty, not me, not Poppy Miller. Some of my old school friends already were, and most of them thought I was a dreamer, or stuck up, or both. A few backed me and I'd always had my parents' support, although for Mum whatever I did was never enough. I got my ear chewed off as soon as I walked through the front door.

'There you are, Poppy. Please tell me you didn't spend the night with that awful Ewan Cooper?'

'No.'

She looked at me, still suspicious.

'No, you didn't spend the night with him? Or no, you're not going to tell me you didn't?'

'No, I'm not going to tell you.'

'So you did? Really, Poppy, he's not at all suitable . . .'

'I know. I dumped him.'

She'd been meaning to go on, primed for what might have been the thousandth mother and daughter row, but fell silent for a few seconds before she managed to adjust to the news.

'Then you've done the right thing, but it's not before time. If you are serious about a career in politics the last thing you need is ghosts from your past coming back to haunt you when you're trying to get on.'

'He was my boyfriend, Mum, that's all. Everybody has boyfriends, and no I didn't let him take any pictures of me in the nude, or send him any dirty emails, or let him talk me into group sex with three other girls, the vicar and his dachshund, so just relax.'

'Poppaea Miller, you can be extremely vulgar at times!'

I'd already reached the top of the stairs, and her voice faded as I closed the door of my room behind me. Even when I'd got my exhibition she'd been disappointed because it wasn't a scholarship, but we both knew that if she hadn't pushed me so hard I'd never have made it at all. What she didn't know, and would never have been able to understand, was that if it hadn't been for Ewan and one or two other boys I'd have cracked up long ago. Maybe it's a weakness, but sometimes I need to be held, and sometimes I need to be fucked.

As I crammed a last few items into my cases I could hear Mum and Dad talking downstairs, not the words, just a low grumble. I knew what they'd be saying anyway, she fussing over what I'd been up to and he dismissing her worries. He was the one who'd really made me work, not by pushing me, but by his casual assumption that I would succeed in whatever I did without really trying, just as he had when he was young.

Mum had calmed down by the time I went downstairs. I suddenly found myself feeling rushed and close to tears, with a choking feeling in my throat as I said my goodbyes. Dad was as calm as ever, but managed a last piece of advice as he loaded my bags into the boot of the taxi.

'Remember three things, Pops. Aim for a good second, the Chamber's more important than college, and don't let yourself get distracted by boys.'

'You told me, Dad.'

I kissed him and got into the cab. The driver was one of Ewan's friends, and kept up a monologue on how lucky my wonderful boyfriend was all the way into Exeter, leaving me feeling heartsick by the time we got to St David's. Staring out from the train at the passing countryside only made my feelings worse, but I let myself have a good wallow until at last my emotions cleared to leave me impatient to reach my destination.

Oxford, city of dreaming spires, nine centuries of academic excellence and a place which produces a disproportionately high percentage of the country's most successful people. I aimed to be one of them, but as I rode the bus towards what was to be my college for the next three years I was feeling more daunted than ambitious.

In Oxford, the station is well away from the university and the area around it looks much like any other town or city in the UK – same architecture, same shops, same billboards. Even as you go up the hill it's not so very different or, at least, not so very different to Exeter, with ancient stone buildings and grand pieces of design mixed in with the modern and anonymous. Only when you get past the main shopping centre at Carfax do you really see how different it is, with the High flanked by twin rows of beautiful old buildings made of tawny stone; each college distinct, St Mary's church towering above it all. Even the shops look as if they haven't changed since the Regency.

I'd been up before, for interviews, which had passed in a terrifying haze and in the company of other candidates, every one of whom was older than me and seemed infinitely wiser. The medieval surroundings and atmosphere of self-assured scholarship had left me feeling not only that I was certain to be rejected but also that I was guilty of gross impudence in even daring to apply. Now at least I knew that I was worthy, but I was still filled with awe as I got off the bus and dragged my cases down the narrow cobbled street onto which the main doors of St Boniface College opened.

Another piece of Dad's advice had been to make sure I got on with the porters, so I gave the two men in the lodge my most ingratiating smile as I asked for my keys. They took a moment to find them, with me imagining that there had been some horrible mistake and that I hadn't really got in at all, before a white envelope was tossed down on the desk in front of me.

'There we are, Miss. You're one of the lucky ones. Old Quad four nine.'

I had no idea what he was talking about, but managed to find my way across a wide cloistered quadrangle, flanked by tall buildings and the chapel, to another quadrangle, also cloistered, but so small that with the sun starting to go down it formed a cool dim well between towering walls. My staircase, number four, was on the far side, and I'd already guessed that my room, number nine, would be at the top. I spent a moment looking helpless in the hope of some gentlemanly passerby offering to carry my cases, but there was nobody about. That left me no choice but to lug them up three flights of stone stairs to a door, that looked as if it should have opened onto a torture chamber in some ancient castle, showed the numbers nine and ten.

There was a modern lock in it, which responded to one of the keys I'd been given, revealing two more doors, both modern, in that they looked as if they'd been made fifty years ago rather than five hundred. Mine was on the left, marked by a brass nine and more importantly a name tag reading P. MILLER, the simplest possible statement, but one that at last brought home to me that I was, finally, an Oxford undergraduate.

I quickly let myself in to a small oblong room with a high ceiling and view across low slate roofs to the whole of central Oxford; spires and domes and towers, high gable ends and long attics roofed with dark slate, tawny walls and sheets of lead or copper, windows and skylights glistening in the autumn sunlight, with here and there a tree poking up from among the buildings, yellow and russet leaves a perfect match for the muted colours of the city.

I stayed as I was, indifferent to my immediate, rather stark surroundings, drinking in a view, as splendid in its way as the moors seen from the hill above my home, and which I knew would stay with me for the rest of my life. The porter had been right to say I was one of the lucky ones, because if everything else came to grief I would still have had my time in such a beautiful place.

When I finally managed to pull myself away from the window I took stock of my room. It was bare and simple, with a bed, a chest of drawers and a desk on which sat a new and expensive-looking computer. A section had been screened off to provide a minute bathroom, without which it would have resembled a monastic cell, appropriately enough given the origins of the university. There was a small empty fridge and a kettle but no tea or coffee, and I decided I'd go on a shopping trip as soon as I'd unpacked.

I was halfway through putting my things away when I caught the sound of music, very faint but clearly coming from the room next door. It was classical, or at least not pop, and unlike anything I'd heard, melodic but oddly dissonant, at once both exciting and disturbing. I immediately resolved to visit my new neighbour the moment I'd finished unpacking.

Nobody could call me shy, but I hesitated before knocking on the door. The name tag was no more informative than my own, saying just V. AUBREY, which didn't even tell me if the occupant was male or female, although it had me imagining the sort of sybaritic young man Evelyn Waugh liked to portray. The music suggested something similar, maybe even more exotic, and if so I wasn't at all sure I wanted to introduce myself in a pair of sloppy jeans and a baggy jumper.

As I stepped away my eyes were drawn to the invitingly large keyhole. One quick peep wasn't going to hurt and would give me an idea of what to expect, although if she, or he, happened to open the door while I was kneeling directly in front of it I would have a bit of explaining to do. I did it anyway, ducking quickly down and putting my eye to the keyhole, through which I could see most of the room, including the desk, and the bed. V. Aubrey was a Victoria, or possibly a Valerie, but very definitely female.

She lay on her bed, stretched out on her back, reading a book, her eyes rapt in concentration on the page. Her face was made up, skilfully but more heavily than I'd have expected, with a rich red lipstick and a lot of eye shadow, while her dark hair was cut into a short bob. All of which gave her a lazy, sensual look I wouldn't have expected in an undergraduate, but more unexpected by far was what she was doing. All she had on was a pair of loose and very lacy French knickers, with one hand down the front, gently massaging herself as she read.

It obviously wasn't a good moment to call, and I retired from the keyhole, my cheeks hot with embarrassment but at the same time trying not to giggle. I moved back into my room, slowly and very quietly, although to judge by the look of sleepy pleasure on her face she wouldn't have noticed unless I'd slammed my door as hard as I could. There was no doubt at all that she'd been playing with herself, something I'd only ever done in the warmth and darkness of my own bedroom, something very private indeed.

I knew I'd intruded, badly, and should have felt ashamed of myself, but my fingers were shaking uncontrollably and I couldn't get the image out of my mind. She'd looked so sultry, and so impossibly calm, completely and utterly relaxed as she teased herself towards orgasm without a care in the world or the slightest suspicion of guilt. I wanted to do it myself, just like her, which was very definitely not how I'd imagined spending my first afternoon at Oxford. I also wanted to watch.

That was out of the question, not only because it was a dreadful thing to do, but because she was a woman, and because she might catch me. Then again, it wasn't really very likely. If she got up I could nip back into my own room long before she got to her door, or if necessary pretend I'd been on my way out. Besides, she was the one who was being dirty with herself, not me. It was still a dreadful thing to do, but the fact that we were the same sex wasn't really an issue. After all, I knew myself well enough to be sure I preferred boys, and I'd only be watching. Maybe it wasn't even that dreadful ...

I picked up my keys so that I'd be able to pretend I'd been on my way out if she did catch me, telling myself I'd just have another quick peek. Very carefully, I opened my door. Hers was at an angle to mine, the keyhole temptingly close. I could duck down with half my body still in my own room, allowing me to retreat in an instant. Still I hesitated, listening, but all I could hear was her music, which now seemed compellingly sexual, drawing me to watch.

My resistance gave way and I put my eye to the keyhole. She was as before; her slim, languid body stretched out on the bed, her mouth a little open and her eyes closed, an image of sensual bliss that had my tummy fluttering. Her hand was still down her knickers as well, but her fingers were now moving to a fast, excited rhythm, making little bumps in the black silk as she circled her clitoris.

She'd dropped her book, which lay open on the bed beside her face, but as I watched her eyes came open again, to scan the page in front of her. A shiver ran through her and she suddenly shifted position, onto her back, lifting and opening her legs. One hand went to cup a high, pointed breast, stroking the stiff red nipple at the top. I'd been in the same position myself often enough, giving me a flush of embarrassment at the thought of how I must have looked.

That didn't stop me. She was going to come, and I was going to watch, however bad it made me feel. I wanted to touch myself too, but that was a step too far. She was a woman, after all, and, however beautiful, however much I might appreciate her body aesthetically, I was not going to play with myself while I watched her. That was out of the question.

Again she moved, as suddenly as before, flipping herself over on the bed into a kneeling position, her long, slender thighs braced apart, her back curved into an elegant swan's neck to push her neatly rounded bottom high, her cheeks bulging in the black silk of her knickers. Now I could imagine what she was thinking, of a man behind her, about to push himself deep inside as she offered her sex in that most wanton of poses.

I'd been in the same position myself often enough, for Ewan and for others, completely open and uninhibited. It felt deeply erotic, and deeply feminine, rude too, with everything showing for my lover's enjoyment, and also submissive. She felt the same, I was sure, because she had reached back and very slowly slid her knickers down over her bottom, just as if she was exposing herself to a man for penetration.

She'd certainly exposed herself to me, and I couldn't help but think of how I'd look in the same pose, my knickers pulled down over my bottom to show off every intimate detail between my cheeks and between my thighs, my sex ready to be entered, just as hers was, moist and open, ready to have my lover's beautiful cock slid in to the very hilt. With that thought my will snapped and I gave in to my vivid sexual imagination, always my weakness.

My hand went between my legs, to find the soft shape of my sex beneath my jeans, my fingers pressing hard to rub at myself, every bit as rude and wanton as she was. I wished I was in the same position, my thoughts running away with me as my excitement rose, imagining us side by side, kneeling on the bed, bottoms up and knickers down with two forceful young men behind us, our boyfriends, erect cocks in their hands, gloating over our exposure as they got ready to enter us.

She was coming, her body shivering with excitement, her fingers busy with her sex, a sight at once so rude and so compelling that it tipped me over the edge. I bit my lip in a frantic effort to stop myself crying out as it hit me, my mind still burning with the fantasy I'd created, now stronger and ruder still. We were still together, poised to be entered from behind, but the young men weren't our boyfriends, just two arrogant bastards from the college, who'd got us drunk and teased us into playing cards for our clothes, got us stripped topless and had us suck their cocks, made us kneel and stick our bums in the air, pulled down our knickers and taken turns to fuck us both.

It was that last awful detail that really got to me, the idea of being shared by two men, and not in private but side by side with my beautiful neighbour so that each of us knew exactly how rude the other had been. I'd lost my balance as I climaxed, sitting hard on the floor and knocking against my door to make it swing back and crash against its hinges. She had to have heard, and I scrambled quickly back into my room on all fours, my legs still shaking from the force of my orgasm.

I was sure she was going to catch me, and my face was burning hot as I scrambled to my feet, my blushes a sure giveaway that I'd been watching her. My fingers wouldn't stop shaking either, and I felt so hot and wet between my thighs I was sure I'd have a telltale damp patch on the front of my jeans. The only sensible thing to do was to get into the shower, but as I stripped off common sense slowly began to return.

She couldn't possibly know I'd been watching her, and all she'd have heard was the bang of my door. Even if she'd guessed, she was hardly going to stride in, wearing nothing but her fancy French knickers, and accuse me of being a Peeping Thomasina, even though that was exactly what I was.

2

My guilty feelings didn't last very long. I'd only just sorted myself out after my shower when she knocked on the door to introduce herself. After that things took off at such a pace that I had no time to fret over my bad behaviour. She wasn't a Victoria, or a Valerie, but a Violet – Violet Aubrey, and she was a graduate, in the second year of a D.Phil. in Fine Art. She was also fascinating; so languid and sensual in her manner that it was easy to see her not as a student of art, but as an artist's muse.

I knew immediately that she didn't have the sort of connections I was supposed to be making, but she knew the college inside out and was keen to show me around. On the Sunday evening I was in her room, sat on the bed with my back to the wall sipping coffee as she explained how to cope with Freshers' Week.

'... says in the Handbook that there's something for everybody, which is true, and I know you can't hope to do everything, but do try to sample as many different things as possible.'

'Thanks, but I know what I need to do, and what to avoid.'

'You're very confident, but do keep an open mind or you might miss out on something that changes your whole life. How do you mean, what to avoid?'

'Anything that could come back to haunt me in later life. I'm going into politics.'

'Oh.'

She didn't sound very happy, let alone impressed, but quickly brightened up again as she went on. 'Keep an open mind, that's all. When I first came up I was such a little mouse I hardly knew what to do.'

'I can't believe that!'

'A lot has happened since then. So you're going to be a university student, are you?'

The way she'd suddenly changed the topic of conversation intrigued me, as if she wanted to avoid talking about something, but so did her question, which I didn't understand at all.

'What do you mean? Aren't we all university students?'

'Some students stick very much with their college, like the rowing club. Others are more involved with wider university life; the Chamber and that sort of thing.'

'Yes, that's me, or it will be once I get my feet on the ground.'

'Somehow I don't think that's going to take you very long.'

She was so easy to talk to that I was tempted to explain my grand plan, but at that moment somebody knocked on the door. She went to answer it, opening the door with her normal casual, friendly manner, only to suddenly stiffen and move hastily out into the tiny lobby between our doors and the 'oak' as she called the big door leading onto the staircase. I only caught a glimpse of her visitor, but enough to see that it was a man, of middling height, in his thirties and so almost certainly too old to be a student. What really struck me was his face, which was calm and distinguished but with a hint of something else; amusement, even disdain.

It seemed very likely that he was her tutor, but her obvious embarrassment at his visit and the urgent whispered conversation between them made me wonder if they were having an affair. I couldn't resist listening, but the heavy door and their low voices made it impossible to catch more than the occasional word so I soon gave up. After a moment staring at the wall, I found myself scanning her bookshelves as I tried to work out what she'd been reading while she was playing with herself.

All I could remember was that the spine had been black with white letters too small to be easily read and that there had been some sort of abstract art design on the cover. Several looked about right, but all of them belonged to a collection of French classics I'd never heard of but at least one of which was presumably quite juicy. *La Femme et le Pantin* by Pierre Louÿs seemed the most likely candidate, but I wasn't even sure what the title meant and if it was in the original language there wasn't much point in borrowing it, as my schoolgirl French couldn't get me much further than asking the way to the post office.

I was just wondering if I dared sneak a closer look when Violet came back in. She looked agitated, and while I didn't want to seem pushy I felt I ought to say something.

'Was that your tutor?'

'My ex-tutor.'

She didn't sound too happy about it, and immediately changed the subject, leaving me intrigued.

For the next few days I had very little time to speculate on Violet's private life and not a great deal of time to see Violet. Freshers' Week is the week set aside for new undergraduates to find their feet, to meet their tutors and colleagues, join whatever societies interest them and generally find out about college life and the university. I knew exactly what I needed to do or, at least, what Dad had told me I ought to do. All his life he'd been a Liberal, always the main opposition party in our neck of the woods, where most people distrusted Labour and thought that Conservatives had cloven hooves concealed within their highly polished shoes. That was all very well, but the chances of belonging to a party in government were close to nil and, besides, I had to go my own way.

The question was: which way? The two main parties were a lot closer than they'd been in Dad's day, so if I was going to abandon his ideals it wasn't easy to decide which way to jump. The Conservatives were on the way up, but with three years before I graduated and perhaps as long again before I could expect to make any real impact it was all too likely that my first chance to challenge for a nomination would come just as they started on their way back down, with maybe ten more years until the situation reversed once more. Labour were unpopular and likely to be out of power within the year, but I might well be able to ride their fortunes back to the top.

I had a week to make my choice and held back, keeping my own opinions to myself while I tried to decide who to join. Meanwhile, I took the opportunity to ignore another piece of Dad's advice, not to let myself get distracted by the boys. Not that I intended to let myself get distracted, but it was obvious to me that I'd have a much better chance of success in my chosen career if I was with a wealthy and supportive male. I had three years to make my choice and, while I didn't want to get a reputation as a slut, I could see no reason not to start early.

The tricky bit wasn't finding a suitable man, but choosing between them. Just walking around the Freshers' Fair presented me with a bewildering choice of first-rate masculine talent. The boat-club stand alone was enough to leave me weak at the knees; crowded with lean muscular young men, not one of them under six foot and some of them in kit that left very little to the imagination. Given a free choice I'd have picked four or five of the best and invited them back to my room to take turns with me, but even if they'd been likely to go for it

I just couldn't risk that sort of thing, not unless I could cope with one of them publishing some 'interesting reminiscences' twenty years later. I couldn't, but testing them out one at a time was a different matter. Nobody is expected to be celibate nowadays. In fact, too puritanical an image can do almost as much damage as the reverse, especially when it comes to getting male colleagues to give you a friendly leg up.

I was still trying to choose between a blond man who might well have been used as the model for a Greek statue and another, darker, taller and with an intense expression and the most piercing eyes I'd ever seen, when my mind was made up for me. Both moved away from the boat-club stall within a few seconds of each other, the blond young god to the Gay Soc stall, where he immediately kissed the man running it, and the tall dark man to a stall dealing with commodities trading and run by a man who looked like a highly intelligent weasel with glasses.

My tall dark man immediately asked a question which triggered a complicated explanation from the weasel. I moved closer, listening with what I hoped was an intelligent expression and waiting for my moment. Eventually the weasel stopped talking and turned to me to speak.

'Can I help at all?'

'This seems unusual for a society.'

His voice was dripping condescension as he replied. 'Not really, although it is really only for the wealthier students.'

'How does it work?'

'Essentially, we form an investment co-operative, allowing us to trade in stock, futures and so forth while keeping our overheads to a minimum and gaining experience on the markets. It's really aimed at students who are going into finance and the minimum investment is ten thousand pounds.'

The last comment was obviously intended to put me off, and as that was more than Dad had given me for the entire year it would have done, if I'd been remotely interested in the first place. I nodded and put a question to my tall dark man.

'Do you think it's a good idea?'

'Yes, undoubtedly, although more for the experience than as a way of providing income. It's also a chance to make contacts in the city.'

'I'm hoping to go into politics, but nevertheless...'

I trailed off, hopefully leaving them with the impression that investing ten thousand pounds was at least an option for me. The weasel went back to his explanation, now making an effort to include me, but I'd made my opening move and left after a couple more minutes. My tall dark man stayed put for at least ten before moving on to the coffee machine. I made straight for him.

'What do you think? Are you going to join them?'

'I think so, for a year at least.'

'I'm not so sure. It seems risky and I'm really looking for a different set of contacts.'

'I'd advise against it then.'

'Thanks. I'm Poppy, by the way, Poppy Miller, first year PPE at St Boniface.'

'Stephen Mitchell. Hi.'

He extended one huge hand, which completely enveloped mine as I took it. It was all too easy to imagine that same grip on my hips or shoulders. Persuading him to take me to bed was going to be a pleasure, but I didn't want to rush.

'What are you studying?'

'Chemistry, at Emmanuel.'

'Not economics?'

'No. I applied for my strongest subject, which was the best way to get in.'

'That's what the careers advisor at school suggested.'

'But you went for PPE?'

For a moment I thought I'd made a mistake by implying he was less intelligent than me and I backpedalled hastily. 'It was a risk. Maybe a stupid one.'

'Not if you want to go into politics. It's very hard to switch courses onto PPE.'

A lie seemed like the best answer. 'I didn't know that.'

'Yes. If you're on a popular course you can change to almost anything, but it's next to impossible to switch onto a popular course, otherwise everybody . . .'

I let him talk, although Dad had explained it all to me a dozen times, and watched his eyes, hoping they'd stray to the front of the bright tight cashmere sweater I'd chosen that morning with the deliberate intention of attracting male attention. Sure enough, he was having considerable difficulty talking to my face and not to my tits, despite his best efforts to be polite. I folded my arms to give him a better view and flicked my hair as if to get it out of my eyes. His Adam's apple bobbed as he swallowed and I knew he was mine.

Social conventions are such a pain. In an ideal world I'd have responded to his interest by pulling up my top and bra to let him have a proper look. He'd have given me a squeeze and a kiss on each nipple to say hello, then it would have been off to bed for an afternoon of good rude sex. Unfortunately, I had to play by the rules.

It took me two days, first a drink together, then an afternoon watching him on the river followed by dinner at Browns. He put his arm around me as we crossed St Giles and I responded, more than happy to show interest. Emmanuel was closer than St Boniface and we soon reached the lodge.

I knew I should kiss him goodnight, with just enough passion to leave him eager, but I was feeling mellow and horny.

There were a lot of people around, but that's never bothered me, just the opposite, and as he took me in his arms and tilted my head up to make our mouths meet I couldn't help but let my lips come open. He needed no further encouragement, his grip tightening and one big hand slipping down to cup my bottom. I let him squeeze for a moment and then gave him a gentle pat of admonition as I broke away. There was doubt in his voice as he spoke.

'Coffee?'

'Why not.'

He wasn't sure what was going to happen, but I was. Having – hopefully – shown him that I wasn't easy, it was time to show him that I was good. I didn't want any coffee either, because one more cup and it was going to be coming out of my ears.

His room was in a Victorian annexe at the back of his college, one of a line ranged along a top corridor that looked like something out of Dickens. He kept his arm around me even as he unlocked the door, and kissed me again as soon as we were inside. This time I let myself melt, giving way to my urgency as our mouths opened together, willing to let him touch where he liked, or to strip me, even to put me straight down on his cock the way really forceful men sometimes do.

I wanted it, but he held off, cautious. He was responding to me though, his cock firm against my tummy as he held me close and getting rapidly firmer. That broke what little resistance I had left. I wanted to see, to hold him, to take him in my mouth. As I detached myself from his grip I looked down.

'You're proud of yourself, aren't you?'

He gave an embarrassed shrug, unable to deny the state he was in.

'Let me see.'

His beautiful eyes grew a little wider in surprise, as if he could hardly believe his luck when I drew down his zip and burrowed my hand inside. He was rock hard, and big, making it difficult to tug him out of his fly, but I soon got him showing, his balls too. I took him in my hand, tugging gently as we kissed once again and tweaking open the buttons of his shirt until it fell open across his chest. He responded in kind, tugging my top up and spilling my breasts free of my bra, his huge hands pawing at my flesh, clumsy and too eager but still exciting.

Only when he began to get really rough did I pull away, moving slowly down his body to brush my lips over his neck and the hard muscles of his chest. He groaned as he realised what I was going to do, and I couldn't help but tease, flicking my tongue over the smooth lines of his six-pack with his cock still held in my hand. I was hoping he'd take me by the hair and make me do it, but he seemed frozen, as if the slightest movement or attempt to take charge might scare me off. That wasn't so bad, allowing me to indulge in one of my favourite pursuits – worshipping a cock.

He was worth it too, really magnificent, both long and thick, very pale and very straight, with firm heavy balls, like the statue of some priapic love god. I've always liked to be at the feet of a well-endowed man, worshipping not him, but his masculinity, licking and kissing at the huge virile member that is about to be put into my body. Now I had a real beauty, and I had no intention of wasting it, first folding my breasts around his shaft and letting him push up between them a few times, before at last taking him in my mouth.

I was squeezing and stroking his balls as I sucked, my urgency now so great that it was hard to hold back, but I had no intention of ending up with a mouthful and nothing else. He was groaning softly and had begun to push, but I forced myself to pull away, instead taking him in my hand and licking at his balls as I pulled gently on his shaft, lost in dirty admiration for his sheer virility. I was down on my knees, adding to my feelings of worship as I began to nuzzle my face against him, drinking in his male taste and scent.

He finally took charge, taking a firm grip in my hair and feeding himself back into my mouth so that I had no choice but to suck. I looked up, straight into his beautiful eyes, now full of lust and I knew immediately that I was going to get what I wanted. Sure enough, he spoke a moment later, growling out his words.

'I've going to have you, Poppy. I hope you're safe.'

I nodded around my mouthful and he immediately let go. Now there was no more waiting. He picked me up and tossed me onto the bed as if I weighed nothing at all, turned up my skirt and pulled my knickers down in two urgent motions, hauled my legs up and twisted the little scrap of cotton around my knees to hold me in place as he guided his cock to my sex, and in. I cried out as he rolled me up, shocked at being handled so roughly and stripped so quickly, and a second gasp escaped me as I was filled.

He began to thrust into me, leaving me panting for breath and clutching at the coverlet as I was fucked, still with my legs held up to keep me helpless in his grip. That was exactly how I wanted it, rolled up and penetrated, unable to resist as his lovely big cock moved inside me. He slowed a little and I began to play with my breasts, deliberately showing off, which brought an evil grin to his handsome face as he watched.

'You are a wicked girl, Poppy Miller.'

'I know. Why don't you turn me over?'

His eyebrows rose a little, but he didn't need asking twice, his huge hands immediately gripping my thighs to flip me over on the bed. I lifted my bottom for him, my skirt was twitched up to get me bare and he guided himself into me until the hard muscles of his belly were pressed to my upturned cheeks. Once again he began to fuck me, faster now, and with ever greater urgency. His hands had locked on my hips, holding me firmly in place, while it was all I could do to gasp out my passion into the bedclothes. I tried to reach back, desperate to get to my climax before he did. I didn't want to be robbed of the glorious sensation of having him moving inside me as he manipulated my body as if I'd been a puppet.

I almost made it, finding my sex and starting to rub, only for him to cry out my name and thrust himself deep, his fingers locking into my flesh as he came. That was that, or it should have been, but I couldn't stop myself, still rubbing at my sex and gasping out my ecstasy even as he withdrew, heedless of the exhibition I was making of myself. I heard him blow his breath out in surprise at how rude I was being, but even that didn't stop me. My muscles had already begun to contract and all I could think of was my overwhelming bliss as I brought myself to a long shuddering orgasm. I'd barely finished when he spoke.

'You don't hold back, do you?'

All I could do was shake my head, with the shivers still running through my body as I came slowly down. I was still in a thoroughly rude position, and began to feel embarrassed at the shock in his voice, for all that I'd been offering myself willingly just moments before.

'Sorry. You don't mind, do you?'

'No. It's just that ... that you're not quite what I'm used to, if you see what I mean. You were great though, don't get me wrong.'

'Thanks.' I kissed him on the tip of his nose and began to undress, still talking. 'What are you used to?'

He shrugged, embarrassed, and a thought occurred to me.

'That wasn't your first time? It can't have been!'

'No, no, nothing like that. I was at Laon Abbey School, which is all boys, but I took my year off in Southeast Asia.'

I'd guessed he was public school, and I didn't need the dirty details to realise that he'd been up to no good with the Asian girls.

'English girls can be just as naughty.'

By then I was naked, and I climbed into the tiny shower cubicle attached to his room. As I washed I was feeling not only thoroughly satisfied, but also rather pleased with myself. I'd shocked him, and hopefully had him thinking of me as a rare catch not to be surrendered lightly. Just possibly I'd gone too far, but he'd come to the door to watch me shower, which suggested otherwise. I gave him a bit of a show, posing for him and paying particular attention to my breasts and bottom as I soaped myself.

The steam and the frosted plastic shower door made it impossible for him to see me clearly, and he'd only just come, so I was really only teasing. I couldn't see him properly either, so when I was finished and had pulled the hair away from my face as I stepped out I was amazed to find him with a full erection and clearly ready for more. With that the last of my doubts evaporated. He was as bad as I was.

'I suppose you want me to look after that?'

'Yes, please.'

'I suppose we'd better go to bed then.'

I took him by his cock and led him to the bed. He let me

undress him, and popped himself into my mouth as he stood proud and naked in front of me before we climbed into bed together. As he turned the light off and took me in his arms I knew that I'd found my man.

3

I'd got off to a great start, not only finding myself a wonderful boyfriend but also gaining the perfect means to avoid getting my private life tangled up with my efforts to get on in political circles. On my own it would have been almost impossible to steer clear of the petty jealousies and dislikes that can make all the difference, but now that I was with Stephen I could stay safely neutral with both men and women, yet still flirt a little if the occasion demanded it.

That's what I thought, anyway. I'd decided to join the Labour Party and keep firmly to the centre ground, which seemed to make the most sense in career terms and was also in accord with my principles. Even after the Freshers' Fair all three main parties had stands at the Chamber, hoping to attract members, so on the afternoon after my night of passion with Stephen I went round and introduced myself to the two girls behind the Labour stall. There were posters up advertising the first debate of the term, on whether prostitution should be legal and under state control. I guessed they'd both be against the idea and had soon made myself one of the girls with a few carefully chosen remarks. We were still talking when a man came down the corridor; very tall, with a mop of light-brown hair and an arrogant, aristocratic face. As he passed by me he spoke. 'Don't do it, girl.'

It seemed to me the perfect opportunity to establish my party credentials, by rounding on him and giving him a brief lecture on social principles and how to speak to women.

'Excuse me, but ...'

He just kept going, ignoring me completely, which triggered genuine irritation. I wasn't going to let anybody treat me like that and followed him out of the door, catching him by the arm as he started down Cornmarket.

'Do you mind ...'

I broke off as he turned around, looking down on me with a smile of easy condescension.

'Not at all. I was just giving you a little advice, very good advice.'

'I suppose you're a Conservative, because if so ...'

'Good heavens, no. I'm strictly independent.'

That rather took the wind out of my sails, and pricked my curiosity.

'Then why would you advise me against joining the Labour Party?'

'I'd advise you against joining any party. Find your feet first, maybe try for election to a post, you can worry about party politics later. Giles Lancaster, by the way, Recorder at the Chamber, which means I'm responsible for writing up the debates.'

'I know what the Recorder does, thank you, but isn't it essential to be in one of the major parties?'

'Not at all. It's far more important to prove your skill in debate, and to get on in the Chamber. There's no better start to a political career than being President, if that's what you want?'

He was obviously somebody I needed to know, and I found myself backpedalling.

'Yes, very much. I'm sorry I snapped, but I thought you were just trying to put me down. Can I buy you a coffee or something?'

'No, but you can let me take you out to dinner. How about Les Couleurs, tomorrow night?'

'That's in Thame, isn't it?'

'I see you've been reading your Handbook, but, if I'm going to be taking you out, shouldn't I know your name?'

'Poppy Miller, first year, PPE, St Boniface, but I haven't said I'll go with you yet.'

'Why wouldn't you?'

I nearly gave him a sharp answer, annoyed by his sheer arrogant self-confidence and rather aware that I'd slept with another man the night before, a man I intended to make my boyfriend, although nothing had been said. On the other hand, being on good terms with the Recorder at the Chamber would be an enormous advantage, and while Giles had wolf written all over him I didn't have to make myself easy prey.

'OK, if it's just dinner.'

He merely grinned, and began to walk away, forcing me to call after him.

'Where will I meet you?'

'I'll pick you up from your porters' lodge. Six o'clock.'

He carried on along Cornmarket, leaving me considering my options. Giles' intentions were obvious, and I wasn't in love with Stephen, so I couldn't help but ask myself if I might have made the wrong choice. Then again, Stephen was aiming for the City, while Giles was presumably intent on politics and so not suitable in the long term. Not that he was likely to want me in the long term anyway, because he seemed more the type to get through as many naïve first-year girls as he could. In that case the best choice was almost certainly to play hard to get, which might make him keener or even earn me a bit of respect. As I started back towards college, I promised myself not to let him get me into bed.

I decided to take Giles' advice and remain independent at least until I had a clearer idea of the pros and cons of joining different parties and, as I now had an excellent opportunity to introduce myself into Chamber circles, I decided to walk down to the river and watch Stephen row. It was a beautiful autumn afternoon, with bright sunlight and just the faintest breeze disturbing yellow leaves on the pavement as I made my way down St Aldate's towards the river. I already felt part of the university, and my sense of not deserving to be there had given way to one of feeling privileged because I was, and again a determination to make the very best of my time.

The Emmanuel boats were already on the river, with Stephen trying out as number seven. He didn't notice me, far too intent on his sport, and I contented myself with standing on the towpath and admiring his body and the power of the way he moved. As I watched I was thinking of the night before, how much pleasure he'd given me and the way he'd taken control once he was too aroused to hold back. I always like that in a man, once things have got going and his desire for me takes over, which is always so much better than having to do all the work myself.

It was also intriguing to wonder what he was used to, and what he'd got up to in Thailand and Malaysia. I had asked, but he'd been distinctly cagey with his replies, making me wonder if the girls he'd been with had been hookers and, if so, whether he'd expect me to behave the same way. That was rather intriguing, as I'd often toyed with the fantasy of being a high-class call-girl and having to do what I was told by the man who'd bought me, although I'd never have done it in real life.

By the time he came off the water I'd managed to work myself into a fine state, which the heat of his body as he hugged me and the scent of fresh masculine sweat made even worse. Unfortunately his college boat club were doing some sort of team-building exercise followed by a meeting to decide on their places in the three boats, or I'd have taken him in among the bushes then and there. As it was I had to content myself with walking back to college with him and, as I was due to meet the Chaplain at half past five, that was that. He had a drinks party for the chemists at his college as well, so I ended up back at St Boniface where I spent the evening in the junior common room feeling frustrated, only to get back to my room to find that he'd been and gone.

It was gone midnight by then, and Emmanuel was locked up, so I went to bed, while I had so much to do the next day that there was no time to see if he was about. I was also concerned that he might suggest going out for the evening, which would be more than a little awkward when I'd accepted Giles' invitation. By the time I'd had my introductory tutorial, spent an hour in the library working on an outline for my essay and had a quick shower I was actually hoping not to run into him, and feeling guilty.

At six o'clock I made my way down to the lodge, half expecting to find both Stephen and Giles there, talking to each other. Neither was, but I only had time to check my pigeonhole when Giles appeared, dressed in full black tie with a scarf of cream-coloured silk draped around his neck. He saw me and nodded to himself, as if appraising me, then spoke.'Very pretty, you have the right-sized bottom for tight jeans, but we'll never get in the door.'

It had never occurred to me that the restaurant would have a dress code, making me too flustered even to resent his remark about my bottom, which was a bit fresh when we'd only just met and not necessarily complimentary either. Instead of answering him back with some equally cheeky comment I found myself apologising.'I'm sorry. I'll get changed.'

I made for my room, feeling distinctly small and foolish. Violet was on the landing, having an intense conversation with the man I'd seen her with before, her ex-tutor, which made it easy to simply give a quick hello as I passed. I was convinced that if I lingered Stephen would turn up at exactly the wrong moment, so I hesitated only an instant before picking out a simple red cotton dress. It was quite short and the straps were too thin to allow me to wear a bra without looking slovenly, but it was the only thing I had that was remotely appropriate for the sort of restaurant where men wore black tie. I hurried into it, changed my shoes and tidied myself up, then hastened back towards the lodge.

Violet and her ex-tutor were still talking, and I caught a snatch of their conversation before they went abruptly silent, first his voice, then hers.

'... go down to the river and make one.'

'That's so cruel!'

She smiled at me, looking embarrassed, and I was left wondering what she could possibly make down by the river and why she should think it was cruel of him to ask her. Her tone of voice had been curious too, both shocked and excited, which was yet more intriguing, but I had no time to dwell on her curious relationships.

Giles was where I'd left him, standing against the wall with one foot propped up on the stonework, as nonchalant as I was nervous. Again he favoured me with a nod of appraisal, and this time seemed to be satisfied.

'That's better. Come on then.'

He set off, talking casually as we made our way along the High and turned into Longwall Street, where he'd parked his car, a black Audi TT, which suggested that either he had money to burn or very generous parents. I didn't want to come across as some awestruck little girl, so didn't say anything and simply slid into the seat as if it was nothing out of the ordinary. He made no comment either, clearly not needing to show off, and didn't speak again until we'd crossed Magdalen Bridge.

'If you're at Boniface your tutor must be John Etheridge?'

I hadn't known that Dr Etheridge was called John, and wouldn't have dared address him by his Christian name, but did my best to answer casually. 'That's right.'

'And let me guess, your essay is on the Victorian labour movement?'

'It's the development of socialist theory in the early twentieth century.'

'Close. He's good. You'll do well with him.'

He was impossibly smug, and I was determined to cut him down to size.

'You're a second year, aren't you? The way you talk anybody would think you were a don.'

He merely shrugged, put his foot down to catch the lights ahead of us and kept it there as we climbed the hill on Headington Road, passing the speed camera at nearly fifty with complete indifference. I was used to Ewan's driving, so I wasn't particularly bothered by the speed, but I was getting more and more determined to at least take the edge off his appalling arrogance. Unfortunately I'd missed my chance with his remark about my bum, and as we drove out of the city he was explaining how the internal politics of the Chamber worked, which I needed to know.

By the time we reached Thame he was being so polite and friendly that I'd changed my mind, telling myself that anybody as good looking and privileged as him was bound to be a bit big headed and that I should swallow my pride and make the best of the situation. Although not to the extent of actually going to bed with him. Not that he'd made any effort to try it on, but I was pretty sure he was just biding his time.

Les Couleurs was just outside the town, a small country house converted into a restaurant and hotel. The forecourt was packed with cars, mostly new and all expensive, while an elderly couple getting out of a vintage Daimler were also in evening dress, making me thankful Giles had taken the trouble to correct my outfit. Despite that, the doorman didn't look at all happy as we approached, but it wasn't me he objected to, but Giles.

'I'm sorry, Mr Lancaster, but as has already been explained to you . . .'

Giles interrupted, more amused than annoyed. 'Don't worry. We're simply here for dinner.'

'Very well then, sir.'

We were shown into a dining room far smaller than I'd expected, with just four tables, although there was another, larger room visible across the hall. I wanted to know what had been going on, and asked as soon as we'd been seated and were alone.

'What was that about?'

'Nothing really. He thought I was trying to make a booking for my dining society.'

'Which society is it? Are you banned or something?'

'Only from central Oxford, but we've got a bit of a reputation, and everyone within twenty miles seems to know I'm a member. The Hawkubites.'

'That's the one that deliberately trashes restaurants, isn't it?'

'Not at all. We get a bit high spirited sometimes, but there's no malice in it and we always pay for the damage.'

'It's still vandalism!'

'It's not vandalism if you're correctly dressed.'

'That's outrageous!'

'That's a quote: Oscar Wilde, who was president in 1878.'

33

There was so much scorn in his voice that I found myself blushing and backing down in my response to his behaviour.

'It's an old society then?'

'We were founded in 1713, which makes us the oldest, whatever the Bullingdon and the Phoenix may have to say about it, and named after a London street gang of the time. The story goes that some of our founders had actually been involved, but I doubt that's true. Now, they were a rotten lot. One of their favourite pastimes was to put people in barrels and roll them down Ludgate Hill, just for sport. Another favourite was to rob a man and then make his wife earn the money back on her back, if you see what I mean, preferably in front of hubbie. So you see, we're not really that bad.'

I shook my head in what I hoped he would realise was a gesture of mature contempt for his behaviour, although he was quite obviously utterly indifferent to my good opinion. A waiter had arrived at our table to hand us menus, big white vellum booklets bound with deep-red ribbon. Our conversation changed to food, which Giles seemed to know a great deal about. He was quick to offer advice, but I made a point of making my own choices. Not that he noticed, except to comment on the wine.

'I dare say the turbot is excellent, but I'm not missing out on grouse, so we'll just have to have separate bottles. That means a half for me, as the boys in blue don't seem to make allowances for gentlemen these days.'

'You didn't seem worried about speeding.'

'Fines and the odd three points I can cope with. Getting banned is another matter. I'll have a half of Fronsac, I think. I suggest you try the Chablis.'

'I prefer Australian, the Riesling.' I was making it up, but he didn't comment and I was left wondering just how much useful knowledge I might be able to pick up from him; political know-how, wine and food, social graces, all things that would be helpful. Stephen was distinctly unpolished by comparison, despite his financial knowledge and having been to public school.

The dinner was delicious, from the single oysters presented in tiny silver cups to whet our appetites right through to a slice of the darkest, richest chocolate cake I'd ever eaten. By then I was every bit as mellow as I'd been after my trip to Brown's, but also telling myself that if men kept on treating me to lavish dinners I was going to have to take up running, or even try out for the Ladies' boat. The one thing that marred my pleasure, as I sipped coffee and nibbled at a mint, was that Giles was sure to proposition me and I'd have to turn him down.

I wasn't sure whether I really wanted to or not because, while his good looks and easy charm appealed, his air of arrogant superiority very definitely did not, but that wasn't the issue. If I gave in I could see all too clearly that I'd just become the latest on what was probably a long list of conquests, and that he'd then move on to somebody else. I couldn't turn him down flat either, or he might decide I was a prude and lose interest, and then there was Stephen.

'Shall we go?'

'Um? Yes, let's.'

He'd broken into my thoughts, making me wonder if I'd seemed rude, but as usual he appeared not to have noticed, so wrapped up in himself that he was blissfully unaware of my nervousness. As we walked out to the car I was expecting him to try to put his arm around me, or at least make some gesture of affection, but he was talking about different ways to prepare grouse and seemed oblivious of the situation we were in, at the end of a date, when surely any red-blooded male feels entitled to at least a kiss and a cuddle, and generally a lot more.

As we drove back towards Oxford he was still talking about grouse, followed by his uncle's estate in Scotland, malt whisky and the Loch Ness monster. By then I was beginning to feel insulted, as if he'd decided I wasn't worth his while, only for him to park in a side street off the Iffley Road, a long way from both his college and mine. It was quite dark, with big chestnut trees overhanging the road and a single dim streetlight, making me think of being eased down to take his cock in my mouth or even fucked over the seat. If I turned him down and he kicked me out of the car it was a long walk back to college in my heels, so maybe, just maybe, it would be easier to give in. He gave a low sigh.

'This is about as close as I can get without being clamped tomorrow morning, but don't worry, I'll walk you back to Boniface.'

'Oh.'

Any other man would have heard the emotion in my voice. Not Giles. He got out, waited for me to join him and double-checked that he'd locked the car, then set off, once more talking as if he was walking beside a male friend and not a – hopefully – pretty girl with no bra and the shape of her breasts clearly outlined beneath her dress. By the time we reached St Boniface I'd even begun to wonder if he was gay, only to have my doubts pushed aside as he spoke.

'So what's it to be: a kiss goodnight, or up to your room for some good dirty sex until five in the morning?'

He'd said it as if he was suggesting we go for a coffee. I was completely taken aback, so much so that I didn't know what to say, or whether to laugh, to slap his face, or to take him in and let him enjoy himself with me until dawn. Another push and I might have given in, but he waited and when I finally found my voice it was to stammer out an awkward, defensive lie.

'Um … it's not a good time … sorry. You know how it is.'

His mouth twitched briefly into a grin, maybe knowing, maybe sympathetic, before he leaned forwards to kiss me.

'Another time then. Goodnight.'

He gave a little bow, perhaps mocking me, perhaps just playful, and withdrew, leaving me feeling confused, relieved and yet full of regret. As I went in I was trying to tell myself that I'd made the right decision, and really handled him quite well, but there was an empty feeling inside me. I climbed to my room and began to undress, all the while imagining how things would have been if I'd asked him up; urgent kisses, my dress pulled up over my head, his cock freed into my hand and then my mouth, my shoes and knickers kicked away and then full sex, maybe in the same rude kneeling position Stephen had taken me in just two nights before.

I knew what I was going to do, and that there was no point in trying to stop myself. A quick wash and I got into bed, naked, my thighs coming up and open as I imagined what might have been. I began to touch myself, circling my clit to make the sobs come, of both passion and regret, wishing he'd been firm with me in the car, parking in some lonely lay-by, pulling out his cock and demanding that I suck him off, or bending me over the bonnet to take me from behind as other cars swept past, their headlights illuminating my near-naked body with my dress pulled up to my neck and my knickers pulled down as Giles thrust into me. I was nearly there, only for my fantasy to be shattered by the sudden bang of the outer door and Violet's voice.

'Sh! You'll wake Poppy.'

A masculine voice answered, very deep. 'Then I'll deal with her too.'

'Don't be ridiculous! She's a nice girl.'

I'd frozen, only to quickly pull the bedclothes up as I realised that all Violet needed to do was duck down and peep in the keyhole to discover that I was no more a nice girl than she was. When I heard her door close I tried to relax, but it wasn't easy, with their voices just audible through the wall, although it was no longer possible to catch what they were saying. Still I tried, too aroused to stop and determined to get there.

My thoughts were a muddle, with a dozen different images now crowding in; Giles, Stephen, Violet and her mystery lover. Before long I'd sorted things out, creating a nice rude fantasy in which Giles and his Hawkubite friends robbed Stephen and then made me earn the money back by taking turns with me in front of him, only for my thoughts to be interrupted once more.

I could still hear Violet with her lover, but their words were now punctuated by urgent gasps, as much pain as pleasure and coming too far apart to be the result of hard thrusts into her sex, while his voice still sounded calm, but full of authority. Whatever he was doing to her it hurt, but it was getting her off too, and I could all too easily imagine the state she was in, maybe spread out in front of him, maybe bent over or on all fours as he tormented her.

She cried out again, louder, and an image came into my mind from an old music video, of somebody dripping molten wax onto their lover's chest. It made sense, and I could now picture the scene next door; Violet naked, her back bowed as she pushed out her chest, her eyes fixed to the candle flame, her body jerking to the sting of the hot drops as they fell one by one onto her naked flesh. Her thighs would be open, exposing herself to him as he got ready to enter her.

As I began to rub again I remembered his words, his threat to deal with me too and I was immediately imagining myself side my side with Violet, our thighs spread, perhaps with our hands tied behind our backs, both vulnerable to his cock and to the steady drip of hot wax, or turned over, bottoms up, playing with ourselves as he tormented us, available for entry at any moment. With that thought I came.

4

My head felt clear in the morning and, while I was a little embarrassed for my outrageous fantasy, I was sure I'd done the right thing with Giles Lancaster. Most likely it was because he was a public schoolboy, maybe it was just part of his personality, but he had a very odd attitude to women and was certainly not to be trusted. Stephen's attitude was also a little peculiar, maybe for the same reason, but he was far more down to earth.

I was keen to see him as soon as possible, and sent him a text suggesting a lunchtime drink as soon as I was up and about. His reply came while I was in hall, queuing for breakfast, to say that he was rowing until eleven but would meet me at somewhere called The Boatman's at noon. I had no idea where the place was, except presumably somewhere by the river, so went back to my room to consult my Handbook, arriving at the top of my stair just in time to meet Violet and her mysterious lover coming out of her room. For once they weren't arguing or having a heated discussion, and I was much too curious to pay attention to the acute embarrassment on her face as she saw me.

'Hi, Violet. Are you going to introduce me?'

'Um . . . yes. This is Dr McLean.'

I knew they'd been talking about me from the snippet of conversation I'd caught the night before, and I couldn't help but remember what he'd said, so that I was blushing slightly as he gave me a polite nod. He would have spoken, but Violet was already hurrying towards the stairs and, as I unlocked the door, I caught her voice, raised in agitation. Whatever was going on between them, she clearly didn't want it to be common knowledge, which inevitably made me even more curious. He was also at least ten years older than her, maybe more like fifteen, and had been her tutor.

It was all very intriguing, and as I leafed through my Handbook I was promising myself that I'd find out more. The Boatman's turned out to be on Jackdaw Lane, at least half-an-hour's walk but through the meadows and along the river. Another, rather obvious, piece of Dad's advice had been to make sure I didn't let my social life get in the way of my degree, so I promised myself I'd complete two hours of research for my essay and then set off. Dr Etheridge had provided me with a reading list, which gave me a good start, although I knew I'd do better if I included references he hadn't suggested as well, which meant chasing up obscure books in the depths of the Bodleian.

By the time I emerged into the fresh air I was feeling that I'd earned a break, and set off for the river with a spring in my step. I got a bit lost, what with different branches of the Cherwell, and ended up having to cadge a lift across where it joins the Thames. The pub was on the far side, with a beer garden sloping down to the river, and Stephen was already there, looking very bronzed and fit in his rowing gear. I greeted him with a kiss, keen to affirm our relationship, provoking a pleased grin and the offer of a drink.

An hour later I was very sure that we were together. He was keen to be nice, very careful of my opinions in case he offended me and also to touch, but gently, as if I was made of bone china and he was scared I'd break. That might have put me off a little, had I not remembered the way he'd handled me once I'd got him too aroused to control himself, but I was determined that if we were to be together he would feel able to assert himself sexually. He'd decided to eat, and I waited until he'd finished before popping the question.

'Would you like a treat?'

'I'm full, thanks, and I've got a tute this afternoon so I'd better not drink too much.'

'Not that sort of treat. Come on.'

He didn't seem to understand, until we were some way back down the lane and I'd pulled him in among the bushes. There weren't many people about and the undergrowth was so dense we'd quickly lost sight of the river, but I went well in just to be on the safe side. He followed, happy enough to let me lead and a little surprised by my behaviour, especially when I sat down on a low branch and pulled up my top.

'That's the way you boys like it, isn't it?'

'Um ... yes. Wow!'

I had to beckon him over, but had quickly pulled his rowing shorts aside to release his cock and balls, first into my hand and then into my mouth.

'You really don't hang around, do you?'

I shook my head, sucking eagerly. He'd begun to swell immediately and I closed my eyes in bliss for the taste and feel of him, also the knowledge that he was growing aroused for me so quickly. There's no better turn-on than a man who responds well, and I'd soon abandoned my idea of simply taking him to orgasm and leaving it at that. I pulled off my top and took him between my breasts.

'You can do what you like with me; you know that, don't you?'

'Anything?'

'Anything.'

'God, you're lovely ...'

As he trailed off he grabbed my breasts, squeezing them

around his cock. I fumbled with the button of my jeans, sure he'd rip them down to get me bare and make me bend over to be taken from behind. I repeated my offer, just to be on the safe side.

'Anything, I mean it.'

This time his answer was to come in my cleavage. I hadn't been expecting it, and he was squeezing so hard it hurt as he finished himself off, gasping out his thanks while he was still doing it.

'You're wonderful, Poppy, so wonderful . . . the best . . .'

He gave me a last squeeze and stood back, looking pleased with himself. It took me a moment to get myself together, and for what he'd done to me to cease to be a shock and become something extraordinarily, deliciously rude. I wasn't finished either, and I wasn't having any nonsense from him.

'I think you'd better use your tongue. Come on.'

I was already pushing my jeans and knickers down as I spoke. He swallowed hard as he saw what I wanted, but, if there's one thing men have to learn, it's that fair's fair.

'Come on, it won't hurt you.'

Again he swallowed, hesitating. I beckoned to him as I let my thighs come open, determined not to accept any excuses, but he suddenly nodded and came forwards. I made myself as comfy as I could with my bare bottom on the rough bark of the branch and he got down between my open knees. He poked out his tongue and he was doing it, not between my legs, but on my breasts, licking up what he'd done.

I watched, amazed. No man I'd known had ever done anything of the sort, and I'd never even have thought of suggesting it, and yet it worked for me, such a rude thing to do, so uninhibited. I began to stroke his hair, soothing him as he licked it up, still offering myself to him with my thighs wide across his body. He slid a finger into me and I closed my eyes, lost in ecstasy. I held him to me and his tongue flicked over the skin of my neck and breasts.

He took his time, cleaning me up completely before he even turned his attention to my nipples, sucking each before laying a slow trail of kisses down across my tummy and to my sex. I pushed my hips out, holding him to me, my eyes closed and my mouth wide, as he found the spot, licking far too well for it to have been his first time. In no time at all I could feel my orgasm beginning to well up inside me.

I took a firm grip in his hair, thinking of what he'd done to me, so wonderfully rude, to come between my breasts and lick up what he'd done, something I hadn't even imagined a man would do for a woman. Yet he had, and I knew he'd be able to taste himself even as he brought me to ecstasy under his tongue, a thought that tipped me over the edge. I held him tightly in place until I'd quite finished, only then releasing my grip and allowing him to rock back on his heels, grinning like a schoolboy.

He found his voice first. 'You are amazing!'

'I'm amazing! Nobody's ever done that to me before.'

'What, licked your . . .'

'No, what you did first, licking my breasts.'

He shrugged, his expression growing shy for an instant before he abruptly stood up, adjusting himself as he spoke again. 'Thanks anyway, that was a great treat.'

'For me too.'

I kissed him and began to tidy myself up. He was getting restless long before I'd finished, and I had to hurry after him to get back to the lane. I took his hand, keen to show affection after what we'd done and he responded with a gentle squeeze, leaving me smiling and happy as we made our way towards the main road.

It was only when we got there that I realised that Jackdaw

Lane was the same one Giles Lancaster had parked in the night before, and then only because his Audi was there. So was he, coming around the corner, straight towards us, so that short of turning around and running back the way we'd come there was no hope of avoiding him. He'd already seen me anyway, and as we came together all I could do was get the first word in.

'This is my friend Giles. He's Recorder at the Chamber.'

To my surprise Stephen didn't answer me, but Giles did, both of them grinning and slapping each other on the back as they came together.

'Lancaster, I thought I might run into you sometime!'

'Mitchell! So you got in then? And they say miracles don't happen any more. Which college has drawn the short straw?'

'Emmanuel. And you?'

'Mary's. It's great to see you though!'

They hugged, patting each other on the back with very real affection, not at all the behaviour I'd have expected from two public schoolboys, but they were obviously old friends.

'Were you two at school together or something?'

It was Stephen who answered me. 'Yes. Lancaster, meet my girlfriend, Poppy Miller.'

I was pleased to hear him announce me as his girlfriend, and with obvious pride, but my answering smile must have looked more than a little nervous as Giles responded.

'We've met.'

After his parting comments the night before I half expected him to suggest a threesome, and I knew I was blushing. Fortunately they were much too wrapped up in each other to worry about me, talking about people I didn't know and places I'd never been, until Stephen finally realised that he needed to hurry.

'I have a tutorial in half-an-hour. I'd better get moving.'

Giles jerked a thumb at the Audi. 'This is mine. I'll give you a lift.'

Stephen glanced at the car, then at me. 'It's a two-seater.'

Giles shrugged and swung himself into the car, rolling down the window to speak to us as soon as he'd turned on the ignition. 'Oh, and Poppy, I've booked you in to speak at the debate next Thursday.'

'To speak? On the prostitution debate?'

He gave me the full title. '"This House believes that sex workers should be employed directly by the state and the state alone." That's the one. You're on third.'

'But I don't know the first thing about sex workers! What side are we on anyway?'

'I'm for the motion, you're against.'

'Against? But, Giles . . .'

'Just bung a pair of dungarees on and give them some crap about male privilege and the patriarchy. Are you sure you don't want a lift, Mitchell?'

'No thanks, I'll walk.'

'Ah, young love! She's a good catch too, faithful as a puppy. I offered to bonk her brains out and she turned me down flat.'

I felt the blood rush to my face, so hot it was as if my cheeks were on fire, and Stephen was more taken aback than I was, standing there with his mouth open. Giles gave a cheerful wave and was gone before either Stephen or I could think what to say.

He found his voice first. 'Sorry about Giles. He can be a bit of a clown sometimes.'

'A clown? He's an arrogant pig and a complete and utter buffoon!'

'He's all right. He was Head Boy at Laon Abbey.'

'Then the rest of the school has my deepest sympathy.'

'Come on, I don't suppose he knew we were together, did he, and you can hardly blame him for trying.'

I began to answer, but bit back my words, my anger with Giles starting to die as I remembered that I hadn't turned him down flat and that the situation would have been a great deal more embarrassing if he'd told Stephen what I'd actually said. A hasty change of subject seemed to be in order.

'I don't mean that. I mean put me up for speaker in the prostitution debate.'

'You should be grateful, shouldn't you? How many people get to speak at the Chamber at the first debate after they come up?'

My resentment began to fade with my anger.

'Not many, I suppose, but that's not the problem. There are some topics it's best to avoid completely, including sex, because if I take a permissive stance I'll get labelled a slut and if I take a repressive stance I'll get labelled a prude or – what's the word – a bluestocking.'

'Not nowadays, surely?'

I shrugged, wondering if he was right. It was Dad who'd advised me to avoid any debate with a sexual theme, but his experience was over thirty years out of date.

Stephen carried on as we began to walk. 'Anyway, you don't have to take an anti-sex approach at all. Why not argue that sex should be a loving experience between equals and not a commodity?'

'That's a point. I could do that. That's what I believe, actually.'

'There we are then.'

'Thanks.'

I went briefly quiet, remembering his own somewhat cryptic remark about Southeast Asia and my own fantasies about being a high-class call-girl. There was actually something quite exciting about inequality, and in having to do something because I'd been paid, or been tricked, even pushed into it or simply taken advantage of, just so long as I genuinely wanted the man. I took Stephen's hand and gave it a squeeze.

'That was lovely, by the way, what we did.'

'My pleasure.'

We walked on, silent, hand in hand, my head full of rude thoughts. Stephen was unlike any other man I'd met, especially when it came to sex, making me wonder what else he had to offer. Looking back, I now realised that my sex life had been fairly straightforward, uninhibited but perhaps a bit unimaginative too. I certainly couldn't imagine Ewan doing what Stephen had in among the bushes, despite expecting me to swallow.

I even began to feel happier about the debate. It was an excellent opportunity to get myself noticed, and as the third speaker out of maybe four or five I could afford to be fairly light-hearted about it, and to concentrate more on making sure everybody remembered me rather than the subject in question. Stephen's suggestion was good as well, and by the time we'd reached the High I had a pretty good idea of what I was going to say.

We kissed goodbye at the bottom of The Turl and he hurried off in the direction of Emmanuel while I went into college. I was in need of coffee, and gave Violet's door a tap as I pushed my key into my own. She answered immediately and I stuck my head in to find her lying face down on the bed, reading, with her legs kicked up and one lipstick-red shoe dangling negligently from her toes.

'Coffee?'

'I've got some. Help yourself.'

'Thanks.'

I came in and poured myself a black coffee from the cafetière she kept pretty much always ready. As she folded her book I saw that it was the Pierre Louÿs, *La Femme et le Pantin*, which I was pretty sure she'd been reading when I'd watched her playing with herself. I couldn't resist a question.

'Is that good?'

She paused, as if to consider.

'It's a classic, if you like late-nineteenth-century erotica.'

'I've never read any.'

She tossed the book down on the carpet where I'd curled myself on the enormous purple bean bag she kept in one corner. I picked it up, feeling awkward.

'But aren't you in the middle of it?'

'I've read it before, plenty of times.'

I was forced to admit my ignorance. 'I don't read French, I'm afraid.'

'No? Hang on.'

She'd answered me much as if I'd admitted to not knowing my alphabet, but quickly got up, reaching down another volume from her shelves, a translation of the same work. I took it, intrigued, but I wanted to tell her about my part in the Chamber debate.

'I'm speaking at the Chamber next Thursday.'

'On government brothels? I hope you're against?'

'Yes, I am actually. Giles Lancaster put my name forward, but for the opposition.'

'Then you'll be with James ... Dr McLean. He's opening, as guest speaker.'

'Great, maybe we can compare notes, if he wouldn't mind?'

She seemed a little uneasy as she answered. 'I'm sure he wouldn't mind, um ... I suppose I'd better tell you about me and James.'

'Not if you'd rather not.' It was a blatant lie, because I was fascinated, and fortunately she didn't take me up on my offer.

'He and I were together, while I was an undergraduate.'

'Here at Boniface?'

'No, at Mary's. He got dismissed.'

'And you?'

'I was the innocent victim, as far as they were concerned. I got counselling.'

She made a face, a little worried, a little defiant, and I hastened to reassure her.

'Don't worry, I don't mind. Why should I?'

She bit her lip, and for an instant looked close to tears. I knelt up, holding her to me for a moment before letting go as she went on.

'Thanks. It was all a bit fraught, as you can imagine. Very fraught, in fact, and it still is.'

'I was wondering. Let me guess; you feel he pushed you into it but you can't let go?'

'No, just the opposite. I seduced him.'

5

I didn't manage to get the full story out of Violet, but as I lay in bed that night reading the book she had lent me I began to feel that I was gaining at least some insight. She'd referred to the book as erotica, but it wasn't so much about sex as about obsessive love, cruelty and manipulation. It was also beautifully written, drawing me into the atmosphere of nineteenth-century Seville and the highly charged emotions of the narrator. Had it not been for the title I wouldn't have been sure who was manipulating who, as the narrator, Don Matteo, was mature, wealthy, confident, everything you'd expect in a preda-tory older male, while the girl, Concepcion or Conchita, was young and seemingly both vulnerable and naïve. Only as the book progressed did it become clear that she had more than a touch of the devil in her, while he was at least to some extent her willing victim.

When I finally put the book down, no longer able to focus properly on the page, my head was full of images of sun-drenched Spanish streets, dark windows and darker eyes hinting at sensual delights only to draw back at the last instant. I felt pity for the man, Don Matteo, yet also sympathy for Conchita and a savage yet also guilty pleasure in the way she tormented him, apparently for no better reason than to take pleasure in his frustration. What I hadn't felt so far was arousal, mainly because the descriptions were a little coy, but also because I had no real desire to treat a man that way myself, nor to be treated that way in turn. I wondered how Violet felt, and if her affair with James McLean really mirrored that of Conchita and Don Matteo.

I woke late, very glad indeed that it was the weekend, made myself coffee and went straight back to the book. Within a few pages I'd reached a much better scene, in which Conchita ensured that Don Matteo knew she was dancing nude for other men, bringing his lust and jealousy to boiling point. She handled him with consummate skill, flirting and feigning innocence, making promises of surrender only to withdraw them at the last moment, and all the while making him seem to be the aggressor. Finally he snapped and simply took her, which proved to be what she had been angling for all along.

That I could appreciate, the idea of teasing a man until he lost control, much the way Stephen had on our first night together but with no more contact than a kiss. I could imagine Violet doing it too, although from what I'd heard through the wall I knew that whatever she might have held back from him in the past she had now given herself over completely. She said she'd seduced him, implying that he had tried to resist but eventually broken his will, leading to his dismissal. No wonder their relationship was stormy, and yet he still came back to her.

I had never had that sort of control over a man, and found the idea compelling, also curious. Violet was pretty, and she had a languorous, sensual way about her, intensely feminine despite having snake hips and no bust to speak of. Evidently Dr McLean's desire for her went beyond the merely physical, which was no surprise given his intelligence and learning. Yet he was also physically attractive and no doubt had plenty of admirers, which meant that there was something about Violet that set her apart, something for which he'd been prepared to risk losing everything.

The obvious answer was that he had fallen deeply in love

with her, but that didn't quite seem to fit. He was too cool, too in control. When I'd listened his voice had been calm and authoritative even as she sobbed out her passion, while if he was desperately in love with her he'd hardly have suggested dealing with me too. Perhaps whatever dealing with Violet involved was what was so compelling about her, in which case it was something that could be done to me too, but which I wouldn't accept because they thought I was a nice girl.

I'd imagined hot wax, but that now seemed trivial, too small a thing to excite such passion. Maybe Dr McLean had some rare and curious fetish that Violet was willing to accommodate, and yet she had been the one moaning with pleasure. It didn't seem to make sense, but it had turned me on, both the last two scenes in the book and thinking about Violet and her lover. As my thighs came up and open I had to push aside a brief jolt of shame for having masturbated more often in the previous week than over the rest of the year, but that wasn't going to stop me.

My hand slid in down my knickers and I closed my eyes, imagining how Stephen would feel knowing that I'd danced naked for other men, perhaps waiting for me outside some sleazy club while I performed a slow dirty striptease within. It didn't work, not with Stephen. He was too nice. Giles was better, so arrogant, yet I couldn't actually imagine him caring one way or the other.

He would if I did it in front of him but he was unable to touch. That worked. I imagined that I'd told him to stop in some quiet lay-by on the way back from Les Couleurs, promising him that he could have me if he did as he was told. We'd leave the car headlights on, making a tiny stage for my performance, invisible from the road. I'd tease him, kissing him and touching him gently, promising everything, until I'd managed to persuade him to allow me to tie him to a tree.

His wrists would be secured behind the trunk with his tie, leaving him helpless as I began to strip in the pool of light. I'd do it slowly, teasing as I gradually exposed myself, before finally showing it all.

By then he'd be struggling in his bonds, demanding that I release him, then begging as I began to dance naked in front of him, posing to show off every rude detail of my body, nothing hidden. I'd come in front of him, my hips pushed forwards as I stroked my breasts and sex, or ruder still, with my bottom stuck out so that he could watch my fingers work and imagine where he'd like to stick his straining cock.

He'd have been erect from the start, and desperate for my touch as he watched me come. I'd have obliged, after a fashion, pulling his cock and balls free, tugging briefly at his shaft, perhaps kissing just the tip. Then I'd leave, walking away with a last taunting wiggle of my bottom, throwing my clothes casually into the car and driving off, to leave him helpless with his raging erection still sticking out of his fly.

I was on the edge of orgasm for real, and ran the whole glorious fantasy through my head one more time, hitting my peak at the point when I finally lifted my bra and holding it all the way to that last cheeky wiggle. It was very good indeed, and only slightly spoiled at the very end by the thought that, whatever the details, I had just come over the thought of Giles Lancaster.

For a long while I lay still, my warm satisfied feeling slowly giving way. It was to all intents and purposes the end of Freshers' Week, with the majority of second- and third-year students arriving, so that the college was full of bustle even at ten o'clock in the morning, with friends calling out to each other and people bumping cases up the stairs outside my door. I knew I was wasting my day and ought to be out and about instead of playing with myself. There would be new people to meet, new things to do, while my essay had to be in on the Wednesday. Then there was the debate, which meant finding out exactly what Giles had dropped me into, meeting Dr McLean and the rest of our team, preparing my speech and generally running around and being enthusiastic. From Monday onwards there would also be lectures to attend, so I really needed to get my act together.

If there's one thing I'm good at it's making myself work when I know I have to. My technique is to promise myself a treat once I've completed a certain amount; my favourite sweets when I was little, pieces of chocolate for my GCSEs, cans of lager for my A levels, and now that I was at Oxford glasses of old port, which seemed appropriate. By the Tuesday evening I not only had my essay done, but also had compiled several pages of notes for my speech, all between lectures, study groups and three brief but passionate liaisons with Stephen.

One thing that quickly became clear as I did my research on prostitution and the state was that Giles Lancaster had set me up, both in the hope of gaining an easy victory for his side and to ensure I made a fool of myself. It was crafty, and pretty low down, but he wouldn't have been giving Niccolo Machiavelli any lessons, because I'd realised what he was up to within a few seconds of typing 'male privilege' and 'patriarchy'. Both terms belonged to the most radical feminist ideologies, used by extremists who'd lost all touch with the fundamental need for equality. Had I based my argument on what I found on the net I'd have been laughed out of the building, which might very well have been the end of my political aspirations.

Stephen's idea was far better, a little idealistic perhaps but that would probably be expected of me. It also made sense, because I've always felt that there should be somebody for everybody, and if people were just a bit less hung up about sex then nobody would need to sell it, or buy it. The only problem was that it didn't really answer the question, except in that state-run brothels might make paid sex seem the norm. That part needed work, but I felt I was ready to discuss my ideas with Dr James McLean.

Violet had passed on a message to say that he and the other two speakers would be meeting in the White Horse rather than the Chamber bar, allowing us to discuss our position without fear of being overheard. Given Dr McLean's reputation and his casual suggestion that I should be dealt with in some unspecified but presumably kinky fashion, I was glad that there would be four of us there, but as it turned out he was polite and friendly, while the other two speakers were also female undergraduates, although third years rather than first. After making the introductions and a little casual chat, he got down to business.

'Do you all know Giles Lancaster?'

We nodded as one.

'Then you'll know the angle he's likely to take; bread and circuses to keep the masses quiet, meanwhile eliminating the crime associated with prostitution by undercutting private enterprise, which in this case means traffickers, pimps and other thoroughly unpleasant people, an idea which has plenty of popular appeal. He used much the same arguments in the debate on the legalisation of drugs last Hilary term, as Komali and Susan will remember, and their side won. I have some ideas on how we combat the approach, but I'd like to hear yours first. Poppy?'

'Um ... OK. Essentially I want to argue that state-controlled brothels legitimise the concept of sex as a commodity.'

'Which you regard as a bad thing?'

'Yes. Sex should be a shared experience between loving, consenting adults, surely?'

'OK. Let me ask you a question. Will you concede that a disabled person, perhaps in a wheelchair, still has a sex drive?'

'Yes, of course.'

'And that they have the right to express their sexuality?'

'Yes.'

'Good. Now let's take it a step further. He, or she, is also ugly and socially inept. How are they going to find their loving, consenting partner?'

'Dating agencies, something online perhaps?'

'Do you really think that would work?'

'Sometimes, maybe . . . OK, not very often.'

'Hardly ever, I expect. Realistically, their only opportunity for sexual expression will be to pay.'

'I see what you're getting at, but you seem to be arguing for the proposal, not against?'

'Not at all. My argument supports sex work as a valid profession, but that in no way implies it should be controlled exclusively by the state.'

'OK, I'm sorry. Obviously that wasn't such a good idea.'

'Not at all. I'm merely playing devil's advocate, but the opposition might very well put forward the same argument.'

'What do you think I should say then?'

'Your point is valid, but needs to be qualified, while I'd also like the four of us to be singing from the same song sheet. One argument in favour of our position, and I expect the one Giles himself would use if he was on our side, is the capitalist argument, which is self-explanatory.'

He glanced between us and I was pleased to see that I wasn't the only one looking blank. After having my own idea squashed so easily I didn't want to speak up again, but Susan was bolder.

'How do you mean?'

'Essentially the argument is that prostitution should be legal, but run like any other business, designed to make a profit but regulated to prevent abuse, the idea being that any state-controlled system inevitably panders to the lowest common denominator, resulting in a dull, uninspiring service, low wages for the producers – in this case the girls who actually do the work – and a top-heavy management.'

'Isn't that just right-wing theory?'

'Yes, it is, which is why I want Giles to think it will be the main thrust of our argument when in fact I intend to empha-sise the social disadvantages of state control: government intrusion, data gathering and its potential misuse, poor service and so forth, topical things that will resonate with the audi-ence and, hopefully, win us the vote. Also, I want to ...'

He carried on, the three of us listening as he outlined a complete plan, leaving only one question I wanted to ask.

'How are you going to make sure Giles thinks we're going to use the capitalist argument?'

'Because, Poppy, you are going to tell him.'

I couldn't have hoped for a better task. Not only was it great fun, making me feel like a secret agent, but it gave me an excellent opportunity to revenge myself on Giles for his behav-iour. The only question was: how to go about it without arousing his suspicions?

Approaching him directly wasn't going to work. He was much too crafty to fall for it, and for all his arrogance he had to be aware that I wasn't best pleased with him. If he came to talk to me it would be different, as I could pretend to let something slip, perhaps after one too many drinks at the Chamber bar, which was where I went after my Wednesday-afternoon tutorial. Giles was there, as I'd expected, but to my surprise so was Stephen. They were talking together, and when I came up to them I was sure there was a hint of embarrassment or even guilt in Stephen's voice as he greeted me. 'Hello, Poppy, everything OK?'

'Yes, fine, I just fancied a drink after my tute.'

Giles was his normal self. 'After an hour of Jarrow John on social philosophy I bet you need one. Let me get it. What about you, Mitchell?'

'Another pint, please.'

'Port, please.'

'You'll get gout. Have a gin and tonic.'

He made for the bar, leaving me to sit down beside Stephen. There was a question I'd been meaning to ask ever since they'd met in Jackdaw Lane. 'Why do you and Giles call each other by your surnames?'

'It's a school thing, at Laon Abbey and most other public schools.'

'That's weird.'

'Not really. It was normal in the nineteenth century, among higher classes anyway, and the tradition has been maintained, that's all, much the same way as judges and lawyers wear wigs or we wear gowns when we matriculate.'

'I suppose so. It just sounds so formal.'

'Maybe, but for me it's something I only do with my closest friends.'

'So I'll know you really like me when you start calling me Miller?'

He laughed. 'I will if you like.'

'No. It would be too much like being told off at school. Are you coming to hear me speak tomorrow night?'

'Yes, of course, and Giles. He'll win, you know, he always does.'

'You might be surprised. Dr McLean has some very strong arguments.'

It would have been the perfect opportunity to drop my little piece of disinformation into the conversation, but Giles had managed to get served in record-breaking time and was already on his way back. Besides that, I couldn't guarantee that it would have been passed on. As soon as I'd got my drink I tried a different tack.

'What are your arguments going to be, Giles?'

'Do you really think I'm going to tell you that, twenty-four hours before the debate?'

'Why not, if you're as good as people make out.'

'I'm good because I don't let my opponents know what I'm doing. So, have you got your dungarees pressed and your copy of Andrea Dworkin ready?'

'No. That line of argument wouldn't have stood up for a minute, as you perfectly well know.'

'Oh, I don't know. Oxford's full of bluestockings, always was.'

'Anyway, we have something far cleverer.'

'You do? Don't tell me, you're going to argue in favour of prostitution as free enterprise?'

I was taken aback, but only for an instant before I had to force myself not to smile. He laughed at my reaction as I made a hurried and deliberately unconvincing denial and that was that, my job done for me. Anything more and he might have realised I was bluffing, so I hastily changed the subject.

'Did you join the Commodities Trading Club, Stephen?'

'Yes, I did. It's invaluable for me.'

Giles broke in. 'He is also up for election to the Hawkubites, aren't you, Mitchell?'

Stephen responded with an embarrassed nod and a questioning glance in my direction.

I hastened to reassure him. 'I don't mind. One thing I learned a long time ago was to let the boys have their nights out.'

He still sounded awkward as he answered me. 'It is an all-male society.'

'I do trust you, Stephen.'

'Thanks.'

'Just don't expect me to bail you out if you get arrested for trashing some restaurant, that's all.'

Giles made a casual gesture. 'Don't worry, we retain a lawyer for that sort of thing.'

'Isn't that rather expensive?'

'Being a Hawkubite is expensive. That's why we don't let the riff-raff in.'

'Despite modelling yourselves on them?'

'As I believe I mentioned before, it's not vandalism if you're correctly dressed.'

'You did, yes. Would you like to come to hall with me this evening, Stephen?'

'Um...I'd love to, but Giles is taking me to meet the committee.'

'Afterwards?'

'Yes, of course.'

'I'll be in my room.'

I swallowed down what was left of my drink and went back to college. Despite what I'd said I wasn't particularly happy about Stephen joining the Hawkubites, who were nothing more than a gang of upper-class yobs. I had meant it though, because if there's one thing guaranteed to wreck a relationship it's trying to reform your partner, especially by stopping him, or her, going around with their friends. Stephen and I were getting on well, and the last thing I wanted to do was put him off by being too bossy.

With my essay out of the way I was keen to finish *The Woman and the Puppet*, which I'd put aside as being too distracting. The final part was a little disappointing, as I'd hoped for something even juicier than the scene in which Don Matteo lost control with Conchita. It did get wonderfully tense, but the climax I'd been anticipating never came, leaving me with a faint sense of dissatisfaction.

By then it was nearly ten o'clock and there was still no sign of Stephen. Violet wasn't about either, so I went for a coffee with my downstairs neighbours, both male second years, one reading botany and the other history. The conversation was pretty dull, but I was hoping Stephen would come back while I was still there, so that he didn't think I'd been sitting in waiting for him. It was half past eleven when I finally made my way back upstairs, and I was unlocking my door when I heard footsteps below, far too heavy for Violet and taking the stairs three or four at a time. Stephen appeared, looking flushed and apologising even as he took me in his arms.

'I'm sorry I was so long. Come here.'

I responded, letting my mouth open to his despite the taste of beer and something else which I couldn't quite put my finger on, something quite strong and musky. He was drunk too, and horny. I quickly pulled him into my room, not wanting Violet to catch me having my bottom groped up against her door, an action he took for assent. My top and bra were up before I'd even managed to get the door closed, and I had to wriggle out of his grip to shut it or she might have seen a great deal more.

'Slow down, Stephen!'

'I want you.'

'I know, but ...'

My words broke to a gasp as he pushed his hand up my skirt to squeeze my sex through my knickers.

'You're wet. Have you been thinking about me?'

I hadn't. I'd been thinking of what Don Matteo had done to

Conchita, but it looked like I was going to get the same treatment, so there was only one sensible answer.

'Yes.'

'Bad girl. Come on, knickers off.'

He'd got hold of them, and tugged them down even as he spoke. My arms were around him, but he pushed me back onto the bed, rolling me up with my knickers twisted in one big hand, much as he had done on our first night together. His spare hand found my sex, rubbing at me, and I gave in. A finger went inside me, just briefly, and he was fumbling at his fly as he clambered onto the bed.

His cock came out, straight into my mouth and I was sucking as he began to explore my body, playing with my breasts and bottom cheeks, fingering me and rubbing a knuckle between the lips of my sex, all the while with my legs held up to keep me helpless and exposed. I was happy like that, and would gladly have let him make me come, but he was erect in no time and keen to have me.

'Come on, bottoms up.'

I didn't get any say in the matter, twisted over and lifted by my hips. His cock settled between my bottom cheeks, rubbing in my crease before he took himself in hand and slid it up, deep inside me. I was ready and took him easily, which was just as well, because he was too drunk and too horny to take his time with me, thrusting deep and pushing himself in and out so fast and so hard that he was knocking the breath from my body.

'You look so good like that, Poppy, so good.'

I looked an undignified mess, my breasts pulled out, skirt up and knickers around one ankle, but I was in no state to complain. He had taken hold of my thighs, lifting me clean off the bed, my thighs spread so wide that his balls were pushing at my sex with every thrust. I was going to come, if he could only keep it up for a few more seconds, and I was begging him not to stop as I let what he'd done to me come together in my head.

He had just pushed his way into my room, stripped my clothes aside to get at what he wanted and fucked me. If I hadn't insisted on shutting the door it would still be open, wide open, allowing Violet a prime view of me being had from behind. I could imagine her, her hand to her mouth in shock and delight as she watched Stephen's cock push in and out of my sex, giggling for the state I was in, her hand sneaking down between her thighs ...

I came, screaming as it hit me, too far gone to care about the neighbours or anything else except the glorious sensations running through my body. Stephen grunted and I knew he'd done it inside me, driving me to a second peak higher even than the first, so long and so intense that I was still gasping out my pleasure even as he withdrew. Only then did it occur to me to wonder if it was his name I'd called out in my ecstasy, or Violet's.

6

We won the debate, by 219 Noes to 191 Ayes, in no small part due to the way I'd wrong-footed Giles Lancaster. His opening speech was good, with a combination of humour and argument that quickly won the audience around and had well over half the heads in the audience nodding agreement. Fortunately for us, Dr McLean was more forceful still, setting out his argument in the sort of clear, authoritative voice that made it hard even to think of disagreeing. He also spoke with complete conviction, making the argument more compelling still, for me as well as everybody else for all that I knew he regarded the debate more as an exercise in logic than as a chance to promote his beliefs.

By the time he stepped down I was sure we were heading for victory, but that didn't stop me feeling nervous as the other speakers went up one by one. The man who had seconded Giles was a bit of a clown, playing to his friends in the audience and probably doing more harm than good, but Susan was too quiet and diffident. Her speech bored the audience, leaving them restless as the only woman in Giles' team came up. She was very good, answering Susan's points in a clear, serious voice, but she was clearly aggrieved by the idea that anything but the state should run anything at all, which meant her argument was full of holes and I was frantically scribbling notes so that I could incorporate elements of the capitalist angle in my own speech.

My stomach was churning at she resumed her seat, but I

managed to reach the podium without falling flat on my face. After that it was surprisingly easy, really no different from addressing the assembly at school. When there are four hundred or so people all looking at you they seem to merge into one, while I knew to avoid Susan's mistake and keep my head up and my mouth close to the microphone. I'd been worried that because I was female and a first year some of the wilder spirits might heckle me, but my entire speech was delivered to a respectful silence followed by a gentle murmur, leaving me relieved but not sure if I'd done well or badly.

Their summation followed, with Giles' final speaker doing little more than reiterate what had gone before. Komali was better, summing up our argument well, but she insisted on qualifying everything in such minute detail that the audience had begun to stir restlessly, making me wonder if we might lose after all. As the voting began it was clear to me that there were plenty of people who'd have voted for Giles if he'd proposed painting the Radcliffe Camera purple, and a roughly equal number who'd have voted against him unless he'd proposed his own resignation. The floating voters swung it our way, leaving me with a warm glow of success as we made for the bar. Dr McLean treated us to a bottle of champagne, and insisted on pouring me the first glass.

'That was an impressive performance, Poppy. I don't think I've ever seen a first-time speaker so level headed.'

I was blushing as I answered. 'I'm quite used to it really. I was President of the debating society at school, and we had to deliver our sixth-form projects in front of senior assembly, nearly eight hundred people. Cheers.'

I took a swallow of champagne as he turned to Komali, filling her glass as he complimented her in turn. Like me, and Susan, she was basking in the warm glow of his approval, provoking a sudden and completely irrational touch of jealousy, which I quickly bit back. He began to recap, going over how each of us might have improved our delivery with authority but also tact, adding to the respect I'd begun to feel for him since we met up in the White Horse.

Stephen joined us, and then Violet. The conversation grew less serious, and after I'd finished my second glass I decided it was time to go and give Giles Lancaster a chance to congratulate me. He was at the far side of the room, surrounded by a group of the cronies he seemed to attract so easily, but excused himself as he saw me approach, his face splitting into his sloppy, schoolboy grin as he greeted me.

'*Ave Poppaea, crapulari te salutant*, which means "we who are about to get drunk salute you" in case your school didn't provide Latin, while Poppaea was . . .'

'I know who Poppaea was. I'm named after her.'

'You are? Good God, there's hope for the masses yet, or is it simply that dumbing down has yet to reach the darker corners of the West Country?'

'You really are a patronising snob, Giles.'

'Ah, but a charming snob, and quite the best-looking one in Oxford.'

'Can I add conceited to that?'

'By all means, but you're making me blush, so if you could spare a moment from your eulogy I have some friendly advice for you.'

'Yes?'

'Not here, in some quiet corner.'

He took me by the elbow, not hard, but as if to support my arm, and led me out of the bar to a quiet corridor.

'What is it?'

'Just this. Don't let James McLean get you alone.'

'Why not?'

'He is not a healthy companion for young girls.'

'Rubbish.'

'Far from it, I fear.'

'What then? I suppose you're going to tell me he's a letch?'

'Far worse, my innocent little poppet, far worse. You wouldn't believe what he likes to do to pretty young students like yourself.'

'Try me. I know he was thrown out of Mary's.'

'But you don't know the full, incomparably juicy scandal, do you? He was kicked out for giving a student the birch.'

'Giving a student the birch? I don't understand.'

'You know, whacking her on the bum with a bunch of birch twigs, on the bare bum.'

'What! You are joking?'

'Oh no I am not. They got caught red handed, by the junior dean and one of the scouts, who walked in on them. Apparently she was stark naked, bent over his armchair, arse in the air. Juicier still, when they were caught she was pretty well done, as red as a cherry while he pulled his pudding over her cheeks.'

'Now you are joking.'

'Not a bit of it. That comes straight from the scout who caught them.'

'I don't believe a word of it.'

'That, my dear, is your privilege, but may I point out that just because up until now your most unusual experience of sex has been one up the bum over the back seat of the boyfriend's motor ...'

'It has not!'

'Not even that? Oh dear. But my point is that others have more peculiar tastes, including Dr James McLean. Unless, that is, I have underestimated you and you share your tastes with your Roman namesake. Tell me it's so, Poppaea, and I will have my slaves fetch dildos and drugs and donkeys!'

'You're disgusting, Giles, and very drunk.'

'But of course, and you, my dear, are a prude, which is a pity.'

He gave a mocking bow and left. I stayed where I was, trying to work out if what he said could be true, because he was perfectly capable of making the whole thing up either with some strange and elaborate motive or just for the hell of it. What decided me was the memory of the strange noises I'd heard through the wall the night he'd visited college, which fitted disconcertingly well with how I imagined a girl might sound as she was beaten with birch twigs for pleasure. It was true, and, while Giles hadn't given away the name of the unfortunate girl, there was only one person it could possibly be – Violet.

I spent the night with Stephen, which should have been wonderful but was spoiled by the images Giles had planted in my mind and worrying about Violet. What I thought I'd worked out and what Giles had told me didn't seem to fit together at all. If she'd seduced him, teased him and tormented him until he lost control, how come she had ended up bent over his armchair having her bottom thrashed? I could just about imagine her accepting a beating as some form of twisted sexual retribution after he'd been kicked out of Mary's, but that didn't make sense when it was the reason he'd been kicked out. Was she being abused and in thrall to the man responsible? Did she actually enjoy being beaten?

The last idea seemed absurd, but was horribly compelling. I knew people did that sort of thing, but I'd always assumed it was just dirty old men taking out their jaded tastes on younger women, and for money, or on some poor girl with such low self-esteem that she felt the only way she could attract attention was to offer herself up for the satisfaction of some elderly pervert's debauched tastes. I couldn't imagine for a moment that Violet was charging Dr McLean, and she certainly didn't suffer from low self-esteem, while to judge from what I'd heard she had been thoroughly enjoying herself.

I simply could not get my head around the idea, but I couldn't get rid of it either. Again and again I found myself imagining the humiliation of allowing a man to whip me, as if he somehow had the right to punish me and not across my back but with my bare bottom stuck out to take the blows. The idea filled me with disgust and outrage, but every time the awful thoughts came I found myself desperately pushing them away as a very different emotion began to creep up on me – desire.

Stephen didn't seem to notice, but then once he'd got going he always handled me like a puppet anyway, which added another dimension to my disturbing thoughts. I'd always liked men to be a bit rough with me in bed, or at the very least to take control, which made me wonder if Violet and I were much the same except in that she had learned to give herself completely while I hadn't, or not yet. It hurt just to think about it, and yet I could remember all too clearly how the idea of letting a man put his penis in my mouth had once not only disgusted me but also seemed unspeakably degrading. Now it was one of my favourite things.

It took all my effort to concentrate on work the next day, both at lectures and preparing for my essay, which wasn't made any easier by my success at the Chamber. Everybody suddenly wanted to know me, to talk to me, and to invite me to lunches and dinners. I could see that if I didn't watch what I was doing I would start putting on weight, so on the Saturday I signed up for the college rowing club, partly to keep fit and partly so that I could see more of Stephen, but also I knew it would help me to keep my mind off the bizarre erotic daydreams Giles Lancaster had inflicted on me.

My strategy worked, with the effort and discipline of trying to learn a new skill keeping me busy and tired, while Stephen was delighted. He'd also been blackballed by the Hawkubites, to my surprise and his own. They'd apparently done it in the old-fashioned style, with the existing members placing either white or black marbles in a bag, all completely anonymous. In Stephen's case there had been a single black marble among the white, but acceptance had to be unanimous and that was that. Giles had been sympathetic, reporting the vote in more detail than he was really supposed to, but had no idea who had voted against Stephen, or why. I commiserated with him, but was secretly glad, both because of what they did and because for a politician having a partner with a past can be nearly as damaging as having a past yourself.

In response Stephen threw himself into his work, his rowing and me. The evening after his rejection we went out drinking, then returned to his room. He was so eager he had me on the floor the first time, then put me into his bed for a second round before we fell asleep and a third in the morning. I didn't leave Emmanuel until gone noon, and missed rowing practice that afternoon, so the following day the coach told me to take a skiff down as far as the Donnington Bridge and back.

I accepted the punishment, blushing a bit in front of all the other Boniface girls I'd let down, but as soon as I was on the river I was happy again. Up until then I'd rowed in eights and fours, in which teamwork is everything, but in the skiff I was alone, with only the cox of the men's third eight on the tow path to yell at me if I slacked. I had no reason to, enjoying stretching my muscles and determined to make a good time in order to re-establish myself with the other girls.

The scene was idyllic; the sun glistening on the Isis, the rich colours of the autumn foliage along the banks, the meadows and the spires and turrets of the university beyond, rising tawny against blue as they had done for hundred of years while the world moved on. A painted houseboat pulling past me to one side fitted perfectly with the scene, the black and green livery set off by baskets of geraniums hung from bow to stern. Even a girl on the bank might have just been listening to stories with the Reverend Dodgson, her simple red dress and her black curls moving in the breeze as she walked, stopped where the straggling twigs of half-grown silver birch hung down over the water and began to pick them.

She was quite a long way away, and only then did I realise it was Violet. I stopped rowing, my mouth wide as I watched, with all the images I'd tried so hard to push from my head crowding back in; Dr McLean looking stern and dutiful as he hefted the bunch of twigs, Violet's face full of sorrow and resentment as she turned up her dress and took down her knickers, her bare bottom, round and neat and pink, just as I'd seen while she brought herself to orgasm with it stuck up in the air, no doubt imagining her lover chastising her as she came.

If the cox yelled a warning I never heard it, only the awful, splintering crash as my skiff hit the houseboat at full speed. We'd been shown how to bale out, and I'd dropped the oars and got my feet free as the boat began to settle sideways, with water sloshing over the side to wet my legs. I tried to jump, but only succeeded in flopping myself out into the water, leaving me, the oars and the ruined skiff spinning slowly in the wake of the houseboat as it moved on.

* * *

Once I'd hauled myself out of the river and listened to the unreserved opinions of the cox, the coach, the owner of the houseboat and the captain of the boat club I could have done with a supportive word from Stephen, but for once he wasn't there. I made for college instead, picking bits of waterweed out of my hair as I walked up St Aldate's and doing my best to ignore the curious stares directed at my dripping, nearly see-through clothes.

Back at Boniface I stripped off and climbed into the shower. Washed and dried, with my hair wrapped in one towel and another draped over me, I collapsed onto the bed, thinking black thoughts that mellowed gradually as my fatigue took over. It had happened in an instant, and I hadn't had to swim very far at all, but the shock combined with being bawled out by people I might have expected to be sympathetic had got to me, draining my energy and leaving me feeling vulnerable, an emotion made keener by thoughts of Violet.

I was in no doubt whatsoever that she'd been picking birch twigs so that Dr McLean could beat her with them, which brought back all my confused, disturbing thoughts. For a long time I simply lay there, staring at the ceiling, my feelings a mess, until at last exhaustion triumphed and I fell asleep.

When I woke up the air was cool and I was in near darkness, leaving me so disorientated that for a moment I thought I was back at home. I had no idea what the time was, but it was dark outside, the only light an abstract pattern of yellow and orange thrown onto the ceiling from streetlamps and windows. I thought I'd heard a noise, but couldn't be sure whether I'd been dreaming or not, until it came again, a knock at my door, then a voice.

'Poppy?'

It was Violet, and I was going to answer, eager for somebody to lend a sympathetic ear and perhaps fuss over me a little, but I was still groggy with sleep and didn't respond immediately. Another voice spoke, James McLean.

'She's probably with Stephen, or asleep.'

At the sound of his voice I decided not to answer, with all my curiosity and concern crowding back into my head. They were up to something, I was sure of it, from the tone of their voices more than anything.

Violet spoke again, doubtful. 'Maybe. Poppy?'

She knocked again, harder, but I ignored her. Stephen said something in a voice too low to catch. Violet giggled in response and a lump had begun to grow in my throat. I lay still, listening as they went into her room, my ears straining as their voices faded but my imagination easily filling in what I could no longer hear.

They'd wanted to know if I was in and they thought I wasn't. That meant they needed to make sure they were safe, and it was all too obvious what they wanted to be safe for. I could picture every detail in my head; Violet nervous as she presented the birch she'd picked for his inspection, Dr McLean calm and full of authority as he took it from her. She would still be in her old-fashioned red dress, languid and beautiful even as she bent to touch her toes, her eyes full of fear or maybe longing, resentment or lust, most likely a mixture. Her bottom would be the highest part of her body, stuck up in a pose at once lewd and slightly ridiculous, with her back curved to make her cheeks part and ensure that she was showing everything once her dress had been turned up onto her back and her knickers pulled down.

All of a sudden I was painfully aware of my own nudity. The towel had got wrapped around me as I slept, leaving my breasts and the curve of my hip naked. I got up, wondering if I should make some noise to alert them to my presence but instead slipped into my bathrobe as quietly as I could. Next door Dr McLean laughed, a throaty chuckle that seemed to me both wicked and knowing. Again I imagined Violet holding her pose, trembling and scared as he deliberately tormented her by holding back the threat of the bundle of spiky little twigs in his hand, and with that I knew I had to look.

I did try to resist, but it was hopeless. It was just too easy to open my door and duck down at the keyhole. As I knew from before there was no risk of being caught, while it was easy to get over my guilt by telling myself that if Violet was being abused then I had a responsibility to find out what was going on so that something could be done.

Our oak was shut, leaving a thin pencil of light striking down from the keyhole to the floor, otherwise only the dull glow from my window. I got down on my knees as I had before, leaning cautiously forwards until I could see, my heart hammering in my chest as I tried to make sense of what I could see; blood-red folds moving as if to a gentle breeze. Then Dr McLean spoke, his voice now clear. 'Do you accept that you need to be punished?'

Only then, as he stepped forwards, did I realise that I was looking at the back of his gown. He was in full subfusc, the gorgeous scarlet and blue of his doctoral gown over immaculate white tie, while in his hand he held the birch twigs, a thick bunch of them tied tight with a bright-red ribbon I recognised as one Violet occasionally wore in her hair. She was seated on her bed, also in subfusc, but the feminine version, a white blouse and black ribbon tie, black tights and skirt, and black shoes. Her hands were folded in her lap and she was fidgeting with the lowest button of her blouse as she looked up to him, her eyes wide and her lower lip pushed out a little in a sulky, resentful pout. She hadn't answered him, and he spoke again. 'Well, Violet, do you accept that you need to be punished?'

'Yes, sir.'

She sounded frightened yet highly aroused and I found myself remembering the night I'd lost my virginity; scared yet eager as my boyfriend fumbled my knickers off with his cock rearing above my open sex. With that came understanding, or at least what I hoped was understanding, because her expression spoke of emotions as intense as mine had been that night.

Dr McLean spoke again. 'So be it. You have made your birch well, so there will be no need for extra strokes, just the usual dozen.'

'And then?'

'And then you will say thank you.'

He sounded amused, also cruel, and I saw Violet swallow. I didn't understand, but there was no mistaking his next command.

'I will have you kneeling.'

Violet obeyed immediately, although she was shaking badly as she climbed onto her bed, adopting more or less the position I'd imagined, only on all fours and so lewder still, but with her back curved to make an elegant swan's neck and her bottom a neat, round shape beneath her skirt she still looked beautiful and strangely enticing.

Dr McLean nodded and stepped forwards, tracing a slow line across the straining seat of Violet's skirt as he walked past her. He put the birch whip down on the curve of her back and took hold of her skirt, tugging it gently up. Violet had begun to bite her lip as her exposure began and even safely beyond the door I could share her emotions; shame and fear but excitement too, and the thrill of being laid naked in front of your lover.

She was in stockings and a suspender belt, framing the seat of her full black French knickers, dark against her pale skin. Dr McLean gave a pleased chuckle as he saw, the same sound I'd heard before; a little cruel, a little amused, full of pleasure for her surrender to his peculiar vice. A brief smile flickered across her face in response, before she hung her head, her eyes closed and her mouth wide as if waiting for some exquisite sexual thrill.

All he did was pull her knickers down, very slowly, the way dirty-minded men like to do it, but without touching her, and yet the sigh that escaped her lips as her bottom came bare suggested far more than the simple naughty buzz I got when it was done to me. He didn't even take them off either, but left them stretched between her open thighs, adding to the effect of a frame around her now naked bottom.

She was ready for it, as bare and vulnerable as he could possibly have wished, or so I thought, but he wanted her still more fully exposed. Reaching beneath her tummy, he tugged her blouse free of her waistband and turned it up all the way to her shoulders before undoing her bra and flipping the cups up from her breasts. She'd begun to sob as she was exposed, her whole body shaking to the intensity of her emotion.

Had I seen a picture of what was going on I would have said she was in a state of misery, shame and fear, but I now realised that I would have been imposing my own preconceptions onto her. She had put a hand back between her legs, stroking herself gently, not the reaction of a woman in a bad state, but of a woman as happy as she was uninhibited. Dr McLean saw what she was doing and reached down to remove her fingers, speaking as he did so.

'Oh no you don't, young lady. You're to be beaten first.'

'Please?'

'Behave!'

'Yes, sir. Sorry, sir.'

'Good girl. Lift your bottom a little more.'

She already had it stuck high in the air, but did her best to oblige, letting her arms slide apart to lay her chest on the bed and making the curve of her back more hollow still. He was grinning as he stepped back, his lust getting the better of his pose of authority. She closed her eyes as he stroked the bundle of birch across her naked bottom, lifted it, and brought it down with a swish and a smack.

Violet yelped as the twigs hit home, but she stayed as she was, allowing him to apply a second stroke, and a third. With the fourth she had begun to kick her feet and toss her hair. Her whole body was shaking, her muscles twitching to the strokes, while again and again she made to reach back for her sex, only to pull back. I wanted to do the same, for all that I was telling myself I could not possibly masturbate over the sight of another woman being whipped, even if she was so obviously enjoying it.

Dr McLean had said twelve strokes and he kept his word, dropping the birch the instant he'd finished. Violet moved immediately, twisting around to come into his open arms, her body shaking with violent sobs and the tears streaming down her face as she hugged him. He held her, stroking her hair and whispering to her, never once attempting to touch her sexually until she had finished sobbing out her emotions onto his chest. Only then did he ease her gently down to her knees on the floor and free his cock into her mouth.

I realised what he had meant by making her say thank you – sucking his cock – and with that my restraint broke. The idea of a woman having to thank a man for whipping her was too much. I ran back into my room, utterly confused, not knowing if I wanted to scream or to masturbate, to hide myself away for ever or to push out my naked bottom and take my hairbrush to my own cheeks, to rush in next door and punch Dr McLean as hard as I could or get down on my knees beside Violet and help her suck him off.

7

For the next three days I barely slept, barely ate, barely worked. Only on the Monday did I force myself to resume my normal life, and even then it was mechanical. I could not get what I had seen out of my head, nor stop myself from imagining how I would have felt in Violet's place, undergoing the same appalling ritual; my acceptance of what was to be done to me, the exposure of my bottom, the pain of the beating, having my smarting cheeks rubbed with cream, and lastly taking my persecutor's cock in my mouth to say thank you for what had been done to me. It was that last detail that really got to me, the idea that I was the one who should be saying thank you when I was the one who'd been beaten, and by sucking his cock. Nothing could be more unfair, more unjust, and yet when I finally gave in to my needs and masturbated over the memory that was what I came over.

Nor was it just about sex. I had never seen a woman give up her emotions the way Violet had after her beating, clinging to the man who had done it and crying her eyes out as he comforted her. While I wasn't sure if I understood, it had seemed to me that her experience had gone far beyond physical pleasure, providing a catharsis for her emotions maybe somewhere between orgasm and religious penitence. I had never imagined such a thing, and my head still rebelled against the idea, but it was also compelling. Not that I was going to try, partly because I knew I could never let myself go so completely with Stephen, which in turn made me wonder at how deep the bond between Violet and James McLean went.

As with when I had first learned about Violet taking the birch, my ruffled emotions gradually calmed with time and the busy routine of my Oxford life. Work was the best way to keep my mind off things, and it was going well, or at least as well as I could have hoped. I'd always known I wasn't a serious candidate for a first, but of the five PPE students at Boniface I came comfortably in the middle. I also got on with Dr Etheridge, having quickly learned that the easiest way to get on was to discuss all sides of an issue and then reach similar conclusions to those he did in his numerous books.

Stephen and I settled into a comfortable relationship, going out together two or three times a week and sharing a bed at weekends, along with the occasional passionate encounter during the day and usually on the riverbank. The only problem was that even in our most intimate moments I would find my thoughts going to Violet and Dr McLean rather than my lover, but I was sure I'd get over that with time.

I managed to redeem myself with the boat club, at least partially, by doing well in the trials and getting into the women's boat at number two, although I had to accept the nickname of the Wrecker from my team-mates.

The Chamber remained my first priority, and I began to work on manoeuvring myself into a position where I'd be able to stand for one of the lesser posts in due time, and then for President. That meant winning support from as many quarters as possible but never committing myself so fully that I alienated anybody. Inevitably I gained a reputation as a Chamber hack, but I'd known that would happen from the start and made a point of being pleasant to my detractors.

I also made a point of being pleasant to Giles Lancaster, as he was not only Recorder but he also had considerable influence. He continued to treat me with easy condescension, but he was seeing more and more of Stephen, which meant I was spared his most barbed comments and having to reject any advances, or so I thought.

He had taken to enlisting my support for the various projects and campaigns he was involved in and had hinted that he'd want me on his team the next time he spoke at a debate, so I wasn't at all surprised to get a note in my pigeonhole inviting me to lunch at a restaurant called The Perch on the Saturday of my fourth week. I'd bought a bike by then, and cycled out, mildly intrigued by his request but no more. Even when I discovered that he was alone I thought nothing of it, and accepted his invitation to join him at a table in the bay of a window overlooking the river. He had ordered a bottle of white wine, and gave an airy flourish of his fingers towards the ice bucket as he sat down.

'I do adore Oxford, don't you?'

'Yes, I suppose I do. I'm beginning to anyway.'

'That is good, because so many of the students view being here, rather than at some ghastly redbrick, as no more than a stepping stone in their careers, while it should be so much more.'

I poured myself a drink. 'How do you mean?'

'To a man like me Oxford is an essential part of life, as it was to my father, and his father before him – my great-grandfather went to some obscure institute in the Fenlands for some unaccountable reason – but with each succeeding generation it has become harder to get in, to the point at which I fear my own children will not only have to be brilliant, which I expect of them, but also impossible little swots, which I'd rather they weren't. It's very sad.'

'But surely merit is the only fair criteria for admission?'

'Certainly, but what is merit? If it is merely the ability to regurgitate what has been drummed into our heads at school, then I want none of it. Memory, my dear, is not to be confused with intelligence. No, it would be better by far if the swots contented themselves with Bristol, Durham and suchlike places, and left Oxford to dream. For you I shall make an exception. One must have beauty. Besides, I believe that Mitchell told me your father was at Boniface?'

'And Grandpa, and his father.'

'A West Country college for a West Country family. I approve.'

It was unlike him to compliment me on anything except my looks and I began to wonder where he was leading me. More likely than not he wanted something, perhaps for me to exert my influence on one of the women's groups. I decided to tease him a little. 'Do you know who you remind me of, Giles? Anthony Blanche from *Brideshead Revisited*.'

To my surprise he smiled. 'Ah, to be compared to one of the aesthetes of the 1920s, even a fictitious one! Thank you, Violet, and yes, I suppose I am rather like him. I even took you to Thame, didn't I? But don't worry, I have no intention of warning you off Stephen, who is essentially sound, despite being a bit of a rugger bugger. But then, you like it rough, don't you?'

He gave me a conspiratorial wink. I found myself blushing and wondering what Stephen had told him.

He smiled and reached out to pat my hand. 'You mustn't be embarrassed, Poppaea. It's not as if you've been up to naughties with Dr James McLean.'

The heat in my cheeks flared higher still, but he carried on blithely.

'No, there's no cause at all for embarrassment, just the opposite. A fine young girl like yourself should be proud to enjoy a spot of hearty sex, don't you agree?'

'I suppose so. I'm certainly not ashamed of myself.'

'That's the spirit! Now, shall we order? The pheasant suggests itself. It would be my first of the season.'

I was glad to change the subject, and he didn't return to it, speaking of game and wine, then drawing me out about sailing on the Exe Estuary, so easy and polite that I'd soon begun to let my defences down. We had a bottle of red with the pheasant, and glasses of something sweet and heavy with slices of treacle pudding, leaving me feeling full and more than a little tipsy as he settled the bill and guided me outside.

'Walk by the river with me.'

'I'm rowing at three o'clock.'

'I'll drive you over.'

'I'm not sure you should drive.'

'I'm certain you shouldn't cycle and, besides, I have a proposition for you.'

'Ah, I thought you might. Chamber business?'

'Nothing so mundane, and not something for common ears.'

He had taken my arm, a gesture so old fashioned I felt sure it was affected, but it wasn't intrusive and so I let him. We'd reached the riverbank and I let him steer me upstream, along a well-worn path that faded gradually as we came out among fields and little copses of willow and hawthorn. He didn't speak again until we were completely alone.

'As I was saying before lunch, you belong here. You are a part of the real Oxford, or rather of the ideal Oxford, and you are also the most spirited, the most sporting and quite the prettiest girl at university.'

'No I'm not, and you know it.'

'Not at all. Some might beat you if you were to compete in some tawdry seaside beauty contest, it's true, but you are fire where they are mere embers.'

I wanted to tell him he was drunk and that I wasn't that easily flattered, but I was too curious and no more sober.

'I'm little Miss Perfect, but what are you after?'

'Very well, you have forced my hand. I shall tell all. The Hawkubites have finally managed to find somewhere to hold our Michaelmas dinner; a new restaurant in Goring-on-Thames, the owners of which are quite delightfully innocent. I would like to invite you as my personal guest.'

'I thought the Hawkubites was a male-only society?'

'It is, and has been for nearly three hundred years, but female guests have attended on a few occasions. It's a great honour, as I'm sure you'll agree, although naturally it comes with certain provisos attached.'

Even drunk I had begun to smell a rat. 'What provisos exactly?'

'Oh, nothing you can't cope with, just keeping to the dress code, enjoying yourself, being a good sport, and of course, keeping what happens to yourself. Stephen, in particular, must never know, as I'm sure you'll agree. The poor boy would only be jealous.'

'And the dress code is? A school uniform perhaps? A saucy French maid's outfit? Or just stark naked? And what's for afters, blow-jobs all round?'

'Ah ha, I detect from your tone that you are not keen on the idea, in which case I have been authorised to offer you a thousand pounds.'

I'd been meaning to tease him, playing along for a while before turning him down on his outrageous offer, but he had gone too far. We were still arm in arm, and with one quick jerk I had detached myself. One sharp kick to his ankle and he was off balance. A push and he was clawing at the air as he fell backwards, his face set in a truly comic expression of panic and surprise. The bank was about five feet high, above open water, which he hit with a splash, and disappeared briefly beneath the surface before coming up spitting muddy water and flailing for support. He did not look at all happy, and I decided to beat a hasty retreat.

I had reacted instinctively, and as soon as I'd calmed down and sobered up began to worry about the consequences of what I'd done. Fortunately Giles proved too much of a politician to be spiteful, and even sent me a bunch of flowers, which was waiting outside my room when I got back from rowing. The note attached was an apology, saying that he had misjudged me and asking my forgiveness. I didn't believe a word of it, but decided to accept on the grounds that if the story got out it was sure to do me more harm than good. I also decided not to tell Stephen, both because Giles could simply deny everything or claim that I'd come on to him and because it wasn't something I wanted to share.

That was the sensible choice, but it didn't help with my feelings. Giles had effectively asked me to prostitute myself, and he had to have thought there was a fair chance I'd accept. I tried to tell myself that it was simply a result of his bizarre, public-school attitude towards women, but he had touched a nerve. Had I accepted it would have meant he'd made me a high-class call-girl, something I'd fantasised over more times than I could remember.

I knew I would never do it, but it didn't hurt to think about it, save for the shame of imagining myself in the hands of the man who had dared to proposition me. Several times I'd considered asking Stephen if he'd like to play out a fantasy, but sex between us had always been too raw and too urgent for that sort of thing. Now I was glad I hadn't, because I was fairly sure it would have got back to Giles, and I definitely couldn't do it in the near future, because if he found out he would assume it was his offer which had triggered my fantasy, an unbearable thought. He might also repeat the offer.

All of it was still in my head as I went through the motions of rowing practice, which was now so familiar that I could follow the cox's calls without conscious effort. I was even commended on my rhythm by the coach, and by Stephen, who had finished just before us and was standing outside the Emmanuel boathouse as we came in. He looked sweaty and masculine, his clothes plastered to the hard muscles of his chest and abdomen, making me smile as I approached him.

'Hi, did you see that? We bumped the second boat before they'd reached The Boatman's.'

'That was good, but you'll have to do better if you want to beat the City boats.'

'We're getting there. Are you going back to college?'

'Yes, the long way round, if you like?'

We'd frequently taken out our passion on each other in the meadows by Jackdaw Lane, and I knew exactly what he meant. My feelings were still a bit raw after my encounter with Giles, and I was going to refuse, only to think of how amused he'd be to know he'd got to me. Instead I smiled and offered my hand to Stephen.

A lot of people were looking at us as we walked across the front of the boathouses, some of them no doubt with a pretty clear idea of what we were up to, but that I didn't mind. As Giles himself had pointed out there's nothing wrong with straightforward, healthy sex, certainly nothing to be ashamed of, although I did prefer people not to know we did it outside quite so often. That didn't seem to bother Stephen at all, his hand closing on my bottom as we waited for a friendly punt to take us across the mouth of the Cherwell.

I was still conscious of watching eyes when we'd reached the far side, and made him walk me quite a way up Jackdaw Lane before letting myself be pulled into the bushes. We chose the same place we'd used the first time, our favourite, where the low elder branch allowed me to sit down and indulge my love of cock worship in comfort. He'd got used to it, and went to stand in place before I'd caught up, making me smile as he spoke. 'I'll have the usual please, Miss Miller.'

'Certainly, Mr Mitchell.'

He turned me on, just from the set of his powerful body and hot scent of his skin, but even as I sat down and began to nuzzle my face against the bulge in his rowing shorts I was having to make myself do it. Only as he began to stiffen did my rising desire push away my ill feelings, as I'd hoped it would. Soon I was nibbling and kissing at the long hard shape of his erection through his shorts, deliberately teasing myself until I was desperate to get him bare and into my mouth.

I was about to do it, but he broke first, muttering something unintelligible and snatching the front of his shorts aside to expose himself. With his cock and balls free to the weak autumn sunlight I took a moment simply to admire him before running the tip of my tongue all the way up, once, twice and a third time before popping him in my mouth. He gave a groan of satisfaction as I began to suck. His hands settled on my head, holding me firmly in place on his erection to stop me teasing, and I got down to work.

He was eager, pushing into my mouth and occasionally releasing his grip on my head to squeeze at his balls and tug on his shaft, until I was sure he would come at any moment. I wasn't ready, and needed more despite the thrill of paying court to his cock, and pulled my top up to hold my breasts as I sucked, sure I was going to end up masturbating in front of him one more time. He saw, his voice hoarse with pleasure as he spoke.

'Bad girl. I'm going to have to fuck you.'

His words were music to my ears. I pulled back immediately,

turning my back to him and bending down with my hands on the branch. He'd twitched up my skirt and pulled my knickers down in an instant, baring me to his erection, but the position I was in and the act of being exposed behind had instantly turned my mind to Violet and the birch.

I tried to make it go away, but even as my body was filled I was imagining a variation of that awful routine, in which I'd be beaten and then fucked as my thank you instead of made to suck cock. To make it worse, Stephen was thrusting into me so fast and so deep that his hard belly was smacking against my bottom, adding to the fantasy. I gave in, telling myself that what he didn't know wouldn't hurt him, but full of guilt as I thought of myself in the same position to Dr McLean, my skirt lifted and my knickers pulled down, my bottom smacked and his cock inside me as I was made to say thank you for my punishment.

There was as much despair as ecstasy in my groans as Stephen pushed into me, faster and faster, but I couldn't stop myself. My hand went back to find my sex and I was playing with myself as I was fucked, already close to orgasm as I imagined the humiliation of being stripped in the woods, beaten and fucked.

I think I must have been mumbling something, or maybe it was because I was playing with myself, but Stephen suddenly slowed down and pulled out, only to enter me again as he spoke. 'You are such a bad girl, Poppy Miller, but I know you like to come first so I'll let you, but you're going to have to pay for it.'

My first thought was that if I was such a bad girl I ought to have my bottom smacked, and I was so far gone I might have asked, but for the rest of what he said. I knew what he meant, that he'd make me suck and swallow, or do it in my face, but my mind reacted differently. He'd said I'd have to pay, but I was immediately imagining that he had paid me, and not just to suck him or bend over for entry, but for the whole crazed fantasy that had been building up in my head.

Again I tried to stop myself, but I was too close to orgasm and he'd begun to repeat the same trick, pulling out and entering me over and over again, adding a final, utterly filthy detail to my fantasy. In my mind's eye I was no longer just with him, or James McLean. I was bent over the same branch, my bottom bare and rosy from a good whipping, a bundle of fifty-pound notes tucked into the waistband of my pulled-down knickers, as Violet watched Stephen, James, Giles and the entire membership of the Hawkubites take turns with me. They'd be lined up behind me, the cocks I'd just sucked erect clutched in their hands, penetrating me one by one, again and again, just as Stephen was doing.

I came, screaming out loud at the awful thought of being made to prostitute myself with a dozen men, for a whipping and sex, without even being taken somewhere private so that they could take me one at a time, but in public and in front of my friend so that they all got to see how dirty I was, and that there was no possible doubt that I'd been paid.

8

Curiously, letting my imagination go so completely helped me to come to terms with what was going on in my head, at least to the point that I realised I would have to accept it as part of me, and cope. After all, I was developing fast in an unfamiliar world in which for the first time in my life I had to take responsibility for my own actions and, by and large, I felt I was doing quite well. I'd been reasonably careful with my money, kept to a fairly sensible amount of drink and avoided picking up any new vices such as smoking or drugs. I was doing fairly well at work and at sport, very well at the Chamber, and all of that because I made an effort to keep my life under control.

There was no reason my sexuality should prove any different. I'd developed an old fantasy, being a high-class call-girl, and found a new one, being whipped, but there was no reason I should give in to either, any more than I had needed to accept the challenge some of Giles' friends had given me in the Chamber bar one evening, to try to drink an entire magnum of champagne in one go. Even my faintly disturbing feelings for Violet didn't need to intrude on real life.

A few days after pushing Giles Lancaster into the river I'd got my head around the situation well enough to deliberately bring myself to orgasm over a complicated fantasy involving being paid to give oral sex to just about everyone I'd met in recent weeks, or at least all the attractive ones. I even included Violet, briefly, and was left feeling satisfied both sexually and because I felt I'd got things under control.

I had, at least for a while, and things stayed pretty much the same for the rest of the Michaelmas term. Stephen and I grew gradually more intimate, until he was calling me Miller as a matter of course and he knew how to please me better than any man before, both in bed and out. Giles Lancaster treated me with at least a measure of respect and didn't make any more rude suggestions, while both of us kept what had happened firmly to ourselves. The regatta went well, if not exceptionally so, and I passed my first collections without any real difficulty. The Hawkubites held their dinner without me, trashed the restaurant as they had trashed so many before. Two of them were arrested, but not Giles.

It was only when I returned to Exeter that I realised just how much I'd changed in the space of just two months. Every-thing seemed smaller, or rather, lesser; my old friendships, my parents' authority, even the buildings, everything but the land-scape. That was bigger, the dark bulk of Haldon and the great sweep of the estuary raw and primitive beside the gentler hills and slow waterways around Oxford.

I spent most of my time at home, consciously avoiding Ewan and his friends, only going out occasionally and then with girls I'd known since childhood. Even there things had changed, and not just what they wanted to talk about, but their whole atti-tude to life. One was getting married in the spring, another was pregnant, both things I couldn't even consider for at least ten years. They had no more understanding of my attitude than I did of theirs.

Christmas was the usual family affair, with aunts and uncles and cousins all together around a colossal turkey, presents and drink and arguments and a long afternoon walk beside flooded meadows. At New Year I tried to recapture something of what I felt I'd lost by going out to a party with all my old school friends, but found myself repeatedly defending my decision to leave Ewan, despite the fact that he was now comfortably shacked up with Carrie Endicott. I left early and listened to the bells ringing in the New Year as I walked home through empty streets.

Hilary term didn't start until the middle of January, leaving me two long weeks with very little to do and everybody I knew was either away or wrapped up in work. In the end I went back up a few days early, only to find Oxford empty and cold. I'd known perfectly well that Violet was spending the break in Florence and wouldn't be there, but I still found myself expecting her to pop her head around the door and offer coffee, while I found myself visiting Emmanuel simply to be where Stephen and I had walked together so often. Like Violet, he was abroad, but in Florida, teaching high-school children to row as a volunteer.

On the third occasion I found my steps taking me to Emmanuel I got such a peculiar look from the head porter that I walked on past the lodge. Not really knowing where I was headed, I carried on along Broad Street and turned up Parks Road. There was frost on the trees and a cold clear sky overhead, but I was well wrapped up, as was the man walking towards me, so that I didn't recognise him until we were just yards apart – Dr James McLean.

'Poppy? How nice to see a familiar face. You're up very early.'

I could have made any one of a dozen excuses but found myself telling the truth. 'I was bored at home. Everything had changed.'

'The loss of childhood pleasures is the price you pay for growing up, I fear.'

'My friends didn't seem to have changed.'

'But you have. I remember feeling the same when I first came up.'

I smiled, grateful for his understanding and he carried on.

'But you must be bored stiff?'

'There's plenty of work I can do.'

'And no play, what with the boats in and hardly anyone about. Come to dinner with me this evening and we'll console each other over a bottle of something.'

'Thank you. I'd like that.'

I had accepted without a second thought, and it was only after we'd parted that I began to have misgivings. Never once in the time I had known him had we been alone, while he had figured so prominently in my fantasies that I wasn't at all sure if I could resist any advance he might make. I told myself I would simply decline, and that I had a dozen good reasons to do so – Stephen, Violet, his age and what he would no doubt want to do to me – but I knew deep down that only the knowledge that I'd be betraying my friends really mattered. Yet that was enough, while I needed company and didn't want to find an excuse after having accepted his invitation.

He lived just east of Oxford on the Eynsham Road, a house I knew Violet had visited frequently, although I'd never been before. As I cycled out along the Botley Road I couldn't help but think of what the two of them got up to, so that by the time I'd crossed the ring road I was imagining some vast and Gothic mansion with ravens flapping around the turrets and heavy iron grilles across the windows.

Nothing could have been further from the reality, a converted barn set back from the road in a neat garden, now colourless but which looked as if it would be beautiful by the spring. The interior was no more threatening, a single open space beneath the original beams with the bedroom and bathroom built into an upper level. Only one feature was remotely suspicious, a huge iron hook bolted through the width of a beam directly above the centre of the living room, but even that looked ancient, so no doubt was original and used for something to do with farming rather than hanging up recalcitrant girls by their wrists for a dose of the whip. He was friendly and relaxed, suggesting juice rather than wine as I would have to cycle back later, although his conversation was typically profound and difficult to follow.

'... did you see the installation outside the Saïd? You must have passed it as you cycled over.'

'Um ... there was a laser show.'

'Now that is a very telling statement. David Warburton says it is art. But is it?'

'I'm not sure. It's very pretty.'

'You are very pretty. Violet is very pretty. But neither of you is art, because no skill went into your creation: presupposing the absence of a creator, that is.'

'It's your subject. Do you think it is?'

'If you look in a dictionary you will see that the primary definition of art is skill, in which case it is not art, or if it is the credit should go to the people who designed the laser lights rather than to David for arranging them.'

'But surely it's the effect that counts?'

'Given the equipment, I expect you or I could have done as well, if not better. You see, David's argument is that it's art because he, the artist, says it's art, and he has managed to convince a great many apparently sensible people to part with a great deal of money on the assumption that it is art. On the other hand, a cynic might argue that he is forced into that argument because he wants to be an artist but has insufficient skill.'

'And what's the answer?'

'The point remains open, but I suspect that should history remember him at all it will not be as an artist but as a charming rogue.'

'A con-artist?'

'Very clever! I'd put that in my review, but he'd probably sue me.'

'Do you write reviews?'

'I write whatever I can persuade people to take nowadays. I am, as you know, in disgrace.'

I found myself blushing, embarrassed for having inadvertently caused him to bring up the subject of his expulsion from Mary's. It was tempting to ask what had happened, to see if he would talk about it, or lie; or, if he told the truth, how he would explain himself. I didn't dare, instead I changed the subject.

'Whatever you're making smells delicious. Do you cook?'

'Yes, but only in so far as a bachelor has to if he'd rather not sink to ready meals and take-aways. It's tagliatelle with porcini mushrooms, and will end up as tagliatelle with mysterious burned bits if I don't attend to it.'

He went to the cooker and I sat down at the table, sipping my juice as we talked. There was nothing sexual in his conversation, no sly innuendos, no hints that there might be something between us, nothing beyond the casually delivered remark that Violet and I were pretty. I wondered if he was trying to lull me into developing a false sense of security before he pounced, but if so he was in no rush. We ate, drank coffee and talked, covering subjects as commonplace as the approaching election and as obscure as French theatre in the late nineteenth century. He seemed to know a little about everything and a great deal about many things, rather like a younger version of my dad, except that he had few firm opinions, preferring to keep his mind open at all times.

It was nearly midnight by the time I left, and he had not made so much as a suggestive remark, despite having drunk the best part of a bottle of strong red wine and a glass of whisky.

I'd been tempted to flirt, just to see if I could provoke a reaction, but thoughts of Stephen and Violet held me back, along with the possibility that I might get more than I'd bargained for. He didn't even kiss me goodnight.

Cycling back towards Oxford, I was conscious of a strange sense of disappointment, almost of loss, as if something important was supposed to have happened but hadn't. I tried to tell myself that his behaviour had been perfectly correct, and it had, between a don and a female undergraduate, only he wasn't a don any more, but an ex-don who'd been disgraced for seducing a much younger girl into kinky sex.

I stopped outside the Saïd to look at David Warburton's light installation, which before had seemed a pretty display if nothing more. Now I found myself wanting to criticise it for being pretentious, or write some suitably scathing comment on the pedestal. Fortunately I had no way of doing so and moved on after a few minutes, wondering why I felt so strange.

The next few days passed slowly. With the empty college and the cold clear air, Oxford had taken on a dreamlike quality for me, very different to the bustle of my first term and yet more compelling. I took to exploring, on long walks beside the different waterways or among the smaller streets of the city's heart, but never far into what I'd come to think of as town. Again and again I found myself following Jackdaw Lane.

On the Saturday I decided to treat myself to lunch at The Boatman's, drinking beer and then gin and tonic to leave me feeling pleasantly tipsy and nostalgic. I visited the little space among the trees where Stephen and I had made love so often, then turned down the bank and past the sight of my boat wreck, where I'd seen Violet picking birch.

The tree was now bare, the twigs black and scratchy against

the eggshell blue of the sky and the silvery bark, each one outlined by a trace of frost where the feeble sunlight had yet to reach. I reached out to touch, imagining I was Violet as I rolled the thin brittle stem between finger and thumb. She'd had to pick a bunch in the knowledge that she would be beaten with it, a thought that set my stomach fluttering.

I could imagine her feelings all too easily, vexation at the thought of what was to be done to her, resentment for having to make her own implement of chastisement, embarrassment for the watchful eyes of people along the river, some of whom might know what she was doing, but those same emotions causing an irresistible thrill and kicking off an arousal that would not be satisfied for hours, until she'd been exposed, beaten and put on her knees to suck her tormentor's cock.

Just the thought had my breathing ragged, and I'd have picked some birch if there had been anybody to deal with me – that wonderful expression James McLean had used, implying that a good thrashing with birch twigs was something I'd benefit from and which he could give me. As he'd deal with my request for a book or an application to join a society, only what he'd be dealing with was my bottom, my bare bottom, after which I'd have to say thank you.

I almost ran to get away from that tree, and would have done had it not been for the two bar staff from The Boatman's smoking in the otherwise deserted beer garden. Instead I walked, frightened by the intensity of my own reaction, despite having thought I'd got it under control. At that moment I realised that fantasy would not be enough. I had to at least try it, and maybe that way I could break the spell.

Unfortunately, or perhaps fortunately, there was nobody to do it for me, as Stephen was still away and I'd never have dared ask Dr McLean. That did nothing to reduce my need. As I continued my walk down river I tried to tell myself that I was being silly, but it was no good. I needed to know how those twigs would feel across my bare skin, and to suffer the whole awful ritual, and I needed it soon.

I walked fast, telling myself I shouldn't have drunk so much at lunchtime and the disturbing feelings would go away if I got some fresh air. The path grew fainter, then gave out altogether and I found myself skirting some allotments that ended at a road. Not wanting to turn back into the city, I crossed Donnington Bridge and set off down the river again, along a well-worn path.

That path was my sole protection against an idea that had begun to form in my mind; too busy and in plain view of the river for what I wanted to do but was telling myself I shouldn't. Not that there was anybody around, but there might have been, and that kept me safe as I followed the river, under the ring road and out onto a spit of land where the two main channels of the Isis join together.

A weir crossed the lesser branch, the high water passing over it with a steady roar, while a long walkway would have allowed me to cross to the far side. I didn't, telling myself I should turn back but knowing full well that I had no such intention. Instead I followed the lesser branch, beneath gently humming pylon lines to where a fringe of trees flanked the water, oak and ash, holly and yew still in leaf, and birch.

I had to do it, my need too great to resist and the risks of being caught too slim to allow me an excuse. There was nobody to be seen, just the empty meadows, still flooded in places, the river and the trees, under which I was completely sheltered. I found the perfect place after a minute or two of searching, an open space beneath a single huge oak with a screen of holly bushes to hide me from sight. Nearby was a clump of birch, the twigs hanging low and inviting.

My fingers were shaking as I began to pick the birch, twig

after twig, all the while telling myself I was only doing it to push my ridiculous fantasies out of my head once and for all, that the pain would soon make me see sense. I knew it was a lie, because as the bunch in my hand grew my arousal was soaring, until my nipples had grown painfully stiff and I felt damp and warm between my legs.

Violet had used a ribbon from her hair to tie the bundle tight and make a handle for James to hold, but I hadn't worn ribbons since I was six. My belt served instead, making a cruder, but perhaps more businesslike birch whip. Just to hold it made me want to take down my clothes and stick my bottom out for punishment, and I scampered back to my hiding place full of embarrassment and anticipation for what I was about to do.

Having made absolutely sure that nobody was about, I put the birch down and unfastened my jeans. I was still glancing guiltily from side to side as I pushed them down, careful not to take my knickers as well, because that was a moment I wanted to savour, as Violet had done. My shaking had grown uncontrollable as I pushed my thumbs into my waistband and closed my eyes.

She'd been in ecstasy as she was stripped and, as I let my bottom come slowly bare, I felt I could appreciate something of the thrill. Certainly it was stronger than just stripping to show off, when I knew I was baring my cheeks not to tease or for the caress of a boyfriend's hands, but to be whipped. Being bare, always a pleasure save in the most mundane of circumstances, now felt vulnerable, almost frightening as I tried to imagine James and Violet watching, her eyes bright with excitement and amusement too, he cool and full of authority as he swished the birch through the air to test its weight.

I picked it up, deliberately bending at the waist to make my position as revealing as possible. That felt good, both exciting and shameful, emotions I'd come to realise could enhance each other in a delightful and unexpected way. I knew how much I was showing behind, which any man about to whip me would be able to see, enjoying my exposure while he himself was fully clothed.

The birch felt evil, somehow wicked, the braided leather of my belt around the hard twigs giving it a harsh rustic feel, ideal for whipping a naughty girl in the country. As I hefted it I let my imagination run, pushing thoughts of James away so that I wouldn't feel guilty for Violet. Instead I was to be beaten by a young farmer who'd caught me trespassing and given me the choice of the police or taking down my jeans and panties for a dozen strokes of the birch.

I'd stood up again, my bottom pushed out, and brushed the twigs across my cheeks. It tickled, making me giggle, and I thought of the farmer teasing me, deliberately taking his time so that he could enjoy my half-naked body and my rising consternation as he held off from punishing me properly. A gentle smack tingled slightly, a firmer one slightly more, stinging in places, but no more than I could have taken on my breasts.

Sure that my farmer boy would want to see everything and remembering what James had done to Violet, I pulled up my top and bra. A moment playing with nipples and holding my breasts as I imagined myself being made to show them off and I took the birch to my chest, just hard enough to sting a little. It felt nice, but my bottom was definitely the proper target and I stuck it out again, this time landing the birch across my cheeks with a solid flick of my wrist.

Now it stung, making me squeal and jump up, rubbing at my smarting skin. It had hurt, and I was telling myself I was a fool, completely mad, but that didn't stop me sticking my bottom out again and giving myself a second stroke, harder still.

Again I jumped and squeaked, but I stayed in position, imagining the farmer's words as he beat me; ordering me to stick my bum well out, telling me he could see my anus and that my sex was wet, but far less politely.

With that thought I simply lost control, smacking at my bottom as I imagined what he'd say; telling me that he liked my bottom and boobs, that my cunt was juicy and he was going to fuck it, even that he was tempted to stuff his oversized cock up the wrinkled pink hole between my open cheeks. My mouth came open in a cry of shame and ecstasy for that awful thought and my hand was between my thighs, rubbing at myself even as I smacked the birch down across my now flaming cheeks.

It hurt, a lot, but I wanted more, to be whipped to ecstasy and have my man's cock put in me, up my beaten bottom as I went into climax, which I was doing. I dropped the birch and sank to my knees, my bottom stuck well out, my eyes shut and my mouth wide in a silent scream, rubbing at myself as wave after wave of pleasure swept through me, until I could stand it no more and collapsed gasping onto the cold wet ground.

9

When I got back that evening it was as if I'd got lost and returned to a different city, with the same buildings but otherwise a complete contrast. The weather had changed, with warm, moist air coming in from the West, and it began to rain as I hurried the last few yards along the High. People had been arriving across the day as well, so that college was bustling with students carrying cases and trunks, with everybody greeting one another and asking after friends. Within minutes I'd seen more people I knew than I had in the previous week, and I'd barely had a chance to change before being whisked into hall by two of my fellow PPE students.

Sunday was busier still, and Stephen returned, late in the evening, coming up to my room just as I'd had a shower and having me on the bed, wet and naked. That really put the roses back in my cheeks and we slept together that night, too happy and excited to be back in each other's arms to worry about being tired the next day. Only Violet had not returned, but she had sent a postcard to say that she was coming back via Arles and Paris.

By the middle of the first week everything was going full swing once more. I had lectures to attend, an essay to work on, and a new term in front of me at the Chamber, hopefully as successful as the last. The second debate of the Hilary term was going to be a repeat of the famous King and Country motion, when a majority had voted against fighting for Britain a few years before the Second World War. It was sure to attract attention and I was keen to speak.

So, inevitably, were a lot of other people, and as luck would have it Giles Lancaster was leading the team against the motion, which was the angle I wanted to take. I was sure he'd want to make me grovel, but equally sure that he'd want me on the team. My best chance seemed to be to make a bold move, so I asked him outright at the bar with half-a-dozen of his cronies looking on and quite a few other people within earshot.

His usual facetious drawl had vanished as he replied. 'I'm sure you'd be very good, but we do have the son of one of the original speakers coming as a guest, and a third-year historian who's planning to do a thesis on pacifism in the 1930s. That only leaves one place available, and you'll have to admit that it's not your subject.'

'That's true, but . . .'

'My thought is that you might prefer to be one of the tellers?'

I hesitated. Counting the votes was a responsible job, and a useful one to have done for when I came to stand for an elected post, while to turn the offer down would make me look bad, as Giles knew.

'Unless of course you don't feel up to it?'

'No, I'm fine. I'll do it, thanks.'

'Good girl. Drinkies?'

His patronising tone was back, but I accepted the drink, wondering if he was simply keen to maintain my support or had some ulterior motive in making the offer. I didn't trust him, but it was hard to see what could go wrong, and nothing in his conversation suggested that it was anything more than a straightforward offer.

I stayed quite late at the Chamber, then wandered back to college, really quite glad that I'd spared myself the time and trouble of preparing my speech and going through it with the rest of the team. As a teller my name would still be on the report, while everybody would see that I was considered responsible. Giles was also right to say that it was not my subject.

The first thing I heard when I reached my floor was music coming from Violet's room, a classical piece as usual. I knocked immediately, delighted to hear her voice as she invited me in. She looked as languid as ever, in a slinky black dress that was presumably Italian, with her curls tied back in a tell-tale ribbon and a book in one hand. She put it down, smiling as I came in.

'Poppy! I was wondering where you'd got to?'

'I was at the Chamber. I didn't know you were due back today.'

'I wasn't, but there was a little problem in Paris and I had to leave early.'

'Ooh scandal! What happened?'

I'd caught the tone in her voice and her answering smile showed that I was right. She got up, kissed me and carried on as she started to make coffee. 'I met the most beautiful boy, at the *Espace Dalí*, he ...'

'Hang on. What about James?'

'James? Our relationship isn't like that.'

'No, but ...'

'He doesn't mind what I do, as long as I tell him. In fact, the more I do the better he likes it, because ...' She broke off, rather abruptly I thought, then carried on, full of mischief and enthusiasm. '... but I was telling you about Zacharie. He was so beautiful, and so perfectly French. I just had to have him, or my trip wouldn't have been complete. The next morning I woke up in his room in a student apartment block in Montmartre, with a view across the whole centre of Paris. Everybody should do that once, Poppy. You should, but probably not the way I did, because he'd just started to plant kisses on my leg when his girlfriend walked in on us. Look what she did!'

As she spoke she had tugged the front of her dress a little way down, exposing the upper slope of one tiny breast. Her pale skin was marked with four vivid red lines.

'What happened!?'

'I thought she was going to kill me! She was screaming at us and if she hadn't been trying to get both of us at the same time it would have been a lot worse. I just snatched my bag and my dress and ran for it, down the passage with heads popping out of all the doorways . . .'

'Naked?'

'Stark.'

I could picture the scene, and my hand had gone to my mouth as she carried on.

'I had to get dressed at the top of the stairs, and I didn't dare go back, so I had to walk back to my hostel barefoot, in a dress that barely covered my bum.'

She shook her head, grinning. I smiled back, again picturing the scene.

'So you left?'

'I had to. I'd written my address down for him on the back of a beer mat, which she might well have found. I didn't feel safe!'

'I'm not surprised.'

'Anyway, that's my exciting story. Italy was wonderful, and it was great to see Arles even in mid-winter. But how about you?'

'Nothing to match that. In fact I was so bored I came up early. James very kindly treated me to dinner one night, at his house.'

Despite what she'd said earlier, and my innocence, I was a little cautious as I spoke. She merely threw me what might have been an enquiring look and carried on, changing the subject. 'I suspect your boyfriend's back though?'

'Oh, very much so.'

'You two amaze me. You have so much energy, always on the river and out on the town.'

'Rather than being chased around Paris by jealous girlfriends?'

Violet laughed. 'She was Catalan, apparently, or at least that's what he said while she was trying to rake her nails down my face, as if it was an excuse!'

'I suppose she was bound to be angry.'

'Maybe, but not with me. I didn't even know she existed until she came through the door. Anyway, why do people have to be so jealous?'

'It's human nature, I suppose. Defending your mate.'

'Yes, but we don't live in caves any more, do we? As long as we're careful it shouldn't matter.'

'And James?'

'Um . . . it's complicated.'

'I always thought you had a stormy, obsessive relationship? Now you're making it sound so casual.'

'Stormy, yes, but that's . . . that's my fault. He's obsessive enough, though, just not about being faithful.'

She was obviously feeling uncomfortable, so I changed the subject, but I could guess at least some of what had been going on.

Over the next couple of weeks I drifted back into much the same routine as I'd enjoyed the term before; the Chamber, work, rowing, Stephen and other friends, particularly Violet. We were in and out of each other's room for coffee more often than ever, but while Dr McLean was quite often around they'd clearly decided to be more discreet about their relationship, with

Violet cycling out to his house on the Eynsham Road at weekends and quite often in the afternoon.

I was tempted to repeat my expedition to some lonely copse to recapture the thrill of taking a birch whip to my bottom, but there never seemed to be time, while I'd got so carried away before that both my cheeks were spotted with little red marks, which took over a week to fade and made changing for rowing both awkward and embarrassing.

More and more of my time was taken up with the Chamber, and in particular preparing for the King and Country debate, which was creating even more interest than had been expected. As a teller I was neutral, which put me in an excellent position to take over the publicity, which in turn allowed me to talk to people from the broadsheets, radio and television, adding further to my list of contacts.

Among my responsibilities was keeping track of opinion, so that I could pass on the likely outcome to the press, a job that would normally have been done by the Recorder had Giles not been leading the opposition to the proposal. I still had to get him to sign off everything I did, and repeatedly found myself needing his advice.

With just over a week to go before the debate I found myself in an awkward situation, with two of the major television companies wanting exclusive broadcast rights. I wanted to auction the rights to get as large a fee as possible, but didn't know if the idea was acceptable under Chamber rules, while I was also determined to get Giles' signature on the documents so that if it all went horribly wrong I wouldn't end up in trouble.

He had a very casual attitude to signing the documents I brought him, often scribbling his big lazy signature across the bottom without even bothering to read it, especially when he'd had a few drinks. On the evening I needed the signature I waited until after ten o'clock before going to the Chamber bar, but he wasn't there. I waited with increasing impatience, only to learn that he'd been in earlier and left. Stephen had also come in, looking for me, which reminded me that I hadn't seen him since the weekend.

I was feeling guilty as I left, and decided to seek Giles out in his rooms in Mary's, then go on to Emmanuel, hopefully for some naughty rough sex. By then it was nearly eleven o'clock, and I knew Mary's would soon be locked up and I'd be unable to get in without a late gate key, but Giles was on the ground floor with a window looking out onto the High. All I needed to do was to knock.

It only took a few minutes to cycle over and, after a moment working out which was his room, I climbed over the low stone wall and nipped across the thin belt of grass and trees separating the buildings of Mary's from the street. His curtains were closed, but not completely, and out of pure curiosity I peeped inside, telling myself I'd make sure he hadn't gone to bed before knocking.

I could only just reach by standing on tiptoe, but he was there, sitting in an armchair, his head thrown back, his face set in an expression of bliss which could only be sexual. It was very definitely not a good moment to call, but I couldn't resist a closer look, to see his cock if he was masturbating or, better still, to find out who was on her knees at his feet.

A quick glance to make sure nobody was watching me from the street and I'd managed to wedge one foot on the slope of a buttress and catch hold of his window sill to haul myself up, balancing precariously. Now I could see properly and, as the scene within became clear, my mouth came wide in shock. Giles was sprawled in an armchair, half-turned to the window, his face set in ecstasy, a large pink erection sprouting from his open fly into the mouth of the person whose head he was holding, not a girl, but a man, my man – Stephen.

As I watched Stephen's head bob up and down on Giles Lancaster's erection I could feel my whole carefully constructed future crumbling around me. He was gay, which made everything we had together a lie, every passionate word he'd spoken false, every claim of affection a mockery.

I just ran, having jumped down from my perch and leaped the low wall onto the High, oblivious to the stares of passers-by, and I headed for the sanctuary of my room. Every inch of the way that awful image stayed with me, of Stephen, who I'd built up as my ideal image of masculine strength and virtue, on his knees with another man's penis in his mouth. I felt I could hear Ewan's mocking laughter and the taunts of his friends as they teased me about college boys all being gay. I thought of how faithful I'd been, politely turning down every man who'd approached me, including Giles himself. I cursed and spat as I remembered the curious taste in Stephen's mouth and realised it had been cock.

By the time I got to college I was in tears, and rushed up to my room so that nobody would see me and ask what was wrong. I couldn't bear to admit to the truth, save only to one person, Violet. She was out, leaving me to throw myself down on my bed, crying my eyes out into my pillow deep into the night until I finally fell asleep with the winter dawn already brightening my window.

Waking up was awful, with the memory of why I was lying face down on my bed with all my clothes on gradually penetrating my cloudy head. Only needing to pee got me to move, and I felt numb as I went through my morning routine and did my best to hide the vivid rings around my eyes. It was nearly noon and I should have been at the Chamber, but I didn't care. Only the recollection that I was supposed to be lunching with an executive from one of the television companies pulled me out of my lethargy.

Violet still wasn't in her room, and I realised she must have spent the night with James, which filled me with an unaccountable jealousy, adding to my woes as I made my way out of college. The lunch passed in a haze, my answers automatic as he talked me into the contract he wanted. I signed, indifferent to the fact that I didn't have full authority, and was left feeling dull and depressed in a corner seat of the Bear.

We'd ordered wine, but he'd barely touched his, leaving the nearly full bottle on the table. I drank it, slowly, and as one glass followed another my feelings of misery and self-pity gradually gave way to a boiling anger. How Giles had managed to seduce Stephen I had no idea, but I knew why. It was to get back at me, for turning him down, for spoiling his smutty night of entertainment for the Hawkubites, for pushing him in the Isis. I wasn't going to take it lying down.

With the bottle empty I got up, none too steady, and started towards Mary's. I couldn't face Stephen, but I could face Giles and intended to before common sense got the better of me. My only worry was that Stephen might be there, because if Giles was out I intended to camp on his doorstep until he came back. He was there, alone, sat in the same armchair, eating quail's eggs and sipping champagne, his eyebrows lifting in surprise as I slammed the door back.

'Ah, Poppaea, do come in, but I see you already have. Is something the matter?'

'You know what the matter is, you bastard!'

'I'm afraid you have the advantage of me.'

'What you did with Stephen, that's what's the matter. I saw you, last night!'

'I was with Stephen last night, yes, at the Chamber bar, and then in the Turf. He was looking for you, but I managed to persuade him away with the promise of a pint of Old Peculiar.'

'I know what you persuaded him away for, you bastard. I saw you together, in here, with ... with him on his knees to you! You fucking bastard, you ...'

He held up his hands and I broke off, so angry I was close to tears again. After a moment of surprise his mouth had spread to a smug amused grin, making me want to smack him with every ounce of my strength. He didn't try to deny it, but gave a soft chuckle as he answered me. 'Well then, my dear, that will teach you to peep in at people's windows, won't it?'

'I came to get your signature on some documents, and it doesn't matter if I looked or not. What matters is what you did, and why. You just wanted to hurt me, didn't you, you utter ...'

Again he raised his hand. 'My dear, Poppy, please. Believe me, young Stephen was sucking my cock on a regular basis long before you appeared on the scene, he was my fag at Laon, you know, and he will probably be sucking my cock long after he is but a distant memory in your pretty head. Unless, of course, you were planning to marry him?'

What he'd said had shocked me so much it had taken the wind out of my sails, and I gave him a straight answer to his question. 'I had considered it, yes.'

He gave an airy flutter of his fingers, one of his most annoying habits, and stood up. 'Let me explain something to you, Poppy, but first, how about a glass of Cognac, or Scotch if you prefer? You look as if you need it, and do close the door and sit down, you are making rather an exhibition of yourself.'

I was going to refuse, but he was already pouring some

deep-amber liquid from a decanter into a glass and I did need it. He passed it to me and I sat down, leaving him to close the door himself before returning to his seat.

'The thing is, my dear, that, while I know it must come as a shock to realise that lover boy enjoys giving a little fellatio, there's really no need to get those pretty cotton knickers you wear in a twist.'

'How do you know I wear ... never mind that. I have every reason to be upset!'

'Nevertheless, an ambitious girl like yourself must learn to make certain compromises. Stephen is an excellent catch, quite bright and with enough know-how and capital to ensure that in a few short years he will become very rich indeed. He would be the perfect husband for an up-and-coming politician, in fact, but nothing is ever perfect in this world and you must allow him his little foibles.'

'Little foibles? How am I supposed to cope with a husband who has sex with other men, and what if he gets arrested for cottaging or something?'

'Really, my dear, you can be so dreadfully bourgeois. Stephen would never dream of doing anything so sordid, but, when he's had a drink or two with me, and one or two other old friends, well, he might care to relive a few happy memories of his youth.'

'Other old friends? You mean you weren't his only lover.'

'How little you know about men! I'm not sure how many other boys Stephen may have amused himself with while he was in the sixth form, but there were over fifty in each year, and most of us were at it.'

'What?'

'There's no need to sound so shocked. After all, what would you have done if you were cooped up in some God-forsaken barrack for weeks on end with a lot of other girls? I bet you'd have been in and out of each other's knickers on a daily basis, if not hourly . . .'

'I don't think so!'

He raised a single eyebrow. I thought of Violet and shut up. He gave another smug little chuckle, as if he'd read my mind, and carried on. 'And you must concede that Stephen is frightfully good looking. Who could resist him?'

'You couldn't, obviously.'

'I freely confess that resisting the charms of my fellow creatures is not my strong point, your own, for example . . . but I digress. The thing is that there's nothing to worry about. I'm not going to take Stephen away from you, that I promise. You haven't told him you peeped, have you?'

'No.'

'Then take my advice and don't. Sometimes it's best to turn a blind eye to these things, and think of all the filthy lucre you'll be able to enjoy, and all the backing you'll enjoy as you climb the greasy pole of the political hierarchy. Unless, of course, you'd care to join in? To have the two of you working on me, side by side and both as naked as the day you were born, now that would be perfection.'

He finished with a long sigh, no doubt imagining the scene. I made to answer, but stopped, knowing that nothing I could say would prick his monstrous conceit.

10

I left Giles' room so angry that I was prepared to throw every-thing away and start again, but as I walked I slowly began to realise that there was a horrible logic to what he'd said. From the first I had known that my chosen career path would mean making sacrifices, and perhaps accepting Stephen as gay was something I ought to do? Looked at rationally it made sense, but in my heart I felt betrayed and used. Also, it would be such a cold thing to do. I could imagine myself, at thirty or maybe forty, sat at my desk working at some constituency matter and knowing that Stephen was out at dinner with Giles, and what would happen between them afterwards. If I accepted that, a little part of me would die.

The thought of visiting Stephen was more than I could bear. My head was full of images of him on his knees sucking cock for Giles Lancaster, and I didn't know if I could let him touch me. I needed to think and I needed to cry, that or drink myself into oblivion. On my way back to my room I picked up a bottle of wine from the JCR shop, and opened it the moment I was through my door.

At the pop of the cork Violet's head appeared. 'Hello, Poppy ... are you all right?'

I burst into tears. She came quickly across the room, to take me in her arms, not asking what was wrong but giving her support anyway. I melted into her, desperate for comfort. She didn't say a word, but began to stroke my hair and pat my back, at which I gave myself over to my emotions completely, clinging tight as I sobbed my feelings out on her shoulder, and twice kissing her before I realised what an utterly inappropriate thing it was to do. I pulled back, grinning sheepishly, wondering why I'd done it and what she thought of me, but there was only sympathy in her eyes and she kissed me in return before letting go.

'Do you want to talk?'

Still choked with tears, my response was a nod. She went to close the door, not mine, but our oak, then sat down on my bed, patting the coverlet beside her. I'd found some tissues and was dabbing at my eyes as I sat down beside her. She filled the glass I'd put out and gave it to me, wrapping an arm around my shoulders as I took a welcome swallow.

'What's the matter?'

'Stephen.'

'Have you broken up?'

I shook my head, wondering how I could possibly tell her, but a moment later it had all begun to spill out. 'He ... he's having sex with Giles Lancaster, for ages ... before we met, sucking him off, maybe more. I caught them at it, in Giles' room!'

She didn't answer, but the pressure of her arm increased slightly as I went on.

'I thought he was my man, *the* man, maybe, and he's gay! It's all been a horrible lie, right from the start! I don't know what to do, Violet. Giles more or less told me I should get over it, but how can I?'

'Have you spoken to him?'

'No. I couldn't face it, but I went to have a go at Giles, because I thought he'd seduced Stephen to get at me, and ... and they've been at it for years, all the time we've been together! Giles said I could still make Stephen a good wife, while they get pissed together and suck each other off! Bastards!'

'But Stephen likes you, doesn't he, in bed?'

'I suppose so.'

'Then maybe he's not gay at all, maybe...'

'He was sucking Giles' cock!'

'Hush, sweetie, let me explain. They were at public school together, weren't they? A lot of men experiment with homosexuality when they're in their teens, especially if there are no girls around, so maybe it's just something he needs to get over? Anyway, he can't be completely gay, can he, not if he likes you? Nobody's going to say you're like a boy!'

She gave me a squeeze and I'd begun to smile despite myself, only for another grievance to push up to the surface of my mind.

'He still went behind my back, and he might have said something!'

'Oh, come on, Poppy, what's he going to say to his gorgeous new girlfriend? "Oh, by the way, I like to give my old friends bjs from time to time."'

'No, I suppose not, but... but he just shouldn't have done it!'

She didn't have an answer for that, but gave me another squeeze and refilled my glass. I swallowed most of the contents in one and took a deep breath. She was trying to be nice and I could see the sense in her explanation, but it wasn't really working. I felt awful, still full of tears, wishing it would all go away, and wishing I could get back at him, and at Giles, more so at Giles.

Violet listened as I began to talk, more or less at random, her arm still around me except when she filled my glass or gave me a new tissue. I knew I was drunk, and vulnerable, my body loose and my emotions a mess but with an urgent need for comfort overriding everything else. When she kissed me it felt so tender I began to cry again, and the words came unbidden to my throat. 'I need a cuddle.'

Her lips met my cheek again, kissing away a tear, and another, before she spoke. 'I'm going to put you to bed.'

All I could manage in response was a weak nod. My body felt limp and unresponsive, and all I could think of as she began to undress me was that my friend was taking care of me. I didn't mind that she continued to kiss me, or the way her fingers touched the nape of my neck and traced the contours of my breasts as she unfastened my blouse. Even when her mouth found mine I couldn't make myself resist, her kiss too sweet and too full of comfort to be denied. I knew she was going to have me, and a tiny part of myself was telling me she was taking advantage, but that was nothing beside the need to be held, and touched, and loved.

With my mouth open under hers there was no denying my surrender. Her touches grew bolder, less tentative. My blouse was open and she had quickly undone my bra, lifting it over my breasts as our tongues entwined, my kisses no less passionate than hers. Her hands found my breasts, as eager to feel their size and weight as any man, then her mouth, taking my nipples between her lips and teeth, suckling me and nibbling gently. At that a moan escaped my throat and we had tumbled together onto the bed, kissing once more as her fingers fumbled for the button of my skirt.

I lifted my bottom, making it easier for her to get my skirt down. She stripped me quickly, pulling down my skirt and knickers and tights as one, down my legs and off. I wriggled out of my blouse and tugged off my bra as she did it, leaving myself stark naked on the bed with her beside me. Seeing I was not merely willing, but eager, she took my hands, guiding them to her bottom as we once more cuddled close. It felt strange, her flesh soft and rounded instead of hard muscle.

She gave an encouraging wiggle and I had given in completely, no longer passive as I began to explore the shape of her cheeks through her dress, wondering if I dared smack her the way I was sure she'd like, because she seemed very much in charge. I thought she'd do it to me, and I'd have let her, but she only seemed to want to kiss and stroke and rub her face against my flesh as she drank in my scent and the texture of my skin.

When she spoke again there was no pretence at all in her words. 'Get in bed. I'm coming in too.'

I pulled the bed covers back and crawled in as she got up, to kick away her shoes and peel her dress off over her head leaving her in stockings, a vest and knickers. She laughed and I realised that I'd been staring, making me blush for the first time, and her beautiful eyes were still full of laughter as she began to tease, lifting her vest slowly to expose her breasts before turning her back and easing her knickers down over her bottom.

Naked, she looked more slender and elegant than ever, her tiny breasts high and pointed, her hips a poem in grace, her sex neat and pink between the V of her thighs, shaved bare. I found myself pushing out my tongue to moisten my lips and again she laughed, then spoke as she put a knee on the bed. 'I've wanted you so long.'

My answer was to open my arms to her and we came together, now naked, touching each other without inhibition. I let her slip a finger inside me, and by the time she'd begun to kiss her way slowly down my body I was so far gone that I simply let my thighs come wide in open invitation. She took her time, nuzzling my breasts and flicking her tongue over my erect nipples before gradually working her way lower, to kiss the swell of my belly and my navel, lingering on the mound of my sex and the insides of my thighs before finally burying her face between them.

Just the thought that she was licking me was almost too

much, and she was amazingly good, using her tongue with a skill and imagination that quickly had me arching my back and clutching at my breasts and her hair, my mouth already wide in ecstasy. Her hands slipped beneath me and I'd started to come, calling out her name and begging her not to stop as wave after wave of pleasure ran through me, until I'd forgotten all about Stephen, and Giles, and everything but what was being done to me, and who by.

Violet had seduced me, just as Giles had seduced Stephen, but I couldn't find it in myself to be angry, or even resentful. I did try to justify my behaviour, telling myself I'd only done it because I was drunk and vulnerable, but, while it was true that I'd never have given into my feelings otherwise, there was no denying that I had wanted it and, equally, that I'd enjoyed myself.

That was an understatement; Violet had not only shown a skill far beyond that of any man I'd known, but she had also been more attentive, so much so that among my muddled feelings and impressions there was a touch of guilt for having returned so much less than she'd given. Three times she'd brought me to climax before we'd finally fallen asleep in each other's arms, and a fourth at some point in the dead of the night.

I didn't feel resentful, and I didn't even feel guilty, or at least far less than I would have expected. What I did feel was concern, because passionate lesbian sex very definitely did not fit in with my efforts to keep a clean image, but I found it hard to care. Instead I felt so happy I wanted to sing, and a great deal stronger about the situation with Stephen. As Violet and I sat drinking coffee the next morning, having adjusted ourselves just enough not to arouse the suspicions of the scout if she came in early, I was telling myself that I'd have to face him sooner or later, and that the only reason for delay was that I had absolutely no idea what to say.

Violet seemed to read my thoughts. 'Are you going to see Stephen?'

'Yes, but I'm not sure what to say, if anything. Giles advised against it.'

'By the sound of things Giles was arguing for his own best interests.'

'I'm sure he was. That's Giles.'

'Then I suggest you think very carefully about what you want to do before you say anything. If you really can't cope...'

'I'm not so sure, after last night.'

I'd begun to blush as I spoke, but she just smiled and carried on. 'What you mustn't do is tell him you saw and give him an ultimatum. That way disaster lies.'

'I figured that one out when I was about fourteen.'

'Exactly, he'd resent you for the rest of his life, at best. If you do want to stay with him, you're going to have to compromise. That'll be the tricky bit. If you don't, you'll just have to put it behind you and move on.'

'I'm not sure. I still feel betrayed, but maybe I'm no better than he is? I mean, because of what he did...we did, but because we went behind each other's back.'

'I know...' She hesitated, looking into her coffee before she went on. 'I don't expect he'll stop, do you?'

Her eyes met mine, full of doubt and need. I knew what she was really asking and responded with a kiss, reassuring her. Despite my concerns, there was no denying that if the moment was right I'd give in to her again, which raised another question.

'What about James?'

'Oh, he won't mind, but I won't tell him if you'd rather?'

'I'd be embarrassed, thanks, but I've decided I am going to tell Stephen, if you don't mind?'

'Not at all. I think you should.'

'So do I, but what do I tell him? I've decided to try to compromise.'

'Maybe you should give him the permission he needs without admitting you know?'

I nodded. It would be a highly calculating thing to do, but life had been like that recently, full of manoeuvring and compromise, first to get on in the Chamber and now in my private life. For a long time I sat sipping coffee in silence, trying to ignore my emotional needs and think of my life as an elaborate and serious game. At last I reached a conclusion.

'I'll do it. Back to business.'

'You do that.'

She didn't sound very convinced, but said no more. I had wasted a lot of time the day before, and needed to catch up. Stephen was sure to be in lectures, so I hurried into my smartest outfit and made for the Chamber. Having taken what should have been Giles' decision into my own hands, I needed to make sure I wasn't going to run into trouble, which meant talking to him. I would also have to tell him I'd accepted his advice, at least in part, but that could be used as a lever to make sure he didn't make life difficult for me about going over his head.

I was standing in the lobby, going over the situation in my head to make sure it all worked when a tall grey-haired man walked in. He looked vaguely familiar, and carried that same air of absolute confidence that distinguished Giles but with a mature dignity rather than arrogance. After a moment looking around he addressed me.

'Excuse me. Do you know where I might find Giles Lancaster.'

'He's probably in the bar. I'll show you the way.'

'I am on familiar territory, thank you, but I'd be delighted to accompany you.'

He smiled and gave the gentlest of steering touches to my back, low enough to make me stiffen a little, but not so low that I could realistically have accused him of patting my bottom. Evidently he was a randy old goat, but if he knew Giles he might prove to be an important randy old goat, so I made no comment.

Giles was in the bar as I'd predicted, and turned to us as we came in. 'Uncle Randolph, you're early, and I see you've already managed to pick up the beautiful and talented Poppaea, a good choice.'

I wasn't at all surprised to learn that the man was Giles' uncle, and put up with the remark, intrigued to know what was going on. The name Randolph had triggered a memory associated with the man's face, although there was usually a 'sir' associated with it and if I was right he might prove very important indeed. I waited until they'd exchanged greetings and Giles indicated me with a gesture.

'Poppaea is one of our brightest young things, and a natural politician, or at least I hope she is. Have you thought over what we were discussing last night, Poppy?'

'Yes, although I wouldn't want to bore your uncle with the details.'

'I'm sure he'd be fascinated, but we'll talk later, perhaps over lunch? Care for a bracer, Uncle Randolph?'

It was barely eleven o'clock, but Giles ordered a round of gin and tonics, including one for me. I stayed with them, and on discovering that Uncle Randolph was up in Oxford to attend a formal lunch with the Vice-Chancellor and various other bigwigs I was able to ascertain that he really was who I'd thought. Evidently Giles' connections were better even than

I'd imagined, and I did my best to be pleasant, although from the way Sir Randolph's eyes kept straying to my chest he was clearly more interested in my physique than my character.

Sir Randolph left us shortly before twelve, after including me in a dinner invitation at his hotel that evening, and I was left alone with Giles. He got straight to the point. 'Am I to take it from the way you've been flirting with Uncle Randolph that common sense has prevailed?'

'I have not been flirting with your uncle, but yes, I'll put up with the situation. I won't tell him I saw you either, but I will drop a hint that I don't mind.'

'Good girl. You really do have the makings of a politician. Speaking of which, here's some advice. Do you go up to London at all?'

'Hardly ever.'

'Well, next time you do, let me know and I shall arrange for Uncle Randolph to take you out to dinner.'

'Thank you, and I really mean that.'

'Not at all. He has a great deal of influence, as I'm sure you know. He is also very discreet, and a little *quid pro quo* would do wonders for your career, you'll find.'

It took me a moment to realise what he was suggesting, but I was used to his behaviour and simply shook my head. 'If I won't go to bed with you, what makes you think I'd go to bed with your uncle?'

'I rather suspect that you will go to bed with me, eventually, but you certainly ought to with Sir Randolph. Is it such a great sacrifice, when you really think about it? Imagine, a candlelit dinner at his Westminster flat, a little flirtation, an elegantly phrased suggestion that you should let your knickers down, a good humping – if perhaps a trifle less vigorous than you're used to – *et voilà*, the corridors of power will open, rather like your cunt. A good exchange, I'd have said, no?'

The term before I'd probably have slapped him, now I merely shook my head. 'I have no intention of trying to sleep my way to the top, which is a fool's game as you perfectly well know.'

'Not in this case. As I mentioned, Uncle Randolph is discreet, while by the time you get senior enough for the press to take an interest he will almost certainly have drunk himself to death. Think about it, Poppy, seriously.'

'And what would you get out of it?'

'Much the same as you.'

'I suppose he'd realise you'd suggested I give in to him?'

'I'd tell him.'

'You really are extraordinary.'

'Why, thank you. But, returning to young Mitchell, what exactly do you propose to tell him?'

'That, while I expect him to be faithful as far as other women are concerned, I don't mind what he does with other men.'

He gave a thoughtful nod before replying. 'I'd elaborate on that a little, if I was you, otherwise he's sure to wonder why you've brought the subject up.'

'I'm sure I could get round to it.'

'Perhaps, but might it not be better to hint that the idea rather turns you on?'

'I don't think so.'

'I think you will find it's your best angle, and, besides, I bet it's true.'

'It is not!'

'No?'

He gave a smug little chuckle.

I had no intention whatsoever of adopting Giles' suggestion, but I couldn't think of anything better and decided not to seek Stephen out until I'd thought it all over. There was plenty of work to do in any case, and I spent the afternoon in the Bodleian, trying to keep my eyes open and wishing I'd declined Giles' offer of a second drink.

Aside from his outrageous propositions, he'd been at his most pleasant, readily agreeing to my decisions over televising the debate and even backdating his signature so that I wouldn't risk getting into trouble. For once I didn't have to wonder what he was after, as it was now plainly to his advantage to keep me on side. Like me, he intended to make a sensible marriage, although not for some time, which meant that I knew more than he would want to become public knowledge. I might not have done it on purpose, but I had manoeuvred myself into an advantageous position.

If I wanted to I could capitalise on that position. As I sat reading about Ramsay MacDonald and the National Government I even allowed myself to imagine how things might be if I took him up on his offer. There was no doubt at all in my mind that if his uncle Randolph got me alone he would try to seduce me, because I know a dirty old man when I see one. I'd never been with anybody more than a few years older than me, and wondered what it would be like; whether he'd be captivated by my youth, as Don Matteo had been with Conchita, or stern and authoritative, expecting me to do as I was told, maybe even spanking my bottom.

I shook my head to rid myself of the image, shocked at my own imagination. He was far too old, and I had far too much self-respect to submit to spanking from some randy old goat, or from anybody, at least, with the possible exception of Dr James McLean. I could imagine him doing it, easily, maybe with Violet holding me and stroking my hair as I was prepared for the birch, my skirt turned up behind and my knickers pulled down, baring my bottom for punishment. He'd whip me, hard, and, as I gave in to my pain and arousal, Violet would ease me gently down between her thighs, to make me return the favour she'd given so well as I was thrashed.

Again I shook my head, but this time it made no difference. The fantasy was too compelling to be easily got rid of, because I had whipped myself, and I had been with Violet, leaving James McLean as the only missing piece of the arrangement. Just to think about him made my stomach flutter, and I knew I'd do it, if only the circumstances were right. They never would be, because the potential cost was too high, but I could dream.

I was feeling more than a little sad as I forced my attention back to the book in front of me. It seemed that there was to be no end to the sacrifices I was called on to make in order to further my career. I knew I shouldn't really have let Violet seduce me, but a little lesbian experimentation at university would probably be excused, in the unlikely event that it ever came out. A threesome in which I got birched and probably had from behind while I licked my girlfriend was another matter altogether, far too outrageous to ever be considered acceptable behaviour.

By the time I left the Bodleian it was dark, and I hurried back to college. There was no sign of Violet, but I found myself hoping she'd come in as I showered and changed, even risking leaving my door unlocked. She didn't, which meant she was almost certainly at James' house, a realisation that provoked a touch of something akin to jealousy, not because they were together, but because I wasn't with them.

As I walked towards the Pillars hotel I was wondering what was going on in my head. Thinking about Violet, and about James McLean, made me feel warm as well as aroused. To think of what they might do to me was frightening, as it should have been, but also strangely comforting. When I thought about Stephen my emotions were too confused to resolve, and I decided not to see him until the weekend, at least, only to discover that I had no say in the matter.

I knew perfectly well that I'd been invited to dinner because Giles and Sir Randolph found me ornamental, but I'd assumed it would be just the three of us. Instead, the great round table in the exact centre of the dining room at the Pillars had twelve chairs drawn up to it, one of which was occupied by Stephen. He greeted me with his usual boyish smile and kissed me as I sat down beside him. I had no intention of making a scene, and could only respond in kind, kissing him back and joining in his conversation as if nothing had happened.

Giles was quick to take advantage of the situation, pretending to study the menu before making a carefully chosen remark. 'I see they have asparagus, but at this time of the year they can only be those horrible stringy green ones they import from goodness only knows where. They're just not worth eating. Fat, pale, British asparagus, that's the ticket. You like those, don't you, Stephen? Do you remember the ones we had in that restaurant in Sevenoaks?'

Stephen nodded approval and Giles went on with a sigh. 'Eight inches long they were, each as thick as an egg, and almost white.'

He smacked his lips, ignoring my effort to throw him a dirty look. I knew that I would now be thinking of Stephen with a cock in his mouth for the entire meal, and silently cursed Giles, promising myself that if I ever got the opportunity to take my revenge on him it would be slow, highly unpleasant and, above all, humiliating.

Stephen was his normal self; friendly, amusing and attentive, which made it very hard to be angry with him. He was also keen to get me back to Emmanuel afterwards, repeatedly dropping whispered hints and squeezing my leg under the table, which made the situation more awkward still. It was very tempting indeed to develop a convenient headache, and yet I was going to have to talk to him in the end, and I did not want to give Giles the satisfaction of seeing me back out.

Sir Randolph did us extremely well, not stinting on either food or drink, so that, while I held back, Stephen had put away enough for three, which I was hoping would put him off sex. Unfortunately he seemed to have an infinite capacity, and was as full of energy as ever when the party broke up.

Giles came up to us as we stood together on the pavement outside the hotel. 'Good night then, Mitchell, and you, Poppy. Have fun.'

He gave us a knowing wink and walked away, whistling, as my cheeks flared hot. I had to say something, but I still had no idea how to broach the subject unless I used the technique Giles had suggested. Stephen put his arm around me as we started down Walton Street, his hand resting on the curve of my hip.

'I'm sorry about Giles, but you know he's a good sort at heart, don't you?'

I tried hard not to sound bitter as I responded. 'He's certainly very helpful.'

'Yes, and knowing Sir Randolph could do wonders for your career, if you go the right way about it.'

I winced, and briefly considered telling him that his precious Giles had suggested I sleep with Sir Randolph, only to reject the idea. For a space we walked in silence, but I had to say something before we reached Emmanuel, or back out. I finally took the bit between my teeth. 'You like Giles a lot, don't you?'

'We've been friends for years, prep school, then Laon.'

'Close friends, I imagine?'

'Oh, the best.'

I went quiet again, wondering if I really dared say the words, but it was as if I could see Giles' superior smirk and hear some remark about me being a typical comprehensive girl and not up to the mark. It had to be done, and I was going to have to use his gambit.

'Is it true that senior boys at public school often tend to experiment together?'

'How do you mean?'

He knew exactly what I meant. I could tell by his tone of voice, and he sounded worried. It was too late to back out.

'I . . . I don't mind, not at all. In fact I rather like the idea. Did you and Giles ever . . . ?'

I left the question open, my heart hammering as I waited for a response.

He gave a nervous laugh. 'You don't want to believe everything you hear!'

'Oh.'

Again we went quiet. He'd as good as denied it, lying to me, and it was impossible not to feel hurt, and yet I knew his own emotions would be just as turbulent as mine.

At last he spoke again. 'How do you mean, you rather like the idea?'

'Um . . . I don't know, it turns me on, that's all. A lot of men like the fantasy of watching two girls together, don't they? So why shouldn't girls enjoy watching men?'

I was making it up as I went along, because the idea had never really occurred to me at all, but there was no denying that it made sense.

Again he laughed, more anxious than before. 'That's true, I suppose. I could tell you some stories, believe me.'

'So I do want to believe everything I hear?'

I'd said it jokingly, trying to take the tension out of the air, and suddenly it was easy.

He laughed again, openly this time, and gave me a

powerful squeeze. 'You're a disgrace, Poppy Miller, do you know that?'

'Yes. Come on, spill the beans. I want to know what goes on.'

'I can do better than that. Come here.'

He'd tightened his grip, steering me in an alley beside what I think was one of the religious institutions. I knew exactly what he was after, but I wasn't at all sure I could give it.

'Stephen!'

'You want to know, don't you?'

'Yes, but why here? We'll get caught.'

'No we won't.'

He was right. The alley divided at the end, one branch leading into utter darkness, the other to a short flight of stone steps and a door that looked as if it hadn't been opened for a century. He kissed me, then pushed me down onto the steps by my shoulders, quite rough. I made to speak, but he was treating me the way he always did when he was turned on, the way I liked so much, making my emotions more confused than ever.

If I didn't know what I wanted, he seemed to have no such doubts, freeing his cock and balls as he took me firmly by my hair. He pushed close, pressing himself to my face. My mouth came wide more or less by instinct, and I was sucking, just as he'd sucked Giles.

He gave a contented sigh, tightened his grip in my hair to make sure he could control the rhythm, then spoke again. 'Let me talk, and don't stop. Imagine we're in Thailand, and I've talked you into picking up a prostitute for a threesome . . . imagine that. We're in an alley, just like this one, but with the noise of the Bangkok streets all around us and neon signs of every colour on a wall high up above us. I want to see you lick her, Poppy . . .'

He didn't know what he was doing to me, his words filling my head not with the image he was describing, but with thoughts of Violet and of myself as the call-girl. That didn't stop me feeling resentful as his cock grew in my mouth amazingly fast, but I couldn't hold my own arousal back.

His voice was already hoarse with passion as he went on. 'Imagine it, Poppy. I'm watching. You're on your knees. She's giggling as she lifts her mini-skirt to show you...'

He broke off with a groan, now rock hard in my mouth, his cock swollen to full erection in the time he'd taken to outline his fantasy. I was imagining Violet doing the same, with her back to the birch tree down beside the river and my bottom as red as a cherry, but his fantasy didn't seem to have anything to do with men sucking cock. I was wrong.

'She's lifting her mini-skirt, to show off her knickers, but they're not smooth and tight at the front. They bulge...they bulge a lot, because she's not a girl at all, she's a ladyboy...a shemale, with a neat little body and lovely full breasts, and...and the biggest, fattest cock you ever saw in your life.'

I'd have pulled back if he hadn't had his cock pushed in so deep and his hand twisted in my hair. It was bizarre, outrageous, and it got worse.

'You'd laugh...you'd think it was so funny, because you'd been angry with me for trying to bring another girl in. You'd suck, deliberately showing off to get me back. I'd be horrified, but when the ladyboy looked at me and pointed down at her cock I wouldn't be able to resist. I'd go down, side by side with you, darling...Poppy darling, and I'd help you, help you suck him off...side by side on our knees sharing a cock...sharing his great big cock, Poppy...I love you, Poppy, and I want to do that so badly, Poppy...so badly...oh how I love you!'

He finished with a groan and he'd come. I pulled back the moment he'd let go of my hair, astonished and completely confused. I'd never imagined his needs could be so strange, even after I'd caught him with Giles, and yet with all that going on in his head he'd told me for the first time that he was in love with me.

11

It was those three little words that made me decide to stay with Stephen – I love you. He had been drunk and at the moment of ecstasy when he said them, so I knew his feelings were real.

Afterwards he'd been embarrassed and keen for me to affirm my feelings and that I didn't mind what he was into. I'd done my best to reassure him, although I didn't really know how I felt at all, because for all my shock, and for all that I couldn't see myself getting used to the idea of him with other men, I had to ask myself if I was really any better, what with Violet and my fantasies about being a high-class call-girl or having my bottom whipped with birch twigs? The answer was very clear – no.

I would stay with him, and compromise my broken desire for the perfect Alpha male with my own less than conventional needs. There would be no sitting at home feeling lonely while he went for dinner and sex with Giles Lancaster. I would invite Violet around and have the same. Obviously we would need to be discreet, but I was beginning to realise that discretion was an essential virtue.

Having made my decision, I threw myself back into Oxford life with renewed vigour, so much so that even Dr Etheridge complimented me on managing to hand in acceptable essays while apparently spending all my time either at the Chamber or on the river. I was also spending more time with Stephen, and snatching the occasional very private cuddle with Violet, but while everything seemed to be going so well I found it impossible to shake off an underlying sense of sadness. I was doing what I had set out to achieve, there was no denying that, and yet it seemed that the better I did the colder my heart grew.

The debate came and went. I played my part, but without any real enthusiasm, and went through the motions of keeping my profile up and generally playing politics with a plastic smile and a sincerity I didn't feel. Giles and his team won, but by the narrowest of margins, which made my position as a teller unusually important. Despite that, I didn't feel that I'd done anything particularly wonderful, and yet over the following few days everybody seemed to be congratulating me, telling me I should stand for one of the elected offices as soon as possible and assuring me of their support.

I hadn't meant to stand until my second year, or at least the Trinity term of my first, but the chance was simply too good to pass up. There was a lot going on as well, with Giles standing for President against left-wing opposition who were keen to present him as elitist and out of touch with ordinary people. That put me in a pivotal role, as one of his few intimates without a privileged background, so much so that by the sixth week it seemed likely that my influence might make all the difference.

My personal feelings aside, it was obvious that I ought to support him. Everybody knew that we were linked, and I was seen as his protégé, at least in part. To support his opponent would be seen as little more than treachery, while I genuinely believed that a left-wing presidency was likely to stifle free speech in debates. Alternatively, I could remain neutral, but that was likely to cut me off from the support of Giles' faction if I stood myself.

It was not an easy decision. I still blamed him for my less

than perfect relationship with Stephen, while I was sure that for all his very open friendship and kind words he saw me as a socially ambitious little tart. There was nothing I would have liked better than to see him fail, and fail miserably, but I would undoubtedly bring myself down with him.

So for the second time in a matter of weeks I swallowed my feelings and my pride, putting everything into his campaign and my own to take over his position as Recorder. He in turn supported me, while my opposition was a minor member of the left-wing group whose support came solely from within her own faction. Long before the vote itself I knew I was as sure of winning as it is possible to be before the result was in, while Giles also looked like securing a comfortable majority.

Even then I didn't stop, visiting people all over the city and making myself pleasant to everybody I possibly could. I was drinking a ridiculous amount of coffee, and far too much alcohol, while I'd cut my work to the basic minimum needed to keep Dr Etheridge happy or, if not exactly happy, at least satisfied. Even at night I got very little peace, as ever since our encounter in the alley off Walton Street Stephen had wanted to be with me more and more, and to explore his sexuality with me.

I never once gave myself away, again and again going down on my knees for entry one way or another as he talked to me, enlarging on any one of a dozen elaborate bisexual fantasies, while my own head was full of thoughts of the way he was using me, of punishment, and of Violet. She at least was understanding, constantly telling me to slow down, making sure I ate properly and always ready with a hug, although more often than not what started as a comforting hug ended up with her down between my open thighs.

The day of the Chamber elections came and all my hard work bore fruit. Giles made it, with a comfortable three-hundred-vote margin, to the utter fury of his opponent, who seemed convinced that he stood on a moral high ground so elevated that no sane individual could have voted against him. All the other results followed much the same pattern. We had conquered the middle ground, or rather, I had conquered the middle ground, most of whom felt that Giles was the lesser of the two evils. My own margin of victory was over six hundred votes.

Giles might have been President, but it was my election and he knew it, taking care to keep me firmly on side and helping me to settle into my new role during the final few days of term. I accepted it all, dizzy with victory and full of confidence. People were speaking of me as an obvious choice for President, and even Giles seemed a little in awe of me. He had stopped making quips about my background and began to stress to his cronies that I was fourth-generation Oxford, effectively bringing me into his own elite circle. Yet on the final afternoon of term, when I went over to Emmanuel after dinner for what I hoped would be a passionate farewell with Stephen, he wasn't there. I waited, staring out over the backs of Emmanuel and down to where the huge old magnolia outside his block was already in flower. He had to pass it to get to his room, but I knew he wouldn't be coming for hours or, at least, not with me.

My second homecoming was very different from the first. Dad was delighted with my achievement, and for the first time in my entire life he actually seemed to be impressed with something I'd done, rather than simply expecting me to succeed. Mum was more critical, worrying about my work suffering because of all the time I'd been putting into the Chamber, but I had passed my examinations comfortably enough.

After the boredom of my Christmas holidays I'd made a point

of angling for invitations from friends, and while Stephen was back in the US teaching rowing I managed enough to keep me busy, including a very important one indeed, to join Violet and Dr James McLean on the Contentin Peninsula in Normandy. I couldn't possibly turn it down, but I was feeling more than a little nervous as I kissed my parents goodbye at Exeter Airport and made for the check-in desk.

I knew the address of the *gite rural* James had hired, and had looked it up on the internet to discover something a little bigger than a chalet set into a hillside that was very nearly a cliff and sloped down to a jumble of little beaches and rocky outcrops. It was certainly very beautiful and, if the satellite picture was anything to go by, also very lonely, with nothing but other single houses, the occasional farm, endless fields and one small village within miles.

It was hot for spring, and stepping from the air-conditioned interior of the plane onto the tarmac at Cherbourg was a shock. The air felt thick and sticky, and as my taxi drove out towards the end of the peninsula the sea looked increasingly inviting. Violet had obviously had the same idea, as when I arrived there was nobody in the house at all, just a note on the kitchen table, a single word scrawled in Violet's big looping hand – 'beach'.

I changed into a bikini and espadrilles, then made my way down a steep path of loose soil running between thorn bushes to a tiny cove flanked by twin outcrops of jagged grey rock. The beach looked wonderful, a crescent of pale sand leading down to blue-green water that barely stirred in the lifeless air, but it was empty, or seemed to be until Violet emerged from beneath a jut of rock. She was stark naked, her pale slender body bare to the sun, her dark curls caught up in the familiar ribbon.

For a moment I just stood and watched, remembering what we'd done together and thinking what we might do in future, especially with no prying eyes or attentive ears to worry about. I'd never seen myself as a lesbian, and still didn't, but there was no denying that she was beautiful, or that she could give me what no man had yet managed to do. Then there was James, and I was biting my lip as I hurried down the last few yards of the slope.

The path ended on a slant of bare rock, hot under my feet. Violet had dumped her clothes at the bottom, shedding them any old how. She was already in the sea, swimming out with her back towards me, and I was tempted to strip and try to catch her, but decided against it, unsure if James was about. I called out to her instead and she immediately turned back, quickly reached the shallows, wet and naked, and walked towards me, smiling a welcome.

We went straight into each other's arms, her body wet and cool against my hot skin, her mouth pressing to mine with her tongue immediately probing between my lips. I resisted, not quite ready and not at all ready to do it in front of James, but she wasn't having any nonsense, whispering into my ear that it was safe even as she pushed my bikini bottoms down around my thighs. I still wasn't sure.

'Where's James?'

'In town, buying dinner. Now come on, I've missed you.'

She pulled up my top as she spoke and I gave in, efficiently stripped and with my arousal already soaring. I shrugged off my bikini and we went down onto the sand together, Violet on top, her thighs open across my body, her eyes feasting on my naked breasts as she squeezed them. I let her feel, my feelings rising higher still, waiting for the moment when she'd go down on me, to kiss my body from my mouth to my sex the way she liked to, only for her to suddenly speak out. 'I think it's about time you returned a little favour, Poppy Miller.'

I nodded, knowing exactly what she meant, suddenly uncertain again, but telling myself it was only fair and that she had me pinned, any excuse to get over myself and do it. My heart was pounding as she moved forwards, her smile now more than a little wicked as she straddled my chest, sat squarely on my breasts as she took me gently but firmly by the hair and pulled me in. She didn't need to make me. A moment's hesitation and I'd done it, poking out my tongue to taste another woman for the first time in my life.

She gave a pleased sigh as I began to lick, pulling my head in tighter and wriggling her bottom against me. I took hold of her hips, doing my best to pleasure her just as she had pleasured me so often. My legs had come up and open as I licked, just because it felt right to be in an available position, but she took it as a hint, laughing as she let go of my head.

'Greedy girl! OK then, but I want mine too.'

Before I could tell her it was OK she had twisted around, presenting me with her bare bottom. She went straight down, taking hold of my cheeks in her hands and burying her face between my thighs. I responded in kind, licking eagerly and stroking the skin of her neatly rounded behind; pale smooth skin, but marked with tiny red spots. She'd been whipped, and she had to know I could see what had been done to her, her beautiful bare bottom spread wide just inches in front of my face, the tiny blemishes all too obvious.

Just knowing was almost enough to make me come, and she was doing amazing things with her tongue, bringing me higher and higher as I imagined her getting it as she was, with me licking while James applied the birch. A moment later she'd tipped me over the edge and I was clinging onto her with my thighs locked tight around her head as my orgasm swept over me. No sooner was I finished than she suddenly sat up, her bottom full in my face.

'Now me, go on, Poppy, do it.'

She wiggled, and I'd begun to lick again for all my shock at having her bum stuck in my face. It was a deliciously rude thing to do, but I couldn't resent it, just the opposite, licking as eagerly as before and delighting in the soft cool feel of her cheeks against my face, still wet with sea water. As I licked, she squirmed herself against me, faster and harder, until at last she finished with a long sigh and I was left gasping on the sand as she rolled off me, laughing.

'That was wonderful. I have missed you so much. You didn't mind having your face sat on, did you?'

'Er ... not really, it was just a bit unexpected.'

Again she laughed, with clear uninhibited joy for my embarrassment. 'I'm glad you came, and you'll love it here. Oxford's so stifling, isn't it? Here we can do as we please and go naked all day.'

'What about James?'

'Don't worry about James. He'd love to see you nude.'

'I bet he would, but what about me!'

'Don't be prissy, Poppy Miller. You're beautiful, and you should be proud of your body.'

She rolled over, to lie face down with her chin resting on her arms. The sand had stuck to her wet skin, making shapes on the muscles of her back and bottom, but I could still see the faint red speckles from her whipping. She had to know I'd seen, and I wondered what to say, but, unlike with Stephen, it wasn't really all that difficult.

'Your bottom is rather red, Violet Aubrey. Whatever have you been up to?'

She laughed. 'OK, let's talk. You know, don't you? James spanks me.'

'He spanks you?'

Just the word was enough to send the blood to my cheeks,

and I'd begun to colour up as I asked the question. The birching was bad enough, but I couldn't get my head around the sheer indignity of a grown woman allowing herself to be put across a man's lap to have her knickers taken down and her bare bottom smacked. It was too much, and I quickly tried to turn the conversation back to something I at least felt I could cope with.

'I thought he birched you?' I immediately realised that I'd given away too much and hastily tried to correct myself. 'I mean, I saw you picking birch twigs one day, and I guessed.'

She raised an eyebrow, grinning. 'Just because I was picking birch? How did you know it wasn't for a flower arrangement?'

'OK, I admit I heard you with James, and when I saw you picking the birch I put two and two together. Anyway, the speckles on your bum look as if they were made by birch twigs.'

She twisted around, wiping sand from one cheek to inspect her skin. 'The bristly side of my hairbrush, actually. I was done this morning.'

A shiver passed through me for the way she said it, that she'd been 'done', as if she was describing some necessary and regular part of her routine. It was all too easy to picture, Violet laid across James McLean's lap, probably stark naked, her little round bottom lifted to the smacks as he took her own hairbrush to her cheeks, probably before easing her to her knees and slipping his cock into her mouth.

She carried on. 'He does birch me, occasionally, and it is rather special, but he usually spanks me across his knee.'

She was almost purring as she spoke, making it completely superfluous to ask if she enjoyed the treatment. I wanted to know more.

'How did it start?'

'Oh, I've always liked it, even before my first serious

boyfriend, who used to do me quite often, once I'd managed to persuade him, but you'd be surprised how many men won't do it, or don't feel right about doing it, which is just as bad. I was hoping I would meet the right man, or preferably a woman, and James had a collection of Louis Malteste illustrations on his shelves, privately bound.'

'That doesn't mean anything to me.'

'I don't suppose it would. Louis Malteste was a French artist, working from the late nineteenth century up until the 1920s. He's best known for fine art and satirical cartoons, but he also did erotic illustrations, many of which involved girls getting their bottoms smacked.'

I felt the blood rise to my face again as she spoke, but tried to hide my reaction behind my hands.

Violet gave me a wan smile, perhaps through her own embarrassment, perhaps as a reaction to mine. She went on. 'When I first saw it I thought it would just be a collections of cartoons from *L'Assiette au Beurre* or something, but I had to check, and when he went to talk to somebody at the door in the middle of a tutorial I sneaked a peek. It was a collection of Malteste's spanking drawings, just those, from several different volumes and some of them damaged, but beautifully displayed.'

'So it was obvious what he was into?'

'Exactly, and he was just the man for me, older and in authority. Even from my boyfriend it always took me somewhere I couldn't reach with normal sex, but from an older man, who had authority over me ...'

She trailed off with a little shiver of pleasure, but sounded more than a little apologetic as she carried on. 'I knew I shouldn't have come on to him, but I had to. Anyway, a lot of first-year girls fancy their tutors, at least when they look like James, and there's nothing wrong with it, is there? It's not as if I was at school, after all, so ...'

She spread her hands and shrugged, a gesture of guilty resignation.

'So you seduced him?'

'Yes, and believe me, he tried to resist. I was awful. At first I thought I should just make it plain that I was available, because I prefer the man to take the lead, so I'd turn up to tutorials in tiny skirts and generally show off. When he didn't take any notice I started to find ways to slip references to corporal punishment into my essays. He still didn't take any notice, but I could see I was getting to him ...'

'How could you tell?'

'Easy. He'd get a whacking big erection during tutorials. I wanted to get it out and play with it, and he knew, so you can imagine what the tension was like. There's another picture, by an unknown artist from the 1950s, which shows a girl sitting on a sofa with her skirt turned up and her knickers around her ankles while she pulls on a man's cock. You can see the turn of her bottom and the flushed skin where she's been spanked. I used to imagine it was us.'

'And you told him?'

'No. I was late one day, on purpose, and suggested I deserved a spanking. He gave me a lecture, pointing out to me that it was not only inappropriate but illegal and that I'd have to go to a different tutor. I broke down, telling him that I loved him and that I needed to be punished by him, all the stuff I'd been building up for weeks. He still wouldn't give in, but he admitted he wanted to do it, and after that there was really no going back. I pretended I'd accepted his decision, but now that we both knew we could talk about it, which used to drive me crazy, and him. He could have had me at any time, but we still managed to hold off, until ninth week.'

'When you were no longer in his care?'

'Exactly. I met him in the High and he took me to lunch.

We both knew it was going to happen, I think, but I must have pointed out that we were no longer pupil and tutor but simply man and woman at least a dozen times before he finally told me that I was an unbearable little flirt, a brat, and a lot more, and that I was going to get what I deserved. After that I swear he could have done me then and there, in the Westgate bar, and I wouldn't have minded. Fortunately he had more common sense, and drove me out to the woods where we'd be safe.'

She paused, smiling at the memory, then went on. 'We found a stile at the edge of a wood, perfect for outdoor spankings. He did me there, in the classic style, over his knee with my skirt turned up and my knickers pulled down. That probably just seems weird to you, but it felt wonderful, perfect, not just horny, but completely right. I suppose you think I need to see a therapist?'

She glanced at me, seeking confirmation.

'No. I understand, sort of . . . maybe. Carry on.'

'He spanked me really hard, and I do mean hard, taking out all his frustrations on my bottom, and maybe even trying to put me off, because I think he knew that if it became a regular thing we wouldn't be able to stop. My bottom was blazing by the end and, believe me, it really hurt, but he wasn't finished with me. He took me deeper into the woods, pulling me along by the hand with my bum still bare. I was made to strip, naked, and make myself a birch, with the handle tied with the ribbon from my hair, and whipped. Then he made me say thank you.'

I knew how, only too well, setting my stomach fluttering uncontrollably as I imagined her sucking on his cock in the woods, naked at his feet with her whipped bottom stuck out behind.

Again she looked at me, her mouth curving up into a little

wry smile as she saw the flush on my neck and chest and my erect nipples.

There was a new tone to her voice as she continued. 'That was the first time I'd been birched or taken anything other than a hand spanking. Sometimes there's a point, when you're being punished, when you can't imagine how you could ever have been mad enough or stupid enough to want what you're getting. It was like that when he birched me, but once I'd got past that barrier it was bliss.'

I wanted to admit that I'd seen, and done it to myself, but didn't dare, while she was still talking.

'After that, well . . . It's like an addiction. I always needed it, but the more I got the more I needed and the more dependent I grew, until if I don't get a good spanking every two or three days and something heavier once a month or so I feel as if I'm going out of my mind. He's the same, but he's stronger than I am, and he had more to lose. In the Trinity term he took me out to the woods several times, always a long way from Oxford, but I wanted more and his resolve began to break down. He started giving me little pats during tutes, then playful punishments, first with my skirt held up for a few slaps on the seat of my knickers, then bare over the knee. Unfortunately, spanking is rather noisy, and he couldn't give me what I needed, so I asked for the birch instead, suggesting that I could pick some twigs as part of a flower arrangement, so that they'd be ready in a vase and nobody would realise what we were up to.'

'But you got caught?'

'Yes, we got caught, by James' scout. He must have heard something, or even seen something, and he assumed I was being abused, so he let himself and the junior dean in with his pass key, right in the middle of a session!'

'I heard.'

'Oh. I'd hoped the rumours might have died down by now,

but obviously not. Anyway, you obviously know what happened, and I'd rather not talk about that bit.'

'OK, but you stayed with James?'

'We were apart for nearly a year, but we both need each other too badly to stop, even though he tried to break away.'

'Is that why you row?'

'Yes, but that's passed now. He's managed to find enough work to keep going and, as you guessed, I get spanked and birched, and other things. So what did you overhear exactly?'

'The two of you talking, strange noises I couldn't make sense of, but I guessed he was doing something kinky to you, because he sounded calm and you, you didn't. And . . .' I was going to admit it. I couldn't hold back. 'And I peeped, through the keyhole. I . . . saw you getting the birch, with James in his gown, and I saw you saying thank you.'

Her mouth had come open in shock and she'd gone pink with embarrassment, but there was no anger in her words as she replied, only a stern, no-nonsense tone. 'You did, did you? Well, I think we all know what ought to be done to you, Poppy Miller!'

12

I was going to be spanked, but I couldn't simply give in. My pride wouldn't let me, and, however much I wanted it, and however much it turned me on, I was also a little frightened and more than a little ashamed of my own desire. At a deeper level I knew full well that the experience would be stronger by far if I had to be talked into it or, better still, just dealt with out of hand so that I could at least avoid the hideous embarrassment of admitting I wanted it, especially to James.

Had Violet simply done me then and there on the beach, it would have been a different matter. I was naked and aroused, while we were completely alone. She could have rolled me over and sat on me, or made me lie across her lap, and I'd have surrendered with no more than token resistance. Yet even then I couldn't bring myself to ask for it, and before she took matters into her own hands we heard James' voice calling from the cliff above us.

I could only see his head, and he was a long way above us, but I immediately found myself blushing for my nudity and scrambling into my bikini as fast as I could, which made Violet laugh. He beckoned for us to come up and Violet gathered her things before taking me by the hand and leading me up the path. I felt small and insecure, both thrilled and scared by the idea that I was expected to take a punishment he would know about, maybe even to have it done in front of him, or worst, and best, of all, by him. As we approached the top of the path my nerve failed.

'You're not going to tell him, are you? About what you told me, and what...'

She laughed, cutting me off. 'Don't you think you deserve it, Poppy?'

'No ... yes, I suppose I do ... maybe ... but seriously, Violet, I'm not sure ...'

'Just relax.'

That was easier said than done, especially as I was sure James would notice the state I was in when we reached the house. He was putting the shopping away; French bread that smelled hot and ready, meats and cheese in paper wrappers, bottles of a local cider.

Violet showed no mercy at all, throwing her clothes onto a settee, kissing him and then coming straight out with a sentence that set my face and chest ablaze with embarrassment. 'The little brat peeped at us. We're going to spank her.'

'Hey, hang on ...'

I stopped, nonplussed, my face crimson, as he looked up in surprise. 'Do you like to be spanked, Poppy?'

Violet answered before I could find my voice. 'Yes, she does. It makes her horny.'

Suddenly I was babbling. 'No it doesn't! I've never been spanked in my life, and I'm not about to start. Come on, you two, I know you like it, but ... but, I don't know ... I mean, I do have some self-respect!'

James closed the refrigerator door and stood up. Violet had been going to say something, maybe to point out that she had plenty of self-respect, and I was already feeling bad for what I'd said, but he silenced her with a gesture, turning to me as he spoke, his voice patient but ever so slightly annoyed. 'I'm sure you do, but in this instance you are confusing self-respect with conformity to the social norm. Let me give you an example. Last time we met, you were wearing a knee-length skirt and a blouse. Does that mean you lack self-respect?'

'Er ... no, of course not. I'd just come from my tutorial.'

'And I don't suppose John Etheridge was shocked when you came in dressed like that?'

'No, of course not.'

'OK, now imagine that we've gone back in time a hundred years to the late-Edwardian period. If you were to visit a don in Boniface dressed like that he would be outraged. The college was all male then and, on the rare occasions when women did visit, they'd never have been alone, and their clothes covered them up from their necks to the ground, and there you are, on your own, with half your legs on show and more cleavage than the most daring of evening gowns. The don would assume that you lacked all self-respect, both for wandering around an all-male college without a chaperone and for the way you were dressed.'

'I suppose so.'

'Undoubtedly. Then consider sex. Just fifty years ago it would have been considered pretty shocking for a female under-graduate to be having open premarital sex with her boyfriend, but nowadays nobody bats an eyelid. Spanking is no different. Society tells us that it is inappropriate for a woman to submit to having her bottom smacked for sexual pleasure, or for any other reason for that matter. Yet even that is changing. For an MP, say, to admit to enjoying erotic spanking would be to invite ridicule, and yet for a film star it would be embarrassing but no more. On the other hand, spanking as punishment was commonplace and is now considered abuse.'

'OK, so attitudes change with the times.'

'And you will accept that they are likely to continue to do so?'

'Of course.'

'So why limit yourself to the moral values of the moment?

Why not choose your own moral values? Because you fear you will be ostracised by society?'

'Yes, I suppose so. I'm aiming for a political career, so I have to be very careful.'

'That's wise, certainly, but do you accept my point about self-respect? After all, Violet enjoys being spanked. Does that mean she has less self-respect than you do?'

He had backed me into a corner, but I thought I had a way out. 'No, absolutely not! But hang on, let me ask you a question. Would you take it from her?'

'Yes, absolutely. I would gain no pleasure from it, but I consider it immoral to do to her what I would not be willing to accept myself.'

'So you don't think it's something women should take and men should dish out?'

'No, not at all. In fact, more men prefer the submissive role, although it's important to understand that in our case Violet needs me to be in authority for her pleasure. She sees the male role as dominant, but that is purely a sexual thing and purely an individual thing.'

I nodded, because I felt the same, but I wasn't ready to admit it, not when it meant ending up over his knee. 'But maybe I don't want to be spanked?'

He shrugged. 'That's your choice.'

Violet had stayed quiet for a long time, and as she spoke she looked as if she was about to cry. 'Don't you, Poppy, really?'

I couldn't lie. 'Yes, I do, you know I do, Violet, but ... but by James, even in front of James! And I am ...'

I'd been going to point out that I was in a relationship with Stephen, but it was pointless, especially when Violet knew what he got up to with Giles.

James shrugged. 'I won't deny that I'd like to spank you,

Poppy, but I have no desire to push you into something you don't want. Still, if you'd like to try, then why not let Violet do it? I'll take a long walk and come back when you're finished.'

With those words he had me trapped, but I still tried to wriggle out of it.

'Violet? But...'

I broke off, sure he knew that she and I had been going to bed together, while at the suggestion of his leaving us to it I'd experienced a sudden and strong sense of disappointment. My voice was a mumble and I was looking at my shoes as I answered. 'That wouldn't be fair.'

'I beg your pardon?'

I forced myself to speak up. 'That wouldn't be fair, if you had to go away.'

'I don't mind, really.'

I shook my head.

Violet spoke up. 'Come along, Poppy, enough nonsense. You're coming with me, and you get it now, and you get it in front of James, because that, Poppy Miller is what you deserve, and what you want, isn't it?'

My heart felt as if it was in my mouth and no words would come. She reached out and took me by the hand, leading me from the main room and into a bedroom. It was very plain, with a single high window looking out at the sky and simple furniture, including a double bed with a bolster and a bright-red coverlet. She sat down on the edge to make a lap for me, her long elegant legs extended to allow me to get over them in that awful position, my head dangling down at one end and my feet at the other, my bottom the highest part of my body. Violet beckoned to me, crooking one slender finger. 'Come on, bad girl, over my knee with you.'

I couldn't bring myself to do it, but her face hardened into a no-nonsense expression and she patted her thigh. 'Come on, over my knee.'

'But, Violet, I . . .'

'Poppy Miller, you little peeper, you will get over my knee, now!'

She almost shouted the final word and I found myself reacting, for all my burning embarrassment. I stepped forwards, trembling violently as I draped myself across her legs and braced my hands and feet on the bare wooden floorboards, lifting my bottom into position for spanking. Her hand settled across my cheeks, just stroking, but I felt them tighten in anticipation.

'Violet, please . . .'

'Hush, darling. Now, we'd better have you bare.'

'Violet! No, not in front of James!'

It was too late. She had peeled down my bikini bottoms, leaving me showing everything from behind, and I was only glad that I was sideways on to the door, where he'd come to stand, watching as I was prepared for punishment. Yet she was right. I'd needed my bikini pants pulled down, because the jolt of excitement as I'd been exposed had been amazingly strong, like a tiny orgasm. At last I understood the expression on her face when I'd watched him give her the same treatment.

Again her hand settled on my bottom, feeling the texture of my flesh, and all of a sudden it had begun, her palm lifted and brought down across my cheeks with a firm stinging slap. I cried out, more in shock than pain, and again at the second slap. A voice in my head was telling me to get up and put an end to the awful indignity of what was being done to me, but I couldn't, instead wriggling and kicking over Violet's lap as the spanking grew harder and she began to tell me off for peeping at them.

'You're a disgrace, Poppy Miller, looking at me through the keyhole, aren't you, an utter disgrace! And now you're going to learn now it feels to have your bare bum showing for somebody else to get their kicks, and more.'

She'd reached under my chest, to jerk my bikini top up. I gasped as my breasts fell free, completing my exposure, and tried to cover myself, snatching for my top and my lowered pants at the same time.

Violet grabbed my wrist, twisting it into the small of my back. 'Oh no you don't!'

I began to struggle, close to panic, but she held me, quickly peeling me out of my bikini altogether before once more setting to work on my bottom. Now I was being spanked in the nude, making my feelings stronger still, and she'd started to do it across the seat of my cheeks, sending a sharp jolt to my sex with every slap.

'No, Violet, not like that!'

She just laughed and carried on, knowing full well what she was doing to me. I was lost to her, on a glorious sexual high for all my utterly humiliating situation, with every slap to my cheeks pushing me closer to orgasm, until I was sure I was going to come and could manage no more than a muffled sob as Violet changed her grip, still spanking me as she began to rub at my sex. I'd given in, my thighs spread to James, who had come into the room, my hips bucking up and down to the smacks and to the motion of Violet's fingers, utterly abandoned as she brought me to one of the longest, hardest orgasms of my entire life.

I was left sobbing and limp over her knee, then in her arms as she took me in, cuddling me and stroking my hair, kissing me as I clung trembling to her body.

At last she let go, to whisper quietly in my ear. 'It would be kind to let James do you. Nod if it's OK.'

I made a face, but nodded, unable to deny her wish.

Violet left me. 'Your turn, James.'

He smiled, calm and full of easy authority as he looked down on me. I stayed as I was, kneeling on the floor and took a moment to rub at my hot bottom cheeks while he got ready for me. For all my moment of ecstasy I felt very small and very sorry for myself as I crawled over his knee and into spanking position once more, but they had me completely and I didn't want it to stop, even if it meant I had to say thank you by taking his cock in my mouth.

My stomach jumped as his hand touched my bottom, a man's hand this time, a lot bigger, and I was sure he'd spank harder, but it was knowing who it was that really mattered, and, as my spanking began, an awful thought came to me – that it was my natural place. With that I burst into tears, not of sorrow or pain, but because I felt perfectly cared for, naked and hot behind over a man's lap, my bottom bouncing to hard purposeful slaps, and yet exactly where I belonged.

Violet spoke quietly. 'Don't stop. I think she needs to cry.'

I nodded, letting it all out as James attended to my bottom, the smacks now firm and regular. As it was done I was babbling apologies for peeping at them, and not realising how badly I needed punishment, and all sorts of things that had nothing to do with them whatsoever. They let me be, James never once letting up as his hand rose and fell over my now aching bottom, until finally my tears had stopped and I'd gone limp in his grip.

'There, that's enough, I think.'

Violet ducked down to hug me, kissing my tear-stained face as I climbed off James' lap. I kissed her back, shaking uncontrollably as she helped me down to kneel beside her.

'Um...'

I knew what she meant, and I nodded. She didn't hesitate,

but quickly peeled down James' fly, releasing his already stiff cock and a pair of heavy balls. I'd been able to feel him against my leg during my spanking, and I'd been pretty sure where it was going, Violet's mouth or mine, maybe both. He wanted both, and there was no resistance in me as we crawled in between his open thighs, to lick and kiss and suck at his erection and at his balls, to thank him for the way he treated us until he had come and we had shared what he had to give.

For all my imaginings and fantasies I had never expected to go so far, least of all on the very first day of my stay, but I was glad I had.

I knew perfectly well that Violet and James had planned to seduce me from the start, both into sex and taking a spanking. It even seemed possible that they'd planned the entire scenario, from the moment I'd met Violet on the beach onwards, but it had been the right thing to do. For the next seven days I existed in a state of unbounded bliss, and it would have been a terrible shame to miss so much as an hour. I'd discovered something within myself that I'd never known existed, although with hindsight I realised that I'd always enjoyed being under the control of a strong man when it came to sex.

We let ourselves go completely, Violet and I, seldom bothering to dress and spending most of every day with our bottoms red. The only times I even bothered to put on knickers was for the pleasure of having them pulled down, something I quickly came to adore. James was no less inhibited, frequently naked, and I quickly came to appreciate his firm but slender body, which might have been nothing like as muscular as Stephen's, but was no less masculine for that.

At first I was careful of Violet's feelings, aware that they were not only together, but that he had sacrificed his career for her, albeit accidentally, and that they needed each other in a way I'd only just begun to understand. Only gradually did I come to accept that the bond between them was different to anything I had experienced before, and stronger. Violet delighted in sharing me with James, and the only thing that would have hurt her was if he and I had tried to exclude her in some way. He was more liberal still, happy to enjoy what we chose to give, or to stand back when we wanted to be together.

I quickly came to accept that he could spank me when he felt I needed it, or simply for his amusement, which helped to keep me in a state of permanent mild arousal that would be brought to a peak three or four times each day. In return we would kneel at his feet and worship his cock together, bringing him to orgasm in our mouths, or he would take Violet in front of me. The only thing he wouldn't do was fuck me, but as the days passed I was growing ever more needy.

There was one other thing I wanted before I went home, to be birched, and hard. When I told them, on my second from last day, Violet simply untied the ribbon from her hair and passed it to me. I knew exactly what to do, the ritual as clear in my mind as if I'd been made to do it a hundred times. All I had on were my espadrilles and a pair of shorts, so I threw a top on and put my hair up in a pony-tail.

The weather had grown a little cooler, with a fresh breeze blowing from the west to make the grass whisper along the cliff tops, a great open space beneath a clear blue sky. Most of the land was open fields, separated by low hedges if at all, but there was the occasional clump of trees standing around build-ings, with birch among them.

I walked far out along the cliff top, enjoying my slowly rising sense of apprehension and half hoping that somebody would see me as I walked back with the finished birch in my hand and guess my fate. Only when I reached a site that I simply could not fault did I stop. A huge concrete blockhouse had been built into a hollow, some relic of war no doubt and now overgrown with bramble and bracken and thorn, and birch.

Standing on the edge of the slope I could easily reach the fresh young twigs, although it meant I was visible to anybody coming along the track. That I didn't mind, eager for any passers-by to see and to know that I was preparing a birch for my own punishment. It was a wonderful thought, keeping me constantly on edge as I plucked twig after twig, imagining not just being seen, but also being birched in public, naked and wriggling under the pain of the twigs as James dealt with me in front of a couple of dozen Frenchmen, every one of them delighted to see me getting what I deserved.

When I had enough twigs I pulled the ribbon from my hair and used it to bind them together into a bundle, one end tied tight to form a handle, the other loose to make the business end of the thing. Just to hold it was both frightening and intensely arousing, just as it had been beside the Isis the first time, only now there was one very important difference – I had a stern handsome man to use it on me.

I turned back for the house, only to see two figures approaching along the track. For one brief moment I thought I was going to have to live out my fantasy of being seen, but it was just James and Violet, who quickly reached me.

'We were beginning to worry about you, but I see you're ready.'

I nodded, offering her the birch, which she in turn made to pass to James. He ignored her, but glanced around the horizon, then into the overgrown dip between us and the wall of the blockhouse before speaking. 'Come with me.'

He began to walk around the structure, until he reached the side furthest from the sea, where a door opened into the grey concrete face, with rungs leading up to it and an iron handrail to either side.

'Perfect. Violet, give me the birch. Both of you, get down there.'

Violet's mouth came open in surprise. 'Me?'

'Both of you, I said.'

I couldn't help but smile at her sudden consternation, even though I would be getting it myself. She looked flustered, and hesitated before climbing down beside me. There was a wicked glitter in James' eye as he again scanned the horizon.

'I think we're safe enough. Take a grip on the handrails.'

I obeyed. Violet hesitated, looking sulky, but did as she was told, taking a firm grasp of the iron rail, setting her feet a little apart and pulling her back in to make her bottom available. I got into the same rude position, our legs overlapped, our hips almost touching. James jumped down beside us and made sure of our exposure, rolling up the light dress that was all Violet had on, then pulling down my shorts and hauling my top up over my breasts to leave us both showing in front and behind.

'Stay as you are.'

He climbed back up the bank, and disappeared, leaving us to share a worried glance at the thought of some French farmer catching us naked. Yet we both held our pose and James was soon back, one hand clutching a bunch of tattered pink bailing twine. Violet gave a weak sob as she realised we were to be tied, and the fluttering in my stomach grew abruptly stronger at the thought of being truly helpless under the whip.

I hung my head, showing my acceptance of his right to do with me as he pleased. First our hands were lashed to the rail, leaving us unable to get away or protect ourselves, then our legs were tied together at the knee, forcing us to keep them set apart with our bottoms flaunted and vulnerable. I'd never felt so exposed, nor so helpless, tied up and near naked to a man with a birch whip in his hand and a tell-tale bulge already growing at his crotch.

He watched us for a while, no doubt enjoying the view, until I'd begun to wriggle with apprehension, then he spoke. 'Two dozen strokes each.'

My muscles twitched at his words and I swallowed the huge lump which had been growing in my throat. I'd wanted it, I still did, but that did nothing to lessen my fear and the awful consternation as he got down behind us, whisking the birch through the air, before brushing it across our out-thrust bottoms, then bringing it down hard across mine.

I screamed, unable to stop myself under the sensation, like a thousand hot pin pricks all at once, and I was wriggling in my bonds, close to panic as Violet was given her first stroke. She was no braver, crying out just as I had done and pulling against my leg. I was genuinely frightened as he lifted the birch once more and, just as Violet had predicted, wondering how I could ever have been mad enough to put myself into such an appalling situation.

The birch struck again and I was jumping up and down on my toes and begging for mercy, all dignity gone under the pain of my whipping. Another stroke to Violet's rear and she was in the same sorry condition, wiggling her bottom in a crazy, pointless dance and pleading for him to slow down. James ignored us, but set up a steady rhythm with the birch, landing stroke after stroke across our wiggling, twitching bottoms. At first I couldn't take it at all, but there was nothing I could do but squirm and squeal and pray I'd soon be pushed over the boundary.

I'd lost count of the strokes when it hit me, a strange warmth, a need to have my breasts and sex touched, and suddenly I was pushing my bottom out to the strokes, no longer hateful but what I needed more than anything else in the whole world.

James saw and obliged, bringing the birch down harder than before, and faster, turn and turn about. Violet had already broken, begging him to whip her harder and gasping with need, her bottom thrust out to the strokes beside mine. One touch and I felt I would come, but suddenly it had stopped and I was left panting and shivering in my bonds.

James threw the birch aside and tugged down his zip, freeing his cock and balls into the sunlight. I needed entry, badly, and held my pose, knowing he could see I was ready. Violet got it first, moaning as she was entered, but after a few firm thrusts he had withdrawn. Now was my time, my sex open to James McLean's erect cock, and I had never wanted a man so badly.

I felt him touch my hips, that alone enough to make me moan. One finger traced a line across my whipped bottom, making my hurt skin tingle and sting. I cried out as his cock touched between my cheeks, and again as I was filled, a moment of pure ecstasy. Five times he pushed into me, short hard thrusts, before he pulled out to leave me sobbing with need as Violet was entered in turn.

He was very fair with us, but very cruel, giving us a few thrusts each before going back, while with our hands tied there was nothing we could do, either to make him pay more attention to us or to bring ourselves off. I thought I was going to go mad when he began to give Violet his full attention, but he was soon done, fucking her hard before touching her in some way that brought her to a screaming, shuddering orgasm.

I soon found out what he'd done as his cock was transferred to my sex, slid deep as he took me by the hips and began to pump into me until I was open mouthed and gasping with ecstasy, only for his cock to be withdrawn and pressed firmly between the lips of my sex. As he began to rub I realised he had brought her to orgasm on the head of his cock and was going to do the same to me.

With that everything came together; the way I'd been sent to make the birch for my own whipping, how he made me pose and stripped my bottom and breasts and sex to the open air, how he tied me to leave me exposed and helpless beside my friend, how he'd whipped me into a frenzy, how he'd teased me with his lovely cock, and how he'd fucked us both and made us come.

They must have heard my screams back in Oxford. I couldn't stop, and he wouldn't. If he hadn't had a firm grip on me I'd have pulled away, because I felt unbearably sensitive and the whole thing was just too much. He knew how to handle me though, keeping me firmly in place and rubbing until at last my muscles went limp and my screams and cries had turned to sobs.

He still hadn't come, seeing to our pleasure first despite being able to do just as he pleased. I was dizzy with reaction, half slumped in my bonds, and Violet was no better, but still I would have surrendered myself in any way he pleased, or done anything he asked once I was untied, for all my exhaustion. Instead he took pity on us, or maybe it was simply that he could no longer hold back, sprinkling our bottoms with hot droplets as he took his pleasure over the sight of what he'd done to us.

After that there were no barriers between us at all. That night the three of us slept together, and in morning he took turns with us again. We stayed in bed for hours, completely lost in each other, before going down to the beach for a final swim. At lunch I found myself unable to shake the deep sense of melancholy that had begun to creep up on me. My flight was late afternoon, and they were leaving the next day, but I was wishing we could stay forever and clung on to each of them in turn until my taxi driver had begun to grow impatient.

It should have been raining, to suit my mood, but I was driven back to Cherbourg in brilliant sunshine. As the plane climbed over the Contentin I was able to make out the house, with James and Violet tiny specks on the beach and kept my head turned until I could no longer see them, or the coast, something I hadn't done since I was a child.

13

The three of us had already discussed our relationship, and while none of us was prepared to abandon what we'd found we all realised that things couldn't be the same. Violet and I would have to wear some clothes occasionally, for one thing, and I couldn't risk anybody finding out that I had become part of a *ménage à trois* with a notorious flagellant ex-don and his equally outrageous lover.

That didn't mean we couldn't see each other, especially Violet and I, or visit James' house, but I would have liked both she and I to move in, which was impossible. I still cycled out to the house on the Eynsham Road the very day I got back, for a brief but passionate reunion, and yet I still felt inhibited and dissatisfied. I was also unsure about Stephen, as my feelings for him had waned just as those for James and Violet had grown, but he was so glad to see me again and so eager to get me into bed that I gave in without so much as mentioning his failure to say goodbye properly the previous term.

After that, things simply picked up where they'd left off, only busier than ever. I had plenty to do as Recorder at the Chamber, while Dr Etheridge made it plain at my first tutorial of the term that he expected me to keep my work up to standard, while with Eights Week later in the term I had to spend nearly all of what little time I had left over on the river. I was doing well, and was determined not to lose ground, so I put everything I had into it, often leaving me so exhausted that it was all I could do to crawl into bed when I finally got back from the Chamber, finished an essay or came in from a boat-club meeting.

Violet was full of sympathy and determined to look after me, chiding me for overdoing it and even threatening me with a spanking. There was nothing I wanted more, and she began to take me in hand each evening, just gently, with me naked over her lap after my shower or with my knickers pulled down, but always bare. When she did it I could feel the tension draining out of my body with each and every smack, until it became more important to me than coffee, drink or conventional sex. As she had pointed out, it was addictive, and I was rapidly becoming hooked. I didn't care, telling myself that a hot bottom did me no harm whatsoever, unlike caffeine and alcohol.

Only at weekends did I manage to get away completely, and James' house quickly became a sanctuary, the only place where I could really relax, although even there my head was always full of the things I knew I'd have to do over the coming days, weeks and months. I couldn't be birched either, which would have done me a lot of good, what with having to change for rowing in front of my team-mates nearly every afternoon and because Stephen would see.

I had thought about telling Stephen, but I wasn't completely sure how he'd take it and couldn't bear the thought of rejection. Nevertheless, I was getting to the point at which sex without spanking could no longer satisfy me and knew that if our relationship was to work I would have to bring it up. It seemed little enough to ask, when he was forever filling my head with disturbing thoughts of Thai ladyboys and Giles Lancaster, but I simply couldn't bring myself to ask for it straight out.

My chance came in the third week, after rowing. As we walked back through the meadows we were discussing our chances in Eights Week. The men's and women's races consisted of each college's boats lining up in a row, one behind the other, depending on their previous year's position. The aim was to bump the boat in front and avoid being bumped by the boat behind and over the week's races move to the front position. The winner would be named Head of the River. Mary's were Head of the River and expected to row over and keep their title, while in the women's table their boat was third and so had an off-chance of gaining them the Double Headship, which had only ever been done once before. Emmanuel were in front of them and Boniface behind, so we both had a lot of interest in the outcome, although he didn't seem to think much of my chances.

'You're good, and I think you'll row over, but Mary's are better and they've got everything to work for.'

'So have we. Three bumps and we're Head of the River.'

'You're not going to catch Emmanuel!'

'If we can catch Mary's we can catch Emmanuel, and St Helen's too.'

'The three best women's boats in the university, over four days? Be realistic, Poppy.'

'I am.'

I wasn't, I was just repeating the coach's propaganda, but if you don't at least pretend to believe in yourself, then who else is going to? In reality the best we could hope for was to catch a dispirited Emmanuel on the second or third day, after Mary's had bumped them, and just conceivably St Helen's in the same way, leaving us second or third with a realistic chance at the Headship if we could get our act together the following year. As Stephen responded with a derisive laugh an idea hit me, the perfect way to end up across his knee without admitting I was into spanking. I acted on it immediately.

'At least we've got a chance, unlike your crew, who're likely to end up in the second division, and I'll tell you something too. If we don't go Head of the River you can spank me, bare bottom, in front of both our crews...'

As he laughed I realised I'd gone too far.

'Not in front of everybody. I was joking. But you can do me, is that a deal?'

I stopped and stuck my hand out. He hesitated.

'Spank you? Really?'

'I mean it. Come on, shake.'

He shook my hand, not very firmly, as if he wasn't quite sure about it, but that didn't stop me feeling as if I'd just dissolved into jelly. Even to use those highly charged words to him had set me trembling, and now he was going to do me, while the two-week wait before it happened was going to bring my state of apprehension to a blissful, agonising peak. Not that I'd go that long without it, because if Violet was in her room when I got back to college I was going to be begging to go over her knee. As it was I had to have something, even if not my favourite.

'Take me into the bushes, Stephen.'

We walked up along the bank of the Cherwell instead of crossing it, so we weren't really safe.

He glanced around before replying. 'There are rather a lot of people about, Poppy. We might get caught.'

He was right, it wouldn't have been all that hard to find somewhere quiet. I reminded myself of my promise not to take that sort of risk and we walked on, now hand in hand. We continued to talk rowing, although my mind was on other things, until we reached the end of Rose Lane. Giles' window was open, and Stephen hesitated, obviously wanting to cross the street to talk to him, but I tightened my grip on his hand.

'You can see him later. I want you now.'

'Well, if it's like that.'

'It is.'

As we walked on I felt I'd won a small but important victory, because for all that I was effectively offering sex on a plate he had chosen to stay with me. I promised myself he wouldn't regret the decision, hurrying him to Boniface and up to my room. The oak was open, which meant that Violet was in, but I made a point of raising my voice to address Stephen, making sure she knew I wasn't alone.

He hadn't changed, and the scent of hot fresh sweat was clear in my senses as I pushed the door closed. I wanted to treat him and, although my head was full of images of him pulling my shorts down for spanking in front of the entire Emmanuel rowing crew, I took a very different tack as I put my arms around his neck.

'How would you like to fuck me while you're sucking on a nice big cock?'

We both knew the answer, and he responded with a groan. I hauled his top up, kissing the hard muscles of his torso and rubbing my face against his sweat-slick skin. For all his gay fantasies he was magnificently male, and my body was responding to him for all the conflict in my mind. I lifted my top, freeing my breasts into his hands and he began to knead gently and stroke my nipples while I continued to stroke and tease, still talking.

'That would be fun, wouldn't it? You could go on top, so I'd be trapped underneath you, and I could watch, close up. I'd watch, Stephen, as he slid his cock in and out of your mouth, with his balls right in my face. I'd kiss them too, Stephen, and suck him. Would you like that, darling? Would you like to watch me suck another man's cock?'

I'd changed tack, not on purpose, but just letting my fantasy build of its own accord.

His answer was more a gasp than words. 'Bad girl!'

'So you would? That's nice ...'

It was, a great deal nicer than imagining him with another man. I pulled the front of his shorts open and burrowed in to find his cock, tugging on it as I carried on.

'I would, for you. I'd go down on my knees to both of you, letting you take turns in my mouth, all the way.'

'Rubbing us together.'

'If you like, and putting both of you in my mouth at once, if you'd fit. I don't think you would.'

I was sure of it, his erection was thick enough to make my jaw ache without trying to accommodate another man at the same time, but fantasy is fantasy. Another man like him and I'd at least do my best, while on a more practical level there was no doubt about the effect my dirty talk was having on him. I guided him down onto the bed, kneeling at his feet in the position I liked best, where I took him between my breasts, squeezing them around his hard, hot shaft as I continued.

'Both together in my mouth, until you came, or you could do me top and tail, with you inside me while you watched me suck him off. How would that be?'

'Better still, side by side with two men, or two ladyboys.'

I bit back a touch of irritation and reminded myself that I was supposed to be giving him a treat.

'You think about that then.'

I took him between my lips, enjoying his cock despite knowing that in his head he was the one with a mouthful. He was still worth worshipping, and I was in the place I felt I should be, on my knees to him with my breasts naked, his erection rearing high over the rim of his shorts, his balls naked to my tongue. I pushed my shorts down behind, baring my bottom as if I'd just been spanked over his knee and was saying thank you.

In a couple of weeks I was very likely to be in that position, paying my forfeit for my supposed overconfidence with a smacked bottom. He was sure to do it hard, because he could hardly fail to with his long muscular arms and powerful chest, hardened by endless rowing. I'd be helpless too, with him holding me around my waist or with my arm twisted behind my back as he spanked me, squealing and wriggling across his knee, my bottom bouncing and bare to the smacks, his cock growing hard against my side.

I couldn't hold back any more, not even to wait for him to lose control and fuck me. My hand went down the front of my shorts and I was rubbing frantically as I sucked, my spare hand stroking my out-thrust bottom and wishing my cheeks were red and hot and sore. He came, and that pushed me over the brink, the two of us riding our orgasms together, united in body if not in mind, but it didn't matter. In a couple of weeks I was going over his knee.

He gave a pleased sigh as I rocked back on my heels. It had been good, and done in anticipation of better to come, but I wasn't at all prepared for the first words he spoke once he'd recovered himself.

'I could make it real, Poppy ... not with the ladyboys, but what you were talking about before.'

I could imagine exactly who he was thinking about as the third party, and it was not going to happen. Physically, Giles couldn't be faulted, and if his personality was a different matter I might have managed to get over that. It was his attitude to Stephen that made submitting to him out of the question, and it would have been submission.

Fortunately I had an excuse, having explained to Stephen my determination not to do anything that might come back to haunt me. As I explained I was very conscious of having already done so, and with a vengeance, but he didn't even know about Violet, let alone James. So he accepted what I had to say and the idea was put on the shelf, to remain a fantasy unless one day it proved possible without risk.

We spent the rest of the afternoon together, increasing my sense of having scored a victory, but I knew he was still seeing a lot of Giles and presumably for the same purpose. He hadn't admitted to it either, as such, although I was pretty sure that he was aware that I'd at least guessed. Not mentioning it had become yet another tactful compromise, and with my own circumstances I could see that a need for discretion was going to become an ever more important part of my life.

As it happened I saw Giles before Stephen did, when I went over to the Chamber after dinner. He was in the bar, as usual, but instead of holding forth to a group of cronies in what had become almost his personal armchair he was at a table in the far corner, alone but for a girl I didn't recognise. She was small, blonde, strikingly pretty and blessed, or cursed, with awkwardly large round breasts, something it was impossible to miss. As I drew nearer I saw that despite a tiny waist she was equally well endowed in the bottom department. I was curious and not about to be put off by the distinctly uninviting glance he threw me as I approached their table.

'Hello, Giles. Hello. Aren't you going to introduce me?'

'Good manners oblige, I suppose. Poppy, meet Lucy Smith. Lucy, this is Poppaea, a dreadful hack who has usurped my position as Recorder.'

She answered in a soft voice, all sex and bemusement. 'But you're the President?'

'A position she will also usurp in due time. Now if you don't mind, Poppy, my sweet, I'm trying to seduce this gorgeous young lady and you are rather cramping my style, as I believe the expression goes.'

It struck me that even Giles wouldn't have spoken the way he had unless the seduction was complete. She giggled, confirming my suspicions and increasing my curiosity. I chose to ignore him, addressing her instead.

'Hi. I'm at Boniface, reading PPE, and you?'

'Maths, at Mary's.'

I'd been half expecting her to say she wasn't at the university at all, because she looked and spoke as if she belonged in a glamour magazine, but I'd met enough mathematicians to know that they can be intelligent in a completely different way to the rest of humanity. She was nice too, eager to be friendly and plainly captivated by Giles, so that after exchanging a few pleasantries I decided it was best to leave them alone after all, and to help things along a bit.

'I'll leave you to it then. Lucky girl.'

Giles said something I didn't catch as I made for the bar, where I ordered a gin and tonic. Instead of joining any of the people I knew, I perched myself on a stool, lost in thought. Lucy was sex on a stick, from a teenage boy's perspective, all boobs and bum and as pretty as a picture, and while I was a little surprised that Giles was interested in her there was obviously something between them. That could only be to my advantage, as far as Stephen was concerned, as with any luck Giles would be getting all he could handle from Lucy and not want to risk her finding out about his dirty habits. I was determined to help push the relationship along in any way I could, a decision made without a trace of guilt. After all, neither Giles nor Stephen had bothered to consult me, or even to tell me.

My chance came sooner than I expected. I'd barely finished my drink when the Secretary came in, making a beeline for Giles. Whatever it was looked urgent and I joined them again, listening as the Secretary explained the looming crisis over

Giles' determination to choose speakers with the most radical views possible.

'...and they're threatening some sort of direct action. The General Secretary is on the phone, and you're going to have to speak to him yourself.'

Giles drew a sigh as he heaved himself up from his chair. 'Wretched little people, they have no concept of the meaning of free speech. Look after Lucy, would you, Pops? I shall not be long, I hope.'

I slid myself into his chair, immediately apologising to Lucy on Giles' behalf. 'I'm afraid that sort of thing happens all the time, but don't let it put you off. You two are together, aren't you? Sorry, I don't mean to be nosy, but...'

'That's OK. Yes, sort of, I suppose.'

'You're so lucky. Everybody likes Giles...not me, of course, because I'm with his best friend, Stephen. We must all go out together sometime.'

'I'd like that, thank you.'

'No, really. I'll come over to Mary's later in the week and sort it out if you like, because if we leave it to the boys it'll never happen. But how come I haven't seen you about? Are you a Chamber member?'

'No, not here. The Student Union, yes. I suppose I keep myself to myself, really, and there's Chess Club, and Pi. Giles is so sweet, isn't he?'

I'd been right. She was a mathematician through and through, brilliant but utterly naïve. Nobody else could have described Giles as sweet, especially after going to bed with him, as she presumably had. I'd never been entirely sure what he was into, but between some of the things he'd said and talking to Stephen I was pretty sure he was a dirty bastard. Fortunately I'd become an accomplished liar.

'Yes, he's lovely. So how did you two get together?'

'He came up to my room and asked me out. I was really surprised. He'd never even spoken to me before, and he is the best-looking man in college. I'm always seeing him about the place with the most beautiful girls.'

The temptation to make some remark about Giles being seen with beautiful men as well as women was considerable, but I kept my thoughts to myself. Instead we began to chat about university life, and the more I drew her out the more surprised I became that Giles had fixed on her. She was quite shy, and distinctly introverted, had got in from a South London comprehensive with perfect A levels and quite simply didn't belong to his world in any way at all, except that they were both at Mary's. He also preferred boys, while she was abundantly feminine. What she did have was a sense of mischief, and it was easy to imagine her letting herself go completely in bed, which was presumably why he found her attractive.

Before long he returned to the table, still trying to seem nonchalant but plainly angry. 'It really is extraordinary. I tried to explain to the wretched little oik that just because I invite a speaker doesn't mean I share their opinions, but he simply wouldn't listen. If we let Suarez speak his gang of layabouts won't work, not that we're likely to notice, and apparently at least half the pinkos in the university will be picketing the gates.'

'Are you going to cancel?'

'Certainly not. Think of the publicity, you foolish girl. We'll be on the national news. There'll have to be a vote though, and that, Poppaea, means work. Sorry, Lucy, but Poppy and I have to persuade at least two hundred people that freedom of speech outweighs personal politics.'

'Can I help?'

'Only by going back to college, pouring yourself a large glass of whatever takes your fancy and getting into my bed.'

She giggled in response, not in the least embarrassed by his suggestion, for all her apparent shyness. Giles gave her his room key and kissed her with real affection, or so it seemed, and she looked back twice across her shoulder before leaving the bar. For a moment he and I were alone.

'She's nice.'

'Nice? She's delectable. Tits like melons and the morals of a rutting polecat. You could learn a thing or two from her. To think I have to talk to these idiots when I could be in bed with her, but still, better get on with it, eh? Unless you fancy giving me a quick bj in the loos first, just as a spot of stress therapy?'

'No, I do not.'

We got down to work, circulating among our colleagues and explaining the same points over and over again. I was also going to have to organise the press, despite having no particular interest in the cause, beyond being in broad agreement with Giles on freedom of speech and wanting to hear what Suarez had to say out of a sort of horrid fascination.

It was gone eleven o'clock before we decided that we'd done all we could, and as I started back for college I was ready for bed. Giles walked with me as far as Boniface Lodge, kissing me goodnight before hurrying on to Mary's and Lucy. I hurried into college, rather pleased with myself despite being so tired. The day had gone rather well, and would be perfect if Violet was still awake and was game for a cuddle.

Our oak was shut and my spirits fell, but I unlocked it to find her door open. She was sitting on her bed, dressed in nothing but stockings and black French knickers, with her hairbrush in one hand and a meaningful look in her eyes. I managed a nervous smile.

'What's this for?'

'I saw you, you bad girl, and I heard you. What was it, being shared by two men? You are a disgrace, Poppy Miller. Now come down across my knee, this instant!'

'Hang on, you mean you peeped at me with Stephen!?'

'Yes, and I saw everything.'

'Exactly, and what happened when I peeped at you?'

She didn't answer, her stern expression fading to uncertainty.

I went on. 'Yes, Violet, I got spanked, didn't I, knickers down, in front of James.'

'That's not the point . . .'

'Oh yes it is.'

I pushed the oak shut and ran at her. She tried to grab me and we went down on the bed together, laughing as we tried to get at each other. I'd meant to spank her, but in just moments we'd both given in, kissing and pulling at each other's clothes and our own. We were soon naked, rolling together on the bed, each eager for the other, but it was Violet who took control, climbing on top of me to apply a dozen firm swats to my bottom as she told me off, then going head to tail and burying her face between my open thighs. I gave her bottom a single hard slap, but I had decided her punishment could wait and as she began to lick I was lost to everything but the pleasure of her body and my own. My work, the upcoming bumps, the flap at the Chamber, even Stephen and Giles and Lucy; nothing mattered, only the slender beautiful girl on top of me, the warmth of my smacked bottom and the wonderful things she was doing with her tongue.

14

The next morning I found myself with no choice but to concentrate on things other than Violet. We were still in bed together, fast asleep, when the first knock sounded on the door. A few moments of panic-stricken adjustment and I was able to unlock our oak, peering out through still bleary eyes to find the rest of St Boniface Women's Boat Club looking horribly keen and athletic.

The cox tapped her watch. 'Seven o'clock in the lodge, Poppy. It's nearly ten past.'

I managed a groan, which I hoped they'd take for enthusiasm, and pushed on my door. It was locked, just as it had been all night. For one awful moment I remained frozen, sure that all thirteen of them would be able to work out exactly why my door was locked, only for inspiration to strike.

'Bother. I've locked myself out!'

A voice at the back piped up. 'I'll run to the lodge.'

She went, leaving me grinning inanely and hoping that none of them would realise that I was wearing Violet's bathrobe. When the porter finally turned up, none too pleased, and used his master key to let me into my own room I was forced to shut the oak so that I could retrieve my own key from Violet's room before changing into my running kit. She thought it was funny, until she saw the worry on my face.

'Don't be upset, Poppy. You haven't done anything wrong, and I don't suppose they'll realise anyway.'

I put my finger to my lips to hush her, for all that she'd

spoken in a whisper. Most of the team were still outside, and I found myself trying to avoid eye contact as we ran from college. Nobody said anything, and by the time we'd got back I had managed to convince myself that they hadn't noticed. After all, they all knew I was with Stephen, and none of them had actually seen me in Violet's room, but I was still angry with myself for not being more careful.

Once I'd showered and changed again I came back down to the lodge, to find a note in my pigeonhole, from the secretary of a society dedicated to supporting human rights in Latin America, concerned about Suarez. I had no choice but to go and speak to her, grabbing a bun with icing on top from the Queen's Lane Coffee House as I passed. She'd asked to meet in the JCR at Mary's, and turned out to have half-a-dozen other people with her, all determined to voice their opposition to the visit. Two hours later I'd managed to persuade them that only by allowing Suarez to speak would they be able to tell him what they thought.

I left them discussing placards and made my way back to Boniface, feeling pleased with myself despite a creeping sense of exhaustion. This time there were two notes, one from Giles, demanding to know why I wasn't at the Chamber, and one from Dr Etheridge, asking me to extend my essay to cover Churchill's influence following his final stint as Prime Minister. That meant maybe three hours' research and another two writing, which meant I wouldn't be able to see Stephen that evening, especially if I was going to support Giles.

As I made for the Chamber I felt as if I was beginning to crack up, but I was soon lost in work as I began to sort out press releases and make calls to ensure that we got as much coverage as possible and that it stayed positive. Giles had been right about the publicity, and I was soon getting calls back, some critical, some supportive, but most wanting more information. By lunchtime I had a severe headache and the computer screen had began to shimmer, forcing me to stop.

There was already a picket outside, all of whom wanted to talk to me in the hope of changing my mind. At that point I'd have cheerfully strangled Suarez had he turned up, but I did my best to placate them with the same argument I'd used before. I was feeling faint, and picked up a pie in the market on my way to the Bodleian, drawing curious glances from a group of Japanese tourists as I shoved it into my mouth before going in.

My headache had got worse and I couldn't even focus on the words in the books I'd chosen, so found myself a quiet library chair and shut my eyes, hoping that a few minutes of rest would make it all better. It was gone three o'clock when I woke up, with a horrible taste in my mouth but no headache. I got down to work, scribbling notes as fast as I could while I worried about the rowing practice I'd missed and what was going on at the Chamber.

When I got back to college there were another four notes in my pigeonhole, all from people demanding to see me immediately and all to do with Suarez. I hurried for the Chamber, now close to panic, and spent a frantic hour searching people out and trying to change their minds. Everybody seemed to want my personal attention, and my sole consolation was that Giles would be working even harder than me, so I was less than pleased to find him in the bar, sprawled in his pet armchair with a pint of beer in his hand.

I put all the sarcasm I could muster into my voice as I approached. 'Don't work too hard, will you, Giles? I've seen most of the people who count, and I've got most of the press on our side or at least neutral, except for . . .'

I broke off as he made a gesture with his hand, only then condescending to lower the glass from his mouth.

'Sit down, Poppy. Relax. Get yourself a drink.'

'Relax? We've got to . . .'

'No we haven't. Uncle Randolph called earlier this afternoon to say that it would be too politically sensitive to have Suarez in the country at present. Naturally I had to cancel.'

'Cancel?'

'Cancel. Be a doll and find some plausible excuse, would you?'

It took me the rest of the week to backtrack on all the work I'd done for the Suarez visit, during every minute of which I was fantasising over cruel and elaborate ways to murder both Giles and his uncle Randolph. By the weekend I'd had all I could take, and accepted Violet's invitation to spend the night at James' house. I slept like a log on the Saturday night, but we spent Sunday in the woods, where I was given a very gentle birching, not even hard enough to prick my skin and leave marks. In suggesting the punishment I had hoped to recapture at least something of what I'd felt in France, but succeeded only in creating the faintest of echoes, which was more frustrating than satisfying.

I did at least feel rested enough to face the following week, the last before Eights Week, which was such hard work that I was wondering if I could have coped at all had it not been for the cancellation of the Suarez visit. That in no way reduced my resentment of Giles, and nor did his claim to have been searching for me during the period I was asleep in the Bodleian. In my view he should have stuck to his principles, rather than caving in after a single phone call from his uncle.

At the time I'd been too taken aback to make my feelings clear, but I was determined to do so and finally got the chance after rowing one day. Stephen was still on the river, and I'd showered and changed in the Boniface boathouse, so found myself passing Mary's on my way back. Giles' window was open, so he was presumably in, while I had just enough time to visit before my tutorial. I wanted to talk to him face to face, so instead of climbing up and sticking my head through the window I went into Mary's.

He was there, and greeted me with his usual friendly condescension, waving to an armchair. 'Poppaea, I thought you might be along. Come to gloat over your re-election?'

'What re-election?'

'Nobody is opposing you, it seems.'

'Oh . . . that's good. No, I haven't come to gloat, I . . .'

'I would, in your shoes, not that pink boating pumps really suit me . . .'

'Will you talk sense for a moment, please? I wanted to know if you're going to cancel any of your other speakers this term.'

His response was casual, unmoved by my sarcasm. 'The cleric, yes, the blood-sports crowd and the fellow from Philadelphia, no.'

'Is that on your uncle's advice?'

'Yes. It's a nuisance, I know, but what must be done must be done.'

'Why? You're not obliged to do as Sir Randolph says, and God knows you don't take any notice of anybody else.'

'Ah, but I am obliged.'

'Why?'

'For the very simple reason, my dear, that without my uncle Randolph's good opinion I might one day have to join the ranks of the wage slaves.'

'Why?'

'You are beginning to repeat yourself, my dear, which is not a good habit. Why do you suppose I'm going into politics? I am doing so to please my uncle Randolph, and I must continue to please him. Otherwise my inheritance will vanish like a fart in a hurricane.'

'So you're willing to abandon your principles just because you're scared he'll disinherit you?'

'Absolutely, and besides, my principles, in so far as I have any, are largely his own, and will remain so, along with my loyalty, until the day he hands in his dinner pail. Speaking of which, I'm prepared to offer you five per cent of what I get from him if you'll shag the old bugger to death. How about it?'

'Do try to be serious, Giles.'

'Seven per cent and your choice of car, that's my final offer.'

'Shut up. I worked really hard on that Suarez thing, Giles, and ...'

'As I remarked before, I did try to tell you. Still, I suppose I should have realised that it would be a step too far, so I apologise. How about that?'

'Thank you, but ...'

'He's hard to judge you see, old Uncle Randolph, and he too has his political masters, but you needn't worry your pretty head any more, because he insists the cleric is out but he's happy with the other two.'

'Thank you, it's useful to know that, but ...'

'Oh, and, while you're here, you'll be interested to know that Mitchell's up for the Hawkubites again, and this time I feel confident he'll be accepted.'

I was going to ask how he could be so sure, only for a thought to occur to me. 'You blackballed him last time, didn't you? You blackballed him because you thought I'd accept the money to be gang-banged and he wouldn't have let you, didn't you?'

'Certainly not! I would never dream of doing such a thing.'

He was trying not to laugh, and I knew I was right.

'You complete and utter bastard! You sneaky, conniving…'

'Poppy, please, you're making me blush.'

'I'm going to tell him.'

'I shall deny it, and who do you think he will believe?'

There was no doubting the answer.

'You.'

I slumped back in my chair, defeated. He chuckled and reached out to a decanter of whisky, poured two and handed one to me. I took a swallow, once again wondering what I could possibly do to bring him down a peg or two. At that moment there was a knock on the door, which swung open even as Giles answered.

Lucy looked in. 'Oh, you've got company.'

'No, no, come in, darling. It's only Poppy.'

Lucy came in, giving me a friendly but shy glance before turning to Giles with an expression of complete devotion. He pulled her down onto his lap, one arm around her tiny waist. It should have been a good time to leave, but I had the excuse of needing to swallow half a beaker of neat whisky in one and decided to confirm the date I'd suggested, as I was sure there was potential in introducing Stephen to Lucy.

'Remember we were talking about all going out together, Lucy. Let's set a date, although it will have to be after Eights Week.'

I'd expected Giles to try to find some excuse to get out of it, but to my surprise he responded with enthusiasm.

'The weekend will be hopeless, what with bumps suppers and things, not that it will be much fun, because the college authorities are refusing to let us burn the boat. Health and safety apparently. Not that I'm even a member of the club, but still. How about the following Wednesday, after we've all had a chance to recover?'

We agreed and I left after a few minutes, now in despair of

finding anything that could shake Giles without causing trouble for everybody else, myself included.

The next few days were pretty much routine, but with an underlying tension for the approach of Eights Week and in my case the near certainty of a spanking from Stephen. Watching other colleges at practice, I felt sure that in the crucial women's bumps Mary's would be able to catch Emmanuel, and probably on the first day. We had at least a chance of doing the same on the second, but were very unlikely to catch either Mary's or St Helen's, who were equally good and likely to row over for the last two days. The result was therefore likely to be St Helen's, Mary's, Emmanuel, Boniface and a session over Stephen's knee for myself.

There was mandatory practice all weekend, depriving me of my fix from James and Violet, while I was supposed to be in bed by ten o'clock every night and lay off alcohol. I tried, after a fashion, but both Chamber business and work had to take priority. Dr Etheridge had very little sympathy with sports, which he considered trivial, but by working late on Sunday night and spending most of Monday morning in the Bodleian I was able to get my essay finished and spend most of Tuesday relaxing.

I'd been praying for fine weather, but while Wednesday dawned clear there was a stiff south-west breeze, which meant we'd be rowing into a wind that would also be pushing us against the bank. The heavier boats were likely to do better, making the women's bumps even less predictable, but it was only when I got down to the bank that I realised how bad it was. I'd often seen the Exe Estuary smoother, while the marshals were looking worried and talking about postponing the start.

Stephen joined me, looking bronzed and fit, and when he

put an arm around me with one huge hand resting on my hip I could feel my stomach fluttering in anticipation of what he might be doing with it in just four short days' time. Twice he'd mentioned my forfeit, jokingly, but while the idea seemed to make him a little nervous I was sure he wouldn't back out.

Even after the rowing had begun I was still thinking about it, despite my best efforts to concentrate on psyching myself up for the race. I hadn't been getting done often enough, even with my regular visits to James, or hard enough because I couldn't risk showing any marks, but that had only made my need stronger, while the thought of a boyfriend as strong and handsome as Stephen who would spank me whenever I needed it was enough to make me weak at the knees. I could only pray that when he'd done me he would develop an addiction just as I had, only for dishing it out.

Only when the time came for Stephen to race did I make the effort to get to the edge of the bank, cheering him on as the Emmanuel boat moved into position. They were ninth, and so could only hope to advance up the table, while there was no real risk of being relegated, but it was still thrilling to watch as his boat closed on the one ahead while simultaneously losing ground to their pursuers. Neither managed to bump and they rowed over, as had Mary's at the front of the line, with over three lengths of clear water separating them from their rivals.

With the women's races starting I made for the Boniface boathouse, where I was given a ticking off by the coach for not being there earlier and told to get ready. I'd seen how even the best of the men had struggled with the wind, and was imagining the embarrassment of running into the bank or even sinking as I got changed, and for all my anticipation I was determined to do my best.

My adrenalin was running high as we warmed up, and a

tight knot had formed in my stomach before we'd climbed into the boat. I could see Stephen outside the Emmanuel boathouse, and plenty of other friends; Giles and Lucy on the veranda of the Mary's boathouse drinking Pimms, even Dr Etheridge, muffled against the wind and doing his best to look disapproving. Violet had promised to come, and to try to drag James along, but they were nowhere to be seen.

I wasn't particularly surprised, as neither of them had the slightest interest in sport, and put everything but my task from my mind as the cox called out for us to manoeuvre away from the bank. The boat was rocking the moment we were in open water, with little waves breaking over the side to wet my legs, and it took all my concentration to handle my oar properly as we got into position.

The cannon fired and we took off, hurling the boat forwards through the water with the wind whipping at my hair and the slack of my top. In just two strokes I knew we weren't going to get caught, a big gap already opening up between us and our pursuers, but I didn't dare look round to see how Mary's were doing. Maybe forty strokes and I heard a bump called, imagining for one wild moment that we'd done it before I realised that Mary's had caught Emmanuel. My heart sank, only to rise again at the thought of catching St Helen's to over-bump and take the Head of the River in true style, but it was a hopeless task and we had to be content with rowing over.

Only as we made our way back up river did I realise that James and Violet were sitting at one of the tables in the beer garden of The Boatman's, which could only mean they'd been there since opening time, because it was packed. I waved and blew a kiss, which Violet returned.

The following day was not only windy, but also wet, making conditions even worse. Fortunately I was used to it, from sailing on the Exe and being dragged out to sea in fishing boats by Ewan and others. Most of the other girls weren't, and the boats behind us ended up sideways across the river in a tangle of oars, which wasn't the first disaster of the day. We bumped Emmanuel, who'd shipped so much water they could barely make headway, but both Mary's and St Helen's rowed over, which meant we had to bump them on successive days in order to go Head of the River. I couldn't see it happening, short of a miracle, and I was already thinking of how I would feel as I lay across Stephen's legs, with one powerful arm holding me firmly in place as he peeled down my shorts to bare me for my forfeit. I'd told Violet already, but couldn't resist repeating myself when she came in for a coffee that evening.

'Do you remember I told you about my bet with Stephen? It looks like I'm going to get it.'

'Lucky girl. And speaking of spanking, you won't be rowing for the rest of term, will you?'

'Only once a week, I've got to study for prelims after all. But if you're thinking about marks: what about Stephen? He's sure to notice, especially as I hope he'll be doing me regularly after this weekend.'

'I wasn't thinking about marks, as it happens.'

'Oh. That's a pity.'

'Marks can be arranged, bad girl, in due time, but James and I have a little treat for you that doesn't involve marks.'

'What? Tell me.'

'No. It has to be a surprise, but Stephen's away throughout the break, isn't he?'

'Yes, as usual.'

'Then don't go down until a few days after he's left, and you will come on holiday with us, won't you?'

A shudder ran through me at her words.

'Yes, of course. Come here.'

I pulled her to me and we began to kiss and to work at each other's clothes, leading to sex, but I insisted on going to bed alone, determined to do my best the next day so that I could feel I'd genuinely earned my punishment for my pride.

Friday was calmer, with just the occasional flurry of rain, and there were none of the upsets of the day before. Stephen's boat finally managed a bump, which put him in a good mood, and he was grinning and waving as I climbed into the boat.

I couldn't resist a remark. 'We're going to do it, just you watch.'

'Best of luck, that's all I'm saying.'

I gave a haughty toss of my head as we pushed off, hoping to ensure that he dealt with me properly, and hopefully taunted me while he laid in. All I needed to do was flip my oar, maybe even miss a stroke, and I'd be getting it, but it had to be genuine and my determination was very real as we lined up.

From the moment the cannon went we threw everything into it, and from the speed with which we were outdistancing Emmanuel I'd begun to think it might just be possible after all. The crowd on the bank were yelling encouragement, and I never even realised that it was more for Mary's than us, until there was a sudden dull crash, yells of alarm and cries of warning, too late as we ploughed into their oars, nearly upsetting the boat.

Mary's had hit a waterlogged plank, invisible beneath water muddy brown in colour from the rain the day before, only catching it with an oar, but that had been enough to break their stroke and slow them down so fast that we'd run into them very nearly at full speed. It was still a bump, which left us needing to catch St Helen's to take the Head of the River.

I was in no doubt where my loyalties lay. Now that I'd

suggested that Stephen ought to spank me it was surely only a matter of time before it happened, while I couldn't possibly let the rest of the team down. I was even convinced we could do it, despite the fact that Mary's had never looked like catching St Helen's, and the way people were talking it was no more than a formality.

Saturday was a beautiful day, making everybody more optimistic than ever, and the entire university seemed to have turned out to watch. I could hardly stand still as the men's races were completed, and was changed and at the boathouse long before I needed to be. Stephen gave me a hug before I got into the boat, but even the feel of his hands on my body wasn't enough to deter me from trying my very best.

We failed miserably, St Helen's crossing the line two lengths ahead of us to retain their title and leave me feeling so dispirited I was close to tears. I went straight to Stephen for a hug, resting my head on his chest. The feel of his body against mine perked me up a bit, and I'd begun to smile at the prospect of what I'd let myself in for as he spoke.

'It's all right, Poppy. You did brilliantly, and of course you don't have to worry about that silly forfeit.'

15

I wanted to worry about my forfeit. I'd been worrying about it for the previous two weeks and now I wanted that worry to intensify over the sure knowledge that I was going to get it, and finally be brought to a glorious, agonising peak when I did. A lot of the fun in erotic spanking is knowing you're going to be done, preferably when and how, and that there's no escape.

At the time it didn't matter so much but, once I'd got over my initial disappointment and realised that we'd done far better than we could have expected, it began to get to me. We had bumps suppers that evening, strictly college affairs with a lot of drink flowing and in the case of Boniface the girls celebrating wildly and teasing the boys, whose first eight wasn't even in the top group. I was all right at first, very much one of the crowd, but as I began to get drunk I began to get horny too, and optimistic.

I wanted my bottom smacked, and, even though it was hard to convince myself that I wanted it smacked by Stephen rather than James and Violet, it was easy to convince myself that he'd only been trying to comfort me before, and would be itching to do me. He'd also be at his own bumps supper, drunk and with any luck as horny as I was. All I had to do was wait until the celebrations had begun to die down and sneak out of college.

To think was to act. The streets were full of people, and it was hardly unusual for a girl to be visiting her boyfriend on a Saturday evening, but I felt deliciously naughty and secretive as I made my way over to Emmanuel. The porter gave me a knowing grin, setting my cheeks on fire as I immediately imagined him as an audience to my coming punishment. He knew I was Stephen's girlfriend, and was no doubt merely thinking of us in bed, but in my mind's eye he was standing in the doorway of Stephen's room, gloating over my humiliation as my bottom was laid bare and spanked.

Stephen was in hall, booming out a rowing song with his friends, a tankard of beer in one hand while he beat out the time with a roast potato stuck on the end of a fork. I came up behind him and put my arms around his neck, kissing him. Everybody around the table immediately dissolved into cheers and laughter, with quite a few suggestions as to what he should do with me, although none of them as bad as what I was hoping for.

Stephen was grinning from ear to ear as I whispered to him. 'Your friends have got the right idea and, remember, I owe you a forfeit.'

Nobody heard me, but they'd guessed what I'd said, more or less. They set up a chant, demanding that I be taken to bed and soundly rogered. Fortunately the dons had long since gone to bed, or we might have been in trouble, and as it was I was blushing furiously as Stephen got up, took me by the hand and led me from the hall to the sound of deafening cheers. His hand enfolded mine completely, and all I could think about as we made for his room was that it would shortly be applied to my bottom. I wanted it hard, and I knew I was drunk enough to take it. With luck he was drunk enough to dish it out. He began to kiss me as soon as we were through the door, but I pulled back, hanging my head as I searched for the words to make my punishment as sweetly shameful as it could be.

'I know you were nice and said you'd let me off, but I was too proud, thinking we could win, and rude about your chances, so I think you ought to take me down a peg or two and give me my forfeit.'

'Don't you worry about that, darling, just get down the way you do.'

'Afterwards. Spank me first.'

'I can't wait, Poppy!'

'Spank me!'

Suddenly he was serious. 'Look, Poppy, I'm really not comfortable with this. I don't know where it's coming from, if you were abused or something, but ...'

'What? No, I was not abused, thank you very much. I just like it, Stephen, now come on, please?'

I was close to tears, with the wonderful fantasy castle I'd been building up for so long crumbling around me. He saw and took me in his arms, but that wasn't what I wanted.

'Please?'

He nodded, but he didn't look comfortable and he didn't know what to do, just patting my bottom a few times as he kissed me. I gave him an encouraging wiggle, but he began to grope instead, and to pull up my dress. That was better, and I clung to his chest, trying to push the bad thoughts out of my head and concentrate on the slow exposure of my bottom. With my dress up, he stuck his thumbs into the waistband of my knickers and pushed them quickly down, baring me. I pushed my bottom out, now quite enjoying the position, and the feel of his big hands on my cheeks.

'That's nice. Now smack it.'

Again he gave me only a few light pats before going back to feeling my cheeks. I couldn't help getting turned on, but I needed my special thing.

'More please, harder.'

Two more pats were applied to my bottom, just hard enough to make my skin tingle.

'That's nice. Again.'

I was clinging to him, my face pressed to his hard muscular chest, my bottom pushed well out. He liked my rear view, taking me on my knees more often than not, and I didn't see how he could resist. James wouldn't have done, not for an instant. I got two more pats, nervous, uncertain, and then he was pulling away.

'I can't wait.'

It was a lie, but I didn't resist as he manhandled me into position, still hoping that as his arousal grew his inhibitions would give way and he would give me what I needed while he was inside me. It didn't happen. He bent me over the bed, my feet braced apart and my hands flat against the wall, an excellent position for a spanking as well as for entry. I'd given up asking, praying he'd just do it, but he simply got himself hard between my cheeks and slid himself in, gripping my hips and taking off as if he was in a contest to see how fast he could come. His belly was smacking against my cheeks with every thrust, but that only made my frustration worse, and for the first time since we'd been together I didn't come.

He did, deep inside me, before collapsing on the bed, his eyes closed and his handsome face set in a blissful, sleepy smile. I almost forgave him, telling myself that he was only being nice and didn't want to hurt me, but it was no good. He had hurt me, by refusing my request after I'd tried so hard to help him with his own fantasies, which didn't turn me on at all. Worse, he'd suggested that my special desire might be the result of abuse, which was not only untrue but also an insult to me, and potentially to my friends, my teachers, my parents, none of whom had ever mistreated me.

I wanted to talk, but he'd quickly gone to sleep, which was

probably just as well or there would have been a row. He was also sprawled across the bed, and I could see that if I stayed I'd have a very uncomfortable night indeed, not just physically either. I needed to go anyway, my head full of bitter thoughts and frustration, as well as dizzy with drink, so I left Stephen as he was and made my way back out into the night.

It wasn't even late, and the streets were still crowded, with happy students drinking outside the pubs and making their way between colleges. There was a taxi setting a group down directly across the street and I ran to catch it, indifferent to the expense.

'Eynsham Road, please. I'll tell you when to stop.'

He set off without a word and I lay back in the seat, feeling sorry for myself. It really wasn't fair, when all I'd wanted was a strong man who would look after me and answer my needs. Stephen had seemed perfect, and now there was a stubborn part of me that wanted to cling on, hoping that with time everything would come together. I could hear Giles in my head, smug and calm and rational as he explained that I ought to accept Stephen as he was, be discreet and a good wife. That was never going to happen. I'd already been unfaithful, and not just with Violet, but also with James, and there was no denying that as I'd hung in my bonds with my whipped bottom thrust out for entry I'd been completely willing, more than willing.

We reached the house, the windows bright with yellow light, a sight so welcome that I was choking back tears as I paid the driver. He took no notice, leaving me on the darkened road with the light above James' door a beacon for my steps. I knocked, waited, and knocked again before James' voice answered. 'Who is it?'

'It's me, Poppy.'

The door opened immediately, allowing James to hustle me

quickly inside and close it behind him. I immediately saw why he'd been so cautious. The main room was in plain view to anybody who came in and in the centre of the floor, her arms above her head and her wrists bound together, was Violet, her lipstick-red high heels barely touching the ground as she swung from the great iron hook set into the beam above her head. Her mouth was slightly open, her eyes heavy-lidded and drowsy with pleasure. She was stark naked but for her extravagant shoes and the ribbon in her hair, her skin slick with sweat, her nipples straining to erection, her hips and thighs flushed pink. As she saw me she managed a happy smile, but James had realised that I was upset.

'What's the matter?'

His voice was full of concern, and Violet immediately straightened up.

The tears began to trickle down my face as I spoke. 'I'm sorry, I didn't mean to barge in on you, but . . .'

James had put his arm around my shoulders, but it was Violet who realised what was wrong. 'Is it Stephen?'

I nodded miserably, knowing that of all the people I knew they were the only ones who could possibly understand how I felt. James quickly released some catch at Violet's wrists and she took me in her arms as I began to babble.

'He wouldn't. I asked him. I tried to make it fun. I begged him, but he wouldn't, not properly. He seemed to think I'd been abused or something.'

'A lot of men don't understand, sweetie, most of them really. I'm sorry. Pour her a drink, James.'

'I've probably had enough.'

They ignored me, Violet helping me to the sofa while James poured out a measure of brandy. I took it gratefully enough, my fingers trembling as I held the glass. Violet had sat down beside me, cuddling me against her chest, with James on the other side stroking my hair. Slowly I began to relax, and to calm down, until my tears had stopped and I'd begun to feel I was being silly.

I could also see what they'd been up to. The ropes were still attached to the hook, and on a nearby table was a large black whip with a thick leather-bound handle and maybe a dozen tails of what looked like suede. Judging from the look on Violet's face when I'd interrupted them the session had been approaching a climax.

'I really choose my moments, don't I?'

Neither answered, still comforting me, but with the hard feel of James' arm across my back and Violet stark naked beside me my thoughts had turned back to what I'd wanted in the first place.

'Why don't you two carry on ... or something?'

James made some soothing remark, too low to catch, but Violet understood.

'Are you sure?'

I nodded, a single urgent motion. She kissed me and began to guide me gently down across James' lap. He hesitated only a moment, sharing a glance with Violet, who spoke. 'She needs it, James, trust me.'

He already had me over his legs, and as his grip tightened around my waist all my ill feeling had already begun to slip away. I closed my eyes, everything concentrated on the position I was in and being held tight by a man who wanted me and knew how to handle me. As he lifted my dress it was as if some huge weight was being lifted and not a few ounces of cotton. I lifted my body, wanting to be fully bare, and again it was Violet who understood immediately.

'All the way up, and lift her bra.'

I nodded my acquiescence, sighing as my bra was unclipped and tugged high, spilling my breasts out against his legs and the material of the sofa. He didn't feel them, but put his hands straight to my knickers, lifting the waistband and peeling them slowly down off my bottom. Again I sighed, and let my legs come apart until my knickers were taut between my thighs, deliberately showing myself off behind. It felt right, completely open to him, and had he chosen to slip a finger inside me before the spanking began I'd have accepted it.

Again his arm tightened around my waist, his hand settled on my bottom, and it had begun, firm and steady, hard enough to sting. I gave in immediately and completely, lifting my bottom to the smacks and gasping out my feelings into the sofa. In no time at all I'd begun to warm, and before long I'd slipped my hand back between my legs, without the slightest embarrassment as I began to masturbate. He understood, he cared. To him my reaction was a precious gift, an act of submission and of love from woman to man, not some unbalanced fantasy rooted in misery and hate, thoughts which had the tears streaming down my face even as I came to climax under my fingers.

I spent the night with James and Violet, and woke in his huge old bed with him between the two of us. When we'd slept together before it had always been Violet who went in the middle, and as I got up to put the coffee on I was wondering whether the events of the night before had triggered some change in the dynamic between the three of us. After I'd come, Violet had asked for the same treatment, and James had stayed firmly in charge of both of us for the rest of the night, rather than Violet dealing with me.

By the time we'd got to sleep it had been nearly three o'clock, and I'd woken to full, hot sunlight streaming in through the windows. It was nearly noon, but I had no desire whatsoever to return to Oxford, or to hurry at all, despite the hundred and one things I was supposed to be doing. None of it seemed important, for all that I knew I'd neglected my revision for prelims to make time for rowing and the Chamber. I felt warm and safe, happy to go naked as I padded between kitchen and bedroom with the coffees, and unconcerned for a life that felt distant in both time and space.

It was neither, and as we sipped at the hot liquid and talked my mood gradually changed, to an urgent need to get as much out of what would probably be my last free day before the end of term. Unfortunately Violet was still half asleep, while James was clearly content to lie there with the two of us snuggled up to his chest, perhaps not surprisingly. He was also keen to make future arrangements.

'Violet says you'd like to see us over the holidays? We'll be here most of the time, and of course you're very welcome to stay, but we're going to take a cottage again and we'd like you to come.'

'Normandy?'

'Not in the summer. We were thinking of the Ardennes, or somewhere in eastern France, even Germany.'

Violet put in a sleepy comment. 'Somewhere with plenty of woodland . . . lonely woodland.'

'Yes, please. I'd love to come.'

I took another sip of coffee and pulled James' arm around my shoulders. It was a wonderful prospect, the three of us all alone somewhere we'd be able to indulge ourselves to the full without the slightest risk of being caught. I was well overdue a birching, or James could punish me the way he'd done Violet the night before. Then again, I wasn't going to need to change in the boathouse for the rest of term, while after what had happened last night Stephen wasn't likely to be seeing my bare bottom.

'Put me on the hook!'

Violet had closed her eyes, but opened one. 'Eh?'

'Put me on the hook. I don't have to worry about marks any more.'

She rolled over, muttering. 'Whip the little baggage, will you, James. It's too early for me.'

James merely chuckled and carried on drinking his coffee, but I wasn't being put off. I climbed out of bed, and made my way downstairs, where the ropes still hung from the hook. Violet's wrists had been in a pair of rope cuffs linked together with strong metal clips, and it was easy to put my own in and snap the link closed. I immediately realised I was in trouble. She was not only taller than me, but had also been in built-up heels, so that I was forced to go on tiptoe. I couldn't open the link again either, leaving me completely helpless. James laughed and I twisted around to find him standing in the doorway of the bedroom, his dressing gown half closed across his chest.

'I'm a bit stuck here.'

'That, Poppy, is the idea.'

'Yes, but I'm not as tall as Violet and I'm barefoot ...'

'So I see. Being like that shows you off rather well.'

'A couple of inches maybe, please?'

'No. Try to enjoy being in an awkward position. It should add to the experience.'

'Yes, but ...'

He had picked up the whip, which looked heavy and painful. I did my best to pose as he lifted it behind his shoulder, looking back at him with my apprehension soaring. He brought it down, the suede thongs landing with a smack across my flesh, but it didn't hurt at all, producing only a heavy, diffuse sensation, certainly nice but in no way painful.

'You can do that again.'

'I intend to. This was going to be a treat before you went down.'

'Violet said, but she wouldn't tell me what. Sorry I spoiled it.'

'There are other things, two of which I intend to try on you today, as you're so keen. Are you sure about marks?'

'Yes . . . I want some.'

As we'd been talking he'd continued to flog me, laying the soft heavy thongs across my back and bottom and thighs to a steady rhythm but with each blow a little harder than the last. I'd begun to feel the blows, quickening my breath and making my body jerk each time. He was reacting too, his dressing gown now open to expose his cock, which had begun to swell. I hung my head, wondering what he'd do to me and delighting in the knowledge that I was helpless to prevent him.

He changed his rhythm, suddenly, bringing the whip around in a long lazy arc to fall across my breasts. I gasped, jumping on my toes against the shock but keen for more, my chest pushed well out. He'd begun to grin as he continued, amusing himself with me by never letting me know where the whip was going to fall until the last instant, using it to make my breasts bounce and my bottom cheeks jiggle, swinging it up between my legs to smack gently against my sex.

I was in heaven, my entire body aglow, my skin warm and starting to prickle with sweat, while the state of his cock made it very clear that he was enjoying the view and my helpless, aroused reactions. Soon he was fully erect, and again and again I thought he would put it in me, but he held off, tormenting me until I was wriggling on the end of the rope and pushing my hips in and out in my need.

At last he returned the flogger to the table and stepped close, but only to make a brief inspection of my bottom and pull at each of my straining nipples, before calling upstairs. 'Violet, the cane, please.'

There was no response, forcing him to call again. 'Violet, would you please bring down my cane, or you'll be getting it first.'

She appeared a moment later, looking worried. So was I. The thing she was holding was a metre length of thin pale-brown cane with a crooked handle, the sort of thing I'd only ever seen in old cartoons which had made me very, very glad I'd been born too late to have one used on me. Now it was going to happen.

I couldn't stop wriggling, and my heart had begun to race as he reached up to take the wicked-looking thing from Violet. She was still holding her coffee mug, lazy and elegant as she leaned on the balustrade, but her eyes were glittering with pleasure and her mouth had come a little open in her excitement at the prospect of me being given the cane. James had come close again, and drew one finger slowly down between the cheeks of my bottom, pushing between to enter me and to tickle my anus. I gasped, pushing against his hand by instinct, and he gave a pleased nod.

'She's ready. Six strokes is traditional.'

He stood back, measuring the cane across my cheeks. I'd kept my bottom stuck out as best I could, determined to behave, but when he brought the cane down it was like having a line of fire drawn across my cheeks. I could take it though, just, and was quickly back in position, the target presented for his attention.

The second was worse than the first and the third worse still, forcing James to wait while I jumped up and down on my toes in a vain effort to dull the pain. I'd got to the point of thinking I was mad to let him hurt me so much, and with the fourth I very nearly called out for it to stop. Only my need to find my barrier kept me in place, and it came with the fifth stroke, no less painful, but leaving me with a sense of regret that it was nearly over.

I got back into position for the sixth, glancing at James' straining cock as I pushed my bottom out. He was going to have me as soon as he was done, whether I liked it or not. My body was ready, my sex wet and vulnerable, brought on heat by a whipping as I dangled helpless on the end of a piece of rope. The cane struck home one more time and I'd been done, caned, with six livid scarlet welts criss-crossing my bottom.

James dropped the cane and came straight to me, his cock in his hand, with Violet laughing and clapping to see the state he and I were in. I felt him between my legs, but not in me, and I knew I was going to be treated to the same delicious fate he'd given us both at the blockhouse. Now it was better still, with my burning bottom cheeks pushed against him and his arm tight around my hips, as he took me to an orgasm that made me scream and left my vision hazy before he slid himself deep into my body for his own satisfaction.

16

I did not want to go back. Unfortunately I had to, and being with Violet made it a lot easier. I stayed with them on the Sunday night, the first time I'd done so, and James dropped us off first thing in the morning. It took a conscious effort not to hold hands as we came into the lodge, and I was sure the porter's smile hinted that he at least guessed something was going on.

There was a note from Stephen in my pigeonhole, asking where I was. I'd had my mobile switched off, and he'd also sent me a text, so had clearly realised that something was wrong. The last thing I needed was an emotional crisis, and I found myself wondering what I should do, and cursing him for being unable to understand my needs. I'd been ready to spend the rest of my life with him, and had suffered enough trying to make one compromise without needing to come to terms with another.

It was possible, just about, because if he was going to keep seeing Giles I could see no reason why I shouldn't have a similar arrangement with James and Violet, although I knew it would never be entirely satisfactory and was also extremely risky. As I'd learned since I'd first gone to bed with Violet, the wonderful thing about same-sex relationships, particularly between women, is that nobody suspects anything unless you're really quite blatant about it. Unfortunately my relationship with Violet was getting to that point, while, if I was to include James, the three of us would need to be very discreet indeed, especially in the long term.

I knew the answer, or at least the answer most people would have given me: to stick with Stephen and stop behaving like a perverted little slut. Dad would have phrased it less harshly, but it would have been what he thought, Mum too; thoughts that weakened what had seemed such an obvious choice over the weekend and added to my indecision about Stephen. In the end I took the coward's way out and sent him a text apologising, but not explaining where I'd been.

With Eights Week past and my position as Recorder assured, I could at least concentrate on prelims. Fail and I was out, and if there was one thing I was absolutely sure of it was that I wanted to remain at Oxford. So I spent the day at lectures and revising, with an ever-growing awareness of just how much I needed to cram into my head in order to be sure of passing. I had no hope whatsoever of gaining a distinction.

My work did at least give me an excuse not to see Stephen and so avoid the awful choice between having to accept sex, lying to avoid it and having a serious talk which might well break up our relationship. There was also the state of my bottom to be considered, as anybody who saw me bare could not possibly fail to realise that I'd been caned, which is not something that's easy to explain away.

I'd forgotten all about Wednesday at the time, but could now see it was going to be a problem. The most sensible choice seemed to be to cry off sick, but as I sat in the Chamber bar on the Tuesday evening, nursing a well-earned glass of port after an afternoon of solid revision, Giles appeared at my elbow, looking even more pleased with himself than usual.

'Presently, Poppaea, you will be thanking me in broken tones for the favour I have done you, and for which I charge not even the use of your pretty mouth.'

I gave him a filthy look, completely wasted as he went on.

'Uncle Randolph will be joining us for dinner tomorrow, and

thanks to my influence he will be making you an offer. Do not turn it down.'

'What is it?'

'Ah ha, you must wait and see. Suffice to say that it could very well be the making of you.'

'No, seriously, what is it? I'm not in the mood for games, Giles.'

'No? That's not what I've been hearing.'

'What do you mean?'

He tapped the side of his nose, but then went on, rather more quietly. 'That is actually a serious point, Poppy. If you must indulge yourself in a lesbian affair, do at least try to be discreet.'

'What lesbian affair?'

It was a pointless denial, my cheeks flaring scarlet even as he spoke, and growing hotter as he went on.

'The one you are having with Violet Aubrey. She's pretty, I'll grant you that, although personally I like something to get hold of in the milk-dispensing department, but I don't suppose that would bother you so much as you've plenty of your own . . . hmm, where was I? Oh yes. Everybody knows the two of you sleep together, apparently because your entire rowing team caught you at it, or some such story.'

'It wasn't like that!'

'That's a pity. I'd loved to have been . . . you don't suppose I could watch, do you?'

'Giles!'

'No? Oh well . . . just be careful. Not that it matters all that much nowadays, but still. Another port?'

I'd sunk my head in my hands. 'Please, yes. And tell me about your uncle.'

'If you insist. He sometimes takes on juniors over the summer, you know, departmental stuff, a chance to chat up the movers and shakers, that sort of thing. You're on the list.'

The offer was simply too good to refuse, but it was for the entire summer and I had no intention of forgoing my holiday with James and Violet. I was going to have to find an excuse, whatever it took, which meant yet another lie, but lies and secrets and Giles' 'discretion' seemed to be becoming an ever more important part of my life. The first thing to do was to find out if James had booked dates, which would allow me to tell Sir Randolph that I had an unbreakable previous engagement.

There was also the problem of the rumours being spread about my relationship with Violet, and the fact that they were not only true but also very mild indeed compared with the truth was not much consolation. Whatever Giles thought, I wasn't at all sure that a lesbian affair while at college would be considered trivial by the media and therefore by the public. I had compromised my position, and I was feeling bitter and guilty as I walked back to college, but I couldn't bring myself to blame Violet. She was in, with her sketch book open and a frown of concentration on her face, but she smiled and looked up as she saw me.

'Hi, Poppy. Coffee, something stronger, or straight to bed?'

'Something stronger, then bed, but I'm afraid there's a problem. Apparently somebody from the boat club put two and two together the other day and now there are rumours going around about us being together. Even Giles knows.'

'They finally realised, did they? Not the juicy details, I hope.'

'No, I don't think so, or Giles would have said something.'

'That's OK then.'

I wasn't so sure about that, but went to my own room to

fetch the bottle of port, and poured two large glasses, before I carried on.

'We'd better be careful, anyway. There's another thing too. Giles' uncle has offered me a volunteer place over the summer, so I need to know our dates for France as soon as possible. Has James booked?'

'Not yet, but it'll be quite early. It's best to avoid August, because all the French go on holiday themselves.'

'The end of July then? I'll say I'm busy until August. This whole making-a-career business isn't as easy as I thought it would be!'

'How do you mean? You've done amazingly well.'

'On paper, maybe, but I'd promised myself I'd be whiter than white, and there are already several things I need to hide, and hide well.'

'Do you regret them?'

'No, not with you, or James. You make me feel alive, and wanted, and safe. I think I'm falling in love with you, Violet, and with James.'

I was blushing as I said it, and a huge lump had risen in my throat at the thought of rejection, but she smiled and reached out to pat my thigh. 'I've been in love with you since the first time I saw you, Poppy.'

We came together, holding onto each other without a word, lost in the comfort of each other's arms. I could feel tears starting, and let them come, knowing she wouldn't mind.

When we finally broke apart she kissed them away, only to burst out laughing. 'Don't go out like that, Poppy, not if you don't want to confirm those rumours!'

I looked in her mirror, to discover that I had a bright-red-lipstick kiss on each cheek, a little smudged where I'd been crying.

Violet found a tissue and wiped my face, talking as she did so. 'Anyway, if it does all go wrong there's always the milk round.

With your record they'll snap you up, and big companies aren't going to worry about your sexuality. In fact, it's probably illegal.'

'Dad would never forgive me. He's been in politics all his life, and twice came within a few hundred votes of taking a seat for his constituency.'

'Sorry to say this, but isn't he just trying to fulfil his own failed aspirations through you?'

'Maybe ... yes, I suppose you could put it like that, but still ...'

'There comes a time when you have to break away from your parents, Poppy. How do you think my parents feel about me?'

'I don't know. You hardly ever mention them.'

'Exactly. Let's just say I told them about James, and they were not impressed.'

'If you ever want to talk about it, you know I'm there.'

She kissed me and went quiet. I wanted to listen, and perhaps return some of the comfort and sympathy she'd given me, but she went back to her port, looking thoughtful before suddenly breaking into smiles.

'Summer's going to be wonderful. There's so much we can teach you, and there are all sorts of games we can play with the three of us together. You just wait!'

I smiled, my imagination already running wild, but she stood up, striking a dramatic pose at the window her head tilted back, one elegant leg raised to rest her foot on the chair.

'Paris, the Bois de Boulogne. We are kneeling, side by side in a verdant copse, naked, our bottoms rosy. Six men have just witnessed our spanking and the first two are feeding their erections into our mouths. James stands by, counting a bundle of Euros.'

'Go on, I've always wanted to be a high-class call-girl!'

'There's nothing high class about it, darling. The spanking

show was just to keep us in order and we've been sold for ten Euros a suck.'

'You are wicked, Violet, that's worse!'

'Better, darling. If you're going to have a fantasy, make it as rude as possible, do it in style. Now, why don't you lock the oak and let's get you out of that dress and into bed.'

Sleeping with Violet felt completely natural, and in the morning I found myself more resentful of the rumours being spread about us than I was afraid. It really was nothing to do with anybody else, and again I had to remind myself that if I was to be a public figure I would have to guard my privacy as carefully as could be, because the media would regard anything I did as everything to do with everybody else. That was not a happy thought, and set my mind onto what she'd said about the milk round as I struggled to revise the next morning.

She was right, in that my achievements at the Chamber alone would stand me in good stead for a job with pretty much any company I showed an interest in, ensuring a good salary in a secure career, barring total economic collapse. It was certainly tempting, and would mean I could abandon all, or nearly all, of the pretence and deceit I was coming to hate so much. Yet the more I considered the idea the stronger the image of Dad's face set in disappointment grew. Anger I could have handled, but that wasn't his way. Disappointment was another matter.

Violet had told me a little more as we lay in bed together in the dark about how her parents had found out first about her love of being spanked and later about what she did with James. Just to listen to her made me feel cold inside, and I was sure I'd never have the courage to admit to it, or to defend myself if I was caught out. Admitting to an affair with another girl would be bad enough, but the thought of their reaction on learning that I'd come to enjoy being turned over the knee to have my bottom smacked was intolerable.

I couldn't put it from my mind, making it hard to revise, and I eventually gave up and went over to the Chamber. Unlike me, Giles had opposition to his bid for re-election, and quite strong opposition. His choice of controversial debates and speakers had generated a lot of interest and also criticism, so that everybody had their own opinion. I was in two minds myself, impressed by his dedication to free speech but far from impressed by his submission to his uncle, although with my own recent thoughts I was wondering if that made me a hypocrite.

Either way, I had decided on the game to play, voicing limited approval for him so as to retain as broad a base of support for myself as possible. His opponent was centre left, which was going to make for a tougher fight than the term before, but his absolute certainty in a narrow band of political convictions had limited his popularity and I was fairly sure Giles would emerge victorious. Another term's worth of speakers with extreme views and debates that drew pickets to our gates more often than not and I would be ready to stand myself, assuming I could pass prelims. Fail, and I was out of Oxford, in which case I might as well go and indulge myself in Violet's fantasy of the night before, selling myself in the Bois de Boulogne for ten Euros a suck.

Tonight was the night of our double date; the four of us were supposed to be meeting in Mary's lodge at six o'clock and then going on to Browns, but with Sir Randolph now one of the party everything had changed. Giles met me and we walked across to the Fellows' car park, where Stephen, Lucy and his uncle were standing beside a glossy black Bentley. Stephen seemed blissfully unaware that there was anything wrong between us, and greeted me with a kiss, which gave me little option but to accept the same from Sir Randolph, but on my cheek. The old boy was beaming as he addressed me.

'Giles tells me you're taking up my offer of summer work? That's splendid.'

'Thank you. It's very kind of you.'

'Not at all. You'll brighten the place up. Term finishes on the twentieth, or so Giles tells me, so have the weekend with your parents, then up to London and we'll get down to business.'

If the lecherous twinkle in his eye was anything to go by I could guess the sort of business he was hoping for. By the look of it I was going to have to spend more of my summer defending my virtue than surrendering it, but I had to have some fun.

'Late July is difficult, I'm afraid, but otherwise that's fine.'

He gave a little tut and a shake of his head. 'Commitment, my dear, is very important.'

Giles broke in. 'Of course she'll rearrange her dates, Uncle. Shall we move on then?'

We did, out of Oxford and away to the south. Giles was driving, and obviously knew where he was going, quickly leaving the main road to thread his way through a series of lanes so tiny and cut so deep that I might almost have been back home. When he finally stopped we were high on the downs, overlooking a broad flat valley, with the distant spires of Oxford glinting red in the setting sun, a scene spoiled only by a set of colossal grey cooling towers in the middle distance. Giles stretched as he got out.

'The Vale of White Horse, in case you didn't know. Magnificent, isn't it, barring Didcot.'

I wondered if he'd merely stopped to admire the view before going on to the restaurant, but he locked the car and started towards what appeared to be a farm. There were no other buildings close by, just open downland in front and a single set of chimneys rising above the hedges and woods behind us.

Stephen took my arm. 'This is a wonderful place. It's called The Barn.'

'That fits. Have you been before?'

'It's owned by the parents of a chap who was at school with us, just opened. We tried it out last Sunday. You'll love it.'

Only as we rounded the corner of a great flint and brick barn did I realise what was going on. It was a working farm, after a fashion, but the yard was scrubbed clean and the buildings had obviously been smartened up. There was a shop to one side, advertising organic produce and with two tables set out beneath big yellow sunshades in front. The barn itself had been converted into a restaurant, with smart glass doors and long tables covered by white linen cloths and cutlery and glassware set out ready for diners. Only three other people were there, a middle-aged couple with an elderly friend or relative, all three intent on their menus.

Giles glanced around, nodding in satisfaction. 'Perfect, isn't it? Very discreet.'

The word 'discreet' sparked a warning in my mind, but I quickly decided I was being silly. With the other guests there, and presumably staff, it was hard to imagine what he could be planning, while in any event he was hardly going to suggest that Lucy and I service the three of them under the table.

He didn't, nor anything else unexpected or rude. The only embarrassing moment came when Sir Randolph had drunk rather too much and began to grow maudlin, advising the four of us to get married and start producing children as soon as possible. Giles was merely amused, but the look of worship in Lucy's eyes as she looked up at him made me fairly sure she'd have accepted a proposal like a shot. Stephen didn't react at all.

The restaurant was good, serving only the farm's own produce and that of their neighbours, even down to English wine, which caused a mutter of complaint from Sir Randolph. Unfortunately, aside from a chef who we never saw, there were only two people about, Giles and Stephen's old school friend, Nigel, and a girl from the village. As the place started to fill up the service grew slower and slower, so that it was nearly midnight by the time we'd finished. Giles had held back on the drink, but kept it flowing for the rest of us, so I was feeling more than a little tipsy as we climbed back into the car.

Stephen was next to me, and put his arm around my shoulder as soon as we got in. I didn't resist, unready to work out my muddled feelings and definitely not prepared to discuss them with Giles in earshot, let alone his uncle. Lucy had definitely had too much, and was soon asleep, her head knocking gently on the window as Giles navigated the twists and turns of the Berkshire lanes. She was still asleep when we got to Oxford, and Giles was supporting her as he left us to escort his uncle to a guest room.

I was left with Stephen, who was unusually silent, but took my hand as we left Mary's. By then it was gone one, the streets were all but empty and I was feeling tired with a busy day ahead, which seemed a more than reasonable excuse to ask him to walk me back to Boniface instead of taking me to bed. I gave a meaningful yawn.

'That was lovely, but the service was so slow. I'm tired.'

He didn't answer, but let go of my hand and slipped his arm around my waist. I thought of the six still vivid welts marking my bottom, and to all intents and purposes marking me as James' girl. Bed really was out of the question. A bit of casual conversation seemed in order, hopefully heading off any rude suggestions.

'Are you going to the Mary's garden party on Saturday?'

'No, I can't actually.'

He sounded oddly sheepish, rousing my curiosity.

'Why not?'

'Um . . . it's the Hawkubites dinner.'

'Oh.'

I wasn't really bothered, having largely abandoned my outrage at their childish behaviour, while it meant I'd been able to spend as much of the weekend as I could afford to sacrifice from revision with James and Violet. We'd reached the bottom of Queen's Lane, and he made to steer me up it towards Emmanuel rather than along the High. I resisted.

'I'm too tired, Stephen. Just take me back to college.'

'Oh . . . please, Poppy. There's something important I need to say to you.'

'Can't you say it here?'

'Not really, no. It's nothing bad. I just wanted to be somewhere special.'

He was almost pleading, and an awful suspicion had begun to creep up on me. I tried to make a joke of it. 'Special? As in your room in Emmanuel?'

'A lot's happened there. It's special for us, isn't it?'

Now he was defensive, making me feel guilty as well as agitated. I wanted to get away, but I felt awful for my own reaction, now sure what he was going to say. We began to walk up the lane, slowly, only for him to come to an abrupt halt.

'No, you're right, and we can always come back here.'

I'd stopped too, not knowing what to say, both of us silent, standing still with the moonlight flooding down across the Bridge of Sighs to stretch weak shadows along the ground. Never had the name been more apt, and I couldn't speak for the lump in my throat as he reached into his pocket.

'Stephen, I...'

He'd gone down on one knee and was holding up a small black box. As he opened the lid I was struggling to find words; to tell him I knew what he did with Giles, that I was no better myself, that I was in love with somebody else, anything to make him stop, but no words would come. I'd begun to cry as I saw the ring, a narrow band of white gold supporting a diamond alight with reflections from the moon and a distant street lamp.

At last he spoke. 'Poppy Miller, please will you be my wife?'

Still I couldn't answer, unable to accept him, desperate for the words that would deny him without causing hurt but knowing it was impossible. I wanted to run, for the earth to swallow me up, anything to put off the moment I had to answer, but he quickly spoke again.

'Please, Poppy. I promise to be everything to you, everything you need.'

He took my hand and pushed the ring down onto my finger.

17

I was engaged, or not as the case might be. Everybody certainly thought I was engaged, because Stephen was anything but reticent about it and the news spread like wildfire among the rowers and, via Giles, around the Chamber. I'd barely finished my panic-stricken attempt at explanation to Violet before people were knocking on my door wanting to congratulate me, and when I came into the Chamber for the debate that evening a huge banner had been strung across the main chamber, with 'Congratulations Poppaea and Stephen' written across it in brilliant-red letters two feet high. Aside from my parents when I'd done something really appalling, only Giles ever used my full name, so I knew he was behind it, and sure enough he emerged grinning from the crowd as I stood there with my mouth open.

'Congratulations! I told him you'd go for it.'

'You knew he was going to propose?'

'Of course. He always asks my advice, young Mitchell, and I'm to be best man, naturally.'

'Oh God.'

He laughed and clapped me on the back, then made for his place to call the debate to order. I'd been revising in the Bodleian, or rather hiding, and was late, while it was the final debate of his programme as President, so it was already standing room only and I was glad of the seat reserved for me as Recorder. He'd been clever, setting a debate entitled 'This House believes that the University of Oxford should return to full independence', which ensured plenty of robust debate while forcing his opponent for the Presidency to toe the Government line and therefore make himself highly unpopular.

I watched with interest, and once the vote had come in with an overwhelming majority in favour of the motion I was sure he'd be re-elected by a safe margin. James had attended, as he often did, but not Violet, and as soon as I'd completed my official work I went over to where he was talking to a group of students, eager to see him and hopefully to explain the situation.

One of the others spoke up as I approached. 'Poppy, congratulations! That's wonderful news, and quite a debate tonight, wasn't it?'

'Yes, and trust Giles to use it to his own advantage.'

'That's Giles for you, but it's likely to be you against him next term, isn't it?'

'Possibly. We'll see. Hello, James.'

He gave me a bold smile but no more. For a while we talked as a group, while I kept a nervous eye out for Stephen, still completely at a loss as to what to say to him. Only the pretence of exhaustion had allowed me to get away the night before, and I couldn't hide forever. Fortunately he didn't seem to be about, and Giles was nowhere to be seen either, leaving me safe to ask James a cheeky question.

'I don't suppose you could give me a lift?'

None of the people with us knew I lived in, but he did and was fully aware that I was suggesting he take me home.

His answering smile was all innocence. 'Yes, if you like, as long as you're happy to go now. I really need to get back.'

'Of course. Excuse me.'

We left, navigating our way across the crowded floor and out of the debating chamber. It was a warm night and there were plenty of people in the garden, including Giles, who was holding court to one of the guest speakers and a dozen others.

He didn't seem to notice me and we were soon clear of the gate and starting up Cornmarket towards where he'd parked his car.

I felt as if I'd made some daring escape, and couldn't resist taking his hand once we'd reached quieter streets. He returned the pressure briefly, then let go to take his mobile from his pocket and call Violet. We collected her and made for his house, the three of us talking eagerly about our plans for the summer until we arrived.

It seemed so natural, as if the relationship between the three of us was no more unusual than any other. When we got to James' house he made us a supper of salad and cold ham, while Violet opened a bottle of wine. We ate and drank, joking among ourselves, and after a while we began to kiss and to touch. Violet and I took turns across James' lap, first with our clothing disarranged and then naked, until our bottoms were hot and we couldn't keep our hands off each other, or him. We went down together for him, kneeling side by side as we sucked and licked at his cock and balls, taking him all the way before tumbling together on the carpet, head to tail as we brought each other to ecstasy.

Satisfied, we showered and went to bed, with James in the middle and the alarm clock set for seven-thirty so that I could be up in plenty of time for the first day of prelims in the morning. Only as I was on the very edge of sleep was my contentment broken, giving way to guilt and worry as the moonlight caught the facets of my engagement ring where it lay on James' bedside table.

My plans for an early start the next day didn't go quite as I had intended. The alarm clock went off on time and I got up, but so did James, who insisted on cooking me bacon and eggs for breakfast before driving me in, with Violet still asleep in bed. He dropped me as close to Boniface as he could get without being sucked into the worst part of the one-way system, where I kissed him and said goodbye.

The rest of the day was swallowed up, first by philosophy, by far my weakest subject, and then politics, by far my strongest and Dr Etheridge's own speciality. I came out feeling weak and badly in need of a drink, but also triumphant. Both my moral and general philosophy sections had contained questions I'd been reading up on only the day before, while the politics question on the distinction between different branches of socialism in the late nineteenth century related directly to at least three of my essays that term. Barring a complete disaster in my economics exam I was sure to be through.

That left the weekend clear, and I wondered if I should go and see Stephen and attempt to sort out the mess of our supposed engagement, either immediately or in the morning before beating a retreat to the safety and comfort of James' house. I was expected back, with hints of a trip to the woods on the Sunday, while as my cane welts had gradually faded my desire for more had risen. To really enjoy it I'd need a clear conscience, which was impossible to achieve with Stephen's diamond winking meaningfully on my finger.

I steeled myself to do it, all the things that needed to be said running through my mind as I made for Emmanuel, only to discover that he wasn't there, which left me feeling somewhat foolish. The big magnolia outside his block provided the perfect place to sit and wait, with its low branches and broad leaves to shade me from the sun. It also meant I couldn't be seen at all easily, for which I was extremely grateful when Stephen finally appeared, with Giles and Lucy. She had a blue velvet gown hung over one arm, still encased in plastic from the dry cleaners.

They were deep in conversation, and I stayed as I was until they'd disappeared inside his block. It was obviously impossible to have anything in the way of a meaningful conversation with Stephen while other people were around, and I was about to leave when they came out again. I was just in time to nip back into the shelter of the tree, and as they made their way through the arch into the main quad I saw that Stephen was holding what looked like car keys.

I had already realised that Giles intended to hire the farmhouse restaurant we'd visited as the venue for the Hawkubites dinner, but a new suspicion began to dawn on me. It wasn't at all the sort of place they generally used. Les Couleurs was more typical, for all that they were firmly banned. The Barn wasn't exceptionally expensive, and didn't even do French wine, or cigars, or cognac, while aside from the tables and possibly the big glass doors it was going to be hard to trash without industrial machinery. However, it was as remote as anywhere in southern England and belonged to people he knew. When we'd been there he and his friend Nigel had spent a long time in private conversation, while there had been a board announcing that it could be booked for private functions. Also, Giles was the one with the car, a two-seater, but Stephen was the one holding car keys, which suggested they'd hired a bigger vehicle. Finally there was Lucy's newly cleaned evening gown. They were planning to gang-bang her.

My immediate reaction was to tell myself the idea was just too outrageous, but it wasn't. I'd spoken to Lucy often enough to know that she liked sex and had very few moral scruples, while she was besotted with Giles and got drunk very easily indeed. My second reaction was that it was none of my business, but there was Stephen, who had just asked me to marry him whatever else might be going on, and the possibility that she hadn't agreed to do it but would simply be filled to the brim with beer and then coaxed into sex. I could imagine Giles doing it, because underneath all his roguish charm he was a complete bastard.

At the very least I had to talk to her and make sure she was allright. I followed, keeping my distance, to the bottom of Parks Road, where Giles and Stephen turned north, leaving Lucy to continue down Holywell Street towards Mary's. I hurried after her, quickly catching up.

'Hi, Lucy. That's pretty.'

'Isn't it lovely? Giles bought it for me.'

'Lucky you!'

'He is generous, but . . . you're engaged!'

I shrugged, eager to avoid the topic. 'Where are you going? He's not taking you to the Hawkubites dinner, is he?'

She hesitated and I immediately knew I'd hit on the truth. All I needed were the details, but I could hardly ask straight out, especially if she was being paid. I decided to bluff.

'It's OK, I know how it works. They invited me in my first term, but . . .'

I trailed off, hoping she'd fill in the gaps. She didn't, but began to colour up a little and I went on hastily.

'It's all right, it's just that Stephen wasn't a member then, or I'd have gone.'

Now she was smiling, but she still sounded a little cautious as she went on. 'I'm glad you understand. People around here are so stuck up. I mean, so it might get a little bit naughty, but what's wrong with that. It's just a bit of fun, isn't it?'

I laughed. 'Yes, of course, but I suspect it might get more than a little bit naughty.'

She giggled, then turned, looking at me for confirmation. I couldn't help but give it, for all I'd never have let a dozen randy men take turns with me, because I knew perfectly well that most people would consider what I did do to be worse. An open question now seemed reasonable.

'You are OK with it, aren't you? You do know there'll be about twelve men?'

I wasn't even entirely sure what she'd agreed to, and expected her to at least betray a little nervousness. To my surprise she merely shrugged and her voice was full of mischief as she answered me.

'Twelve's good.'

She glanced at me, bright eyed and smiling.

'Can you keep a secret?'

'Yes, of course. Tell me.'

I've had fifteen.'

'Fifteen?'

'The South City team, after they got promoted. They threw a big party at this hotel, you see, and I was working in a lap dancing club to earn some money for my fees, so I got asked along, and well ...'

She trailed off, but I was quite able to fill the details in for myself, imaging her naked and drunk as she entertained an entire football squad, and I'd been worried about Giles taking advantage of her. That was obviously not a problem, especially when she'd as good as admitted selling herself, and with no more than a trace of embarrassment. To me it was a dark, very private fantasy, to her, simply part of life's reality. She'd needed the money, so she'd done it, as simple as that, and I wondered if I'd have been quite so choosy if I hadn't always had my parents to rely on. I couldn't help but be impressed.

'Good for you, Lucy.'

'It was in the papers, not my name, because I used to call myself Peaches, but a shot of my face. I thought I'd lose my place here, but nobody noticed! Nobody who mattered anyway.'

'You know what they say: today's news, tomorrow's chip wrappers.'

It looked as if Giles had been eating fish and chips.

Lucy invited me to have dinner in hall at Mary's, after which I walked back to college. I was exhausted, and would have liked nothing better than to be pampered by Violet and put to bed with a warm bottom, but she was still with James. The temptation to pull myself together and cycle out to his house was considerable, but I badly needed a good night's sleep and I was unlikely to get one in their company, however good their intentions.

I decided to be virtuous and go to bed, despite the soft summer-evening light still filtering through the gaps in my curtains. It can only have been a few moments before I was asleep, only to wake with a horrible start from a dream in which I'd overslept and missed my economics exam, ensuring that I failed prelims. For a few awful moments I couldn't decide whether or not it was real, before my head cleared and I realised that it was not only two days to go before the exam but also the middle of the night.

My body was prickly with sweat from the surge of adrenalin and I'd been asleep for over seven hours, as much as I normally take. I decided to have a shower, hoping the hot water would make me drowsy again but it made little difference and I found myself lying in the darkness with the sheets pushed down against the warmth of the night, thinking vague thoughts about my life; first wondering if it might be possible to reach a compromise with Stephen after all, perhaps with Giles to mediate between us, then trying to come to terms with my jealousy at the thought of what was going to happen to Lucy at the Hawkubites dinner, and, lastly, wondering what would have happened to me if I'd accepted two terms before.

The simple answer was that I'd have been had by all twelve or so of them, but I had no idea how these things actually worked. As they were paying me I'd presumably have been expected to do as I was told, a thought that sent a shiver of mingled resentment and excitement right through me. Maybe I'd have been expected to do a striptease first, or serve in the nude, or with nothing on but a little frilly apron and high heels. Certainly they'd have expected to touch, unexpectedly cupping my breasts from behind, or making me stand still with my hands on my head while they felt me up, my bottom too, maybe even smacking my cheeks.

Only when they'd got drunk enough to overcome their inhibitions would I really be put to work; maybe put under the table to take them in my mouth one after another, or sent into some back rooms where they'd come in one by one after drawing lots for who was going to have me first. Then again, if the articles I'd read about footballers were anything to go by, they'd bend me over a table in full view and make me take them on two at a time, one up me from behind and one in my mouth. I remembered the awful term they used for it – spit-roasting – as if I was a pig skewered on their cocks and another shiver ran through me, more powerful than the first.

I was going to have to do it, because I couldn't stop myself. My thighs came up and open and I was searching my mind for some fantasy that might at least allow me to retain some tiny shred of dignity as I began to masturbate. A couple of touches to my clit and I'd given up even on that, reminding myself of what Violet had said about making a fantasy as rude as possible. She was right, especially in the darkness and quiet of my own room with nobody to know my thoughts or watch as I stroked at my breasts and rubbed my sex.

As I closed my eyes I was wishing there had been people to watch, lots of them, perhaps the Hawkubites, or better still the men in the rowing club, from all three boats. That made 24 big, active young men. I imagined how it would be if it was traditional for the girls to be fucked at bumps suppers, with all eight of us bent over a table, our rowing shorts pulled down and our tops up over our breasts, first to be spanked with an oar, then fucked and made to suck, three men to each girl, or, worse, to have the third take us up our bottoms.

The thought had me arching my back in ecstasy and biting my lip. I'd never done it, but I'd thought about it, and teased myself with a finger. In my mind it was easy, with me mounted on one man as he lay on the table, another in my mouth, my bottom spread to a third, my cheeks rosy from my spanking and the tight pink hole between vulnerable to his erection. I imagined my friends to either side, gasping out their feelings as they were given the same treatment, and myself, pop-eyed and dizzy as my bottom hole was penetrated and filled.

I was biting my lips as I came, determined not to scream as wave after wave of ecstasy ran through me, my back arched tight and my hands clawing at my breasts and at my sex. At the very last moment the image in my head changed, to France, with James up my bottom and two local men filling my mouth and sex, men who paid the grand sum of ten Euros to have me any way they pleased. That was better still, and I brought myself to a final shuddering peak before letting my body go limp on the bed, my mouth curving slowly up into a satisfied, shame-faced smile.

When I woke up for the second time that morning it was broad daylight and time to get up. I had my day mapped out, revision in the morning, then down to James' for lunch. There was also Stephen, but I still didn't know what I wanted to say. If he was going to join in with the others when they had Lucy it put our engagement in rather a different perspective. I'd had no idea if he intended to stop misbehaving with Giles or not, but if he expected to join in with gang-bangs then I was in a strong position to bargain. All I needed to do was tell him what I knew and make him agree to an open relationship.

It made sense, but it didn't feel right and I was still trying to decide whether or not I could go through with it as I left hall after breakfast.

Dr Etheridge was in cloisters, talking to another don and I gave him my usual friendly greeting, only for him to raise a finger. 'One moment, Poppy. Might I have a word? Excuse me, David.'

He sounded even more formal than usual, and my first thought was that I'd failed my prelims, but the papers couldn't possibly have been marked, let alone passed on to him. Nevertheless, I was feeling distinctly nervous as I followed him to his rooms.

He sat down, eyeing me for a moment over his glasses before speaking. 'As you know, Poppy, I am, at least technically, your moral guardian as well as your tutor, and it is a moral matter I wish to discuss.'

The blood had begun to rise to my cheeks as I realised he must have heard the rumours about Violet and myself, and I was desperately trying to choose between denying everything and standing my ground as he went on.

'You are, I believe, close friends with your neighbour, Miss Aubrey?'

That one at least was easy.

'Yes.'

'And also with her, ah ... um ... associate, Dr McLean?'

'Yes.'

'And you have in fact stayed at his house on numerous occasions?'

'A few times, yes.'

'You are, um ... perhaps unaware of his, um ... reputation?'

He obviously was having serious difficulty in choosing his words for embarrassment. I was not about to admit that I knew James liked to spank girls, let alone that he did me.

'Reputation, Dr Etheridge?'

'Yes. The thing is, Poppy, that he is something of a, um ... a roué, a sexual predator.'

I pretended to look shocked. 'He's always behaved very well towards me.'

He had, by keeping my bottom warm, so it was true enough in a way.

'I am very glad indeed to hear that, and yet, in my position as your moral guardian, and also with respect to your career, I really must advise you that you would be better off if you were to see less of him or, better still, disassociate yourself from him entirely.'

'Oh. Thank you.'

It was all I could say, but I felt sick to the stomach. I'd had no idea I'd been so obvious or, as Giles would have put it, indiscreet, and Dr Etheridge was still talking.

'As to your personal relationship with Miss Aubrey, well, in this day and age it is not for me to criticise, but I do feel that you should consider your situation very carefully. You are, I believe, engaged?'

'Er ... yes.'

'Congratulations, but do bear in mind what I have said.'

'Yes. I will. Thank you.'

'You may go.'

I went, blushing furiously as I clattered down the stairs and around cloisters. He knew, or had guessed, far more than I'd expected. James' reputation was obviously worse than I'd realised, while I wondered if the students in the room below and to either side of me and Violet could hear us at night, for all the massive stone walls and thick floors. It didn't bear thinking about, but at least the subject of spanking hadn't come up directly, or the interview would have been ten times as embarrassing.

Everybody seemed to be looking at me, and I was sure they knew. I had to get out of college and find somewhere to calm down. There was only one thing for it, to go to James' early, despite Dr Etheridge's well-meant advice. I fetched my bike from the sheds and was waiting for a gap in the traffic before turning into the High when I saw Giles coming towards me. He was a friendly face, of a sort, and I paused, waiting until he came up with me.

'Hi, Giles. I have just had the most embarrassing interview with Dr Etheridge.'

'Oh yes, what's old Jarrow John been on at you about then? Caught you talking to the Conservatives, did he?'

'No, it was about Violet, and James McLean.'

'Ah. Well, you must admit, he does have a point. I was actually going to have a word with you about that myself.'

'Why? I can choose my own friends, Giles.'

'No doubt, but you are spending rather a lot of time with him, and staying at his house, so I hear.'

'Is there any privacy around here?'

'Not when you make a habit of cycling smack through the middle of town to go and see a man best known for birching young girls on their bare bottoms, no. The man's a liability, Poppy.'

'That's rich, coming from a man who gets regular blow-jobs from his male friends, not to mention running a club dedicated to trashing restaurants.'

'That's different, gay sex simply isn't an issue nowadays, while a reputation as a bit of a hell-raiser can do a man more good than harm.'

'A hell-raiser? You offered me a thousand pounds if you could spit-roast me!'

'The Hawkubites are extremely discreet, while I was sure you could be relied on in order to protect your own career.'

'And Lucy?'

'Lucy?'

'Yes, Lucy. You're taking her to the Hawkubites dinner tonight, aren't you? Don't lie to me, Giles.'

For once I'd got him off balance, and he was weighing his words as he answered me. 'She is invited to the dinner, yes, but as a guest. I felt it was time to bring the club into the modern ...'

'Bullshit! You chose Lucy because she's got enormous tits and fewer inhibitions than a rabbit on E. I know, Giles, because I spoke to her.'

'Good heavens, you are full of surprises. Quite the little detective.'

'Yes, aren't I? You saw her picture in the papers, didn't you, after she'd been caught out with the South City squad, and that's why you went out with her in the first place, isn't it? Because you knew she'd be willing.'

'Now you've lost me, I'm afraid.'

'Don't deny it, Giles.'

'I do, absolutely. I didn't know anything about that, although it does sound rather fruity . . . then again, no. I mean to say, with soccer yobs? I'm surprised at her. But no, that's not why I chose her. I chose her because I can recognise a slut when I see one.'

'Giles, she's your girlfriend!'

'Don't be prissy, Poppaea. She loves to be called a slut while we're at it, and I bet you do too. I had other reasons too, first because there isn't an ounce of malice in her juicy little body, and second because she will undoubtedly end up as a mathematics don and therefore can be relied on for discretion every bit as much as you can. I had to find somebody anyway, as you turned us down.'

'Why?'

'Because I said I would, Poppy, I gave my word, something you perhaps would not understand. But all that is beside the point, which is that James McLean is a pervert.'

'That's what they used to say about gay men, Giles, and not so very long ago.'

'Maybe so, but this is now and there's a world of difference between the occasional discreet encounter between men of the same age and a supposedly responsible don pushing his female first years into dropping their knickers for a thrashing!'

'That's not how it happened.'

'Maybe so, or maybe not, but do you think that matters? What matters, Poppy, is how people perceive him, which is as a dirty old man who likes to beat young girls.'

'And I suppose you've never done anything of the kind?'

'I haven't birched any first years. Look, Poppy, I've nothing against a spot of swish myself, but you know as well as I do that sort of thing is anathema to ninety-nine per cent of our *hoi polloi* electorate. It's really very simple. If you are serious about pursuing a political career, and in that I include the benefits you'll gain from working for my uncle, you cannot possibly be seen to associate with men like James McLean. You're going to have to make a choice.'

18

Even though he hadn't said it openly, Giles had effectively given me an ultimatum. My instinct was to reject it out of hand, as I had done with more than one boyfriend who'd tried to curtail my life or ambitions. Unfortunately, Giles was right. I'd done my best to keep my relationship with James and Violet a secret, but unless I cut all contact it could now only be a matter of time before it became common knowledge. The affair would then become a skeleton in my cupboard, a great, big grinning skeleton in a mortarboard and gown with a birch in one hand.

I couldn't afford to take the chance, but just to think about telling James and Violet it was over was enough to put an ache in my chest, not just an emotional pain, but a physical one. The fact that they would be understanding only made it worse, while I knew I'd break Violet's heart. Yet it was a sacrifice that had to be made, unless I was willing to abandon everything I'd worked for; not just since I'd come up to Oxford, but at school, along with all the time and money my parents had put into my education since I was a little girl.

At least I would still have Stephen, but I found that knowledge less consoling than it might have been. We got on well enough, but didn't really work together sexually, while I wasn't in love with him and never had been. Even if I ignored all that, looked at logically he was a liability, because as a female politician I would suffer just as surely if my husband was caught indulging himself with a couple of ladyboys on a Thai sex holiday as I would if I was caught with my knickers down across the knee of a disgraced don or my lesbian lover.

I knew that what I should really do was put it all behind me and look for some other strong dark man, although the way my luck was going he would undoubtedly turn out to be a transvestite or a flasher. Even if I could have been sure he was Mr Perfect I wouldn't have done it, because the idea felt cold and soulless, even more so than making a compromise with Stephen.

In the end I decided that there was only one thing to do. I would cycle out to James' house and explain the situation to them, making very sure to explain that I was in love with both of them and how much it hurt. What I was not prepared to give up was our time in France, but when it came to Oxford James and I would have to stay apart. Violet was different, because she would still be my neighbour until the end of term and it was pointless to pretend that we weren't going to end up in bed together.

I was in tears as I cycled out down the Botley Road, and kept having to stop and wipe my eyes. When I got to James' house I dismounted and stood for a long time, trying to pull myself together and to decide on how best to go about what I had to say. Finally I went to the door, which was opened by Violet, who took one look at the state of my face and opened her arms for me. I dissolved in tears, explaining to her in broken words what had happened and telling her how much I loved her.

James listened quietly to one side, speaking only when I'd finally let go of Violet. 'You are making the right decision, Poppy. I'm not a man you should be seen with, and I have no right to ask you to stay.'

'I want to, James, but ...'

'I know, and we will be together in France. There, don't cry.'

He took me in his arms, holding me until I chose to step

back. My vision was hazy with tears and my throat was sore, but I managed a smile as Violet held out a single printed sheet. It had the details for our holiday, and I folded it carefully before sliding it into the pocket of my jeans.

'I'd better go.'

'Must you?'

'I have to. I need to be alone.'

It was half a lie, because I wanted desperately to be with them, but I couldn't bear to stay. After one last cuddle I climbed back on my bike and started towards Oxford again, only to turn down the river, unable to face anybody at all. I rode fast, following the river, past the boathouses, under Donnington Bridge and the ring road, past the private little copse where I'd first tried out the birch, and beyond mile after mile, until at last I began to worry about getting back before dark.

I stopped on a low rise outside somewhere called Cholsey, maybe ten miles south of Oxford. Ahead of me I could see the long line of the Berkshire Downs, chalky green cut by the darker lines of hedges, with here and there patches of wood and houses, including what showed as a tiny grey shape but had to be The Barn. I thought of Giles and Stephen and their friends, getting drunk and enjoying themselves with Lucy while I stood alone and miserable. Had things gone differently, I knew it would be me in her place, soon to pleasure twelve men in an evening and in doing so create a secret that would last the rest of my life, one among many shared between a small group of discreet friends.

For a long moment I considered cycling over and picking up our conversation where we'd left off. I'd thought of several new things to say in my defence, but I knew it would only lead to further upset and embarrassment. Yet it was very hard indeed to turn away. I felt rejected, for all that I could have been there had I chosen, and very curious indeed, especially about Stephen and Lucy.

I thought of the big glass doors and how easy it would be to watch from the darkness and slip behind one of the buttresses that supported the building if anyone came. Both the loos and the door to the kitchen were reached from inside, so there was no reason anybody should come out anyway, until they'd finished. By then I'd be long gone, and, if wanting to watch made me feel intrusive, Stephen was my boyfriend, my fiancé even, and there can't be a woman alive who could be aware that her partner was going to what would almost certainly turn out to be a gang-bang and not want to know what happened.

For the best part of half-an-hour I stood there, my eyes on the distant barn, my curiosity and resentment warring against prudence and a touch of fear for what might happen if they caught me. Not that Stephen, or even Giles, would let me be dragged in and added to the entertainment, but it would be horribly embarrassing. Yet if I turned back I would never be sure what had happened, and in the end my curiosity won.

I hadn't seen any movement while I was watching, but as I approached the bottom of the downs I caught a glint of rich yellow sunlight as the glass doors were opened. Stopping once more, I saw a man who was presumably Nigel put out a sign-board and go back in. A moment later a minibus pulled up and began to disgorge people, too small to make out individually, save for Lucy, much shorter than the others and with her blonde hair and blue gown.

They could undoubtedly see me, but I was equally sure they could not recognise me, and cycled on until I reached a T-junction. A road ran along the bottom of the slope, with the down rising bare and empty above me, The Barn now invisible beyond the swell of the hill. I knew there would be a bright moon, so hid my bike in the hedge and started slowly up, growing more nervous with every step, but also more determined.

A long strip of woodland gave me shelter, then a beech hanger with an old chalk quarry carved into the hillside among the trees. One huge beech had been brought down by the winter gales, the thick grey trunk lying across the lip of the quarry. Even at that moment I thought of how perfect it would have been for me to be bent over and spanked, but it also provided the ideal place from which to watch The Barn without risk of being seen.

Everybody had gone inside, and the parked minibus was the only evidence that anyone was there at all, but at least two hundred yards of open field separated me from the nearest building. With the sun now a glowing red-orange ball above the Vale of White Horse I waited as dusk settled gradually over the land, bringing a faint chill. The moon was already up, and I watched as the vivid green and greys and chalky tones of the landscape gradually faded to a greyscale, with the yellow rectangle of The Barn's doors the only colour left.

A glance at my watch told me that just over an hour had passed since the Hawkubites had arrived. Sure that they'd be busy with their main course, I made for the buildings, my heart pounding as I ran across the short turf, praying that nobody would emerge from the door until I was safely concealed. As I drew closer I could hear laughter and voices raised in conversation, already with a drunken edge, and I was sure I could make out Giles' arrogant drawl among them, and Stephen's bass.

I made the wall of The Barn, throwing myself into the deep shadows beside the buttress nearest to the door. Only a sliver of deepest ultramarine remained in the western sky and the stars were fully out, creating a magnificent panorama about my head as I paused to get my breath back. Nobody had seen me, and I could not make out individual voices clearly above the general hum of noise. Somebody was telling a joke about three nuns at confession, with a smutty ending that raised a chorus of laughter.

With the bright lights inside it had to look utterly black beyond the doors unless somebody came close enough to touch, and yet I was very careful indeed as I poked my head out from behind the buttress. I could see into the room, a little at first, then more as I realised that none of them was paying the slightest attention to anything beyond the long table around which they were seated. Giles was closest, his back to me, with other men ranged to either side, all dressed in formal black tie. Stephen was near the end and Lucy at the tail of the table. Her face was flushed with excitement, her eyes bright and her mouth wide as she laughed at some comment or joke. Her gown was so low cut it could barely contain her breasts, but I'd half expected her to already be naked. To one side a whole pig was roasting slowly on a spit, a bizarre and even macabre sight in the circumstances.

Nigel was there, also in black tie, but wearing an apron. He was sharpening a wicked-looking knife in preparation for carving, while the others were helping themselves to vegetables from dishes already set out on the table. I'd obviously arrived before the entertainment, and was about to slip back into the shadows when the men to either side of Lucy reached out, took hold of the front of her gown and tugged it sharply down. She'd obviously agreed to let them do it, and burst into giggles as her breasts were exposed.

The men began to laugh and clap to see her topless, and one of those who'd stripped her reached out to take one heavy breast in his hand, weighing her as if he were a judge at a county show admiring a prize melon. In response she put her hands behind her head and pushed out her chest, revelling in their attention as her breasts were fondled and her nipples brought to erection. I couldn't take my eyes off her, or stop myself imagining how I'd have felt in her place, with my breasts bare in front of a dozen men as I was touched up to arousal.

They only stopped when the meat was served, but Lucy stayed as she was, plainly happy to be naked and doing full justice to the food. She was plainly drunk, and happy, laughing at their remarks and careless over how she ate, twice dripping gravy onto her bare chest to leave a splash mark and a trickle that ran slowly down to wet a nipple. At that, the man who'd touched her before leaned forwards to take her in his mouth, sucking at her and licking up the gravy from her skin.

I thought they'd have her then and there, but Giles yelled for order and told the man to be patient. At that they settled down a little, but Lucy stayed bare chested and flirting with all of those near her, Stephen included. I moved back into the shadows, trying to sort out my muddled feelings and fight down my own arousal. They'd got to me, badly, for all my hurt and anger, a purely physical need and yet not one I could deny.

Renewed laughter soon drew me back to the door, but it was only a man who'd climbed onto the table, to dance wildly for a few seconds before disappearing over the edge, where he lay giggling foolishly on the floor, unhurt but too drunk to get up easily. At the other side of the room Nigel had moved the remains of the pig and began to clear up. One or two of the men were taunting him, but his response was an ingratiating smile which only made them worse.

I watched as the dinner continued, alternately hiding behind the buttress and peeping out from the side. They ate a summer pudding with cream, and cheese, drinking all the while, until at last Giles banged on the table and stood up. I didn't catch all that he said, his words lost beneath the continuing hubbub, but his final words came across clearly enough.

'... my own little trollop, Lucy Smith!'

She stood up, delighting in their attention as eager hands

reached out to paw her breasts and boost her onto the table top under her bottom. They began to clap, wildly at first, and then to a ragged rhythm. She began to dance, and to strip; the lewdest, most blatantly sexual display I had ever seen, designed to appeal to men's most basic needs, but it wasn't her I was watching.

As Lucy's show began, Giles had pushed back his chair and casually flopped out his cock and balls. I watched, amazed, as Stephen came down the room, on his hands and knees, to take Giles' cock in his hand and start to lick at the bulging sac beneath. The other men just laughed and clapped, while one, a great hairy redhead who I recognised as the number-two oar from Mary's first boat, demanded the same service from Nigel, and got it.

Most of them now had their chairs pushed back, some watching Lucy strip, others their friends. Giles had put his cock in Stephen's mouth, his erection growing fast, but his eyes were on Lucy. She had come down the length of the table and was now dancing for him, in nothing but heels and stockings and knickers, more than happy to watch her boyfriend sucked hard by another man. I knew I couldn't have done it, and part of me was appalled, yet the urge to touch myself was rising to the point at which I had to make a conscious effort to keep my hand from between my thighs.

Giles was soon hard in Stephen's mouth and Lucy nude, showing off her breasts and bottom and sex in pose after dirty pose. Most of the men had their cocks out, and another had made his neighbour go down on him, which didn't bother the others in the slightest. When Lucy took a candle and slid it into herself they all cheered, and at that Giles dismissed Stephen with a casual slap to one cheek and stood up.

'I think she's ready, boys, and so are we. I think I can safely claim the privilege of going first?'

Nobody disputed him, and he had quickly lifted Lucy down from the table. She took hold of his cock, tugging on it as they kissed, before Giles swept his end of the table clear with a single abrupt motion. Lucy was giggling crazily as she was laid across it, with her bottom sticking out and up on her elbows to make her mouth and breasts available. Giles went to her head first and she took him in, sucking and pulling urgently on his shaft.

A hard shiver went through me at the thought of being made to do the same for him, and again as he went round behind her and eased himself in deep. Her eyes were closed in bliss and her mouth was still wide, allowing another man to fill it with his erect cock. I shook my head, trying not to imagine myself in her position, bent over a table with a man at each end while another ten queued for their turns.

Not that it seemed likely she would have to cope with all of them. The redhead was still busy with Nigel and didn't look as if he'd last much longer, while Stephen was on his knees, one man's cock in his mouth as he tugged at another. Yet he was still watching Lucy from the corner of his eye, while he had his own cock in his hand. I wanted to scream at him, and yet dozens of times I'd helped him with fantasies little different to what he was doing, and with him inside me.

Appalled by my own reactions as much as by what was going on, I threw myself back into the blackness of my refuge. I felt wet and urgent, my nipples painfully stiff, the aching need inside me and my battered emotions so strong I was sobbing. I had to come, however ashamed of myself it made me, and I'd given in, my fingers on the button of my jeans when I heard the crunch of tyres on gravel. Somebody had turned in at the lane.

I froze, pressed hard against the rough flint of the barn wall, not daring to move.

The car stopped. There was the thump of a door, then a female voice, high and slightly petulant. 'Private Function. Oh dear, that is a nuisance.'

They were reading the board, no more than three yards away, and I tried to press myself into the wall.

A man spoke, low and grumbling. 'I said we should have called to book a table.'

'Never mind, dear. We can make a booking now, and perhaps we can take a menu away as well.'

They were going to enter the restaurant, and I felt myself starting to panic even though I wouldn't be the one in trouble.

I could hear their footsteps, getting closer to my hiding place, stopping, then the man's voice. 'Good God!'

I ran, blind to everything but the need to escape as I dashed across the gravel and out onto the turf of the downs. The woman's voice called after me, but I only ran faster still, stumbling over the rough grass, sure the couple would call the police and determined to get as far away as possible as fast as I could. A backward glance showed them at the door, talking to somebody, but I didn't stop running until I'd reached the line of trees, and then only because I had no choice. The downs were silvery with moonlight, but in among the beeches it was pitch black.

Behind me, The Barn was no longer visible, hidden by the curve of the hill, although I could see the beech hanger where I'd hidden before. I'd run perhaps a quarter of a mile in what seemed like an instant, and I was grateful for all the training I'd done as I moved into the trees. As I moved down the hill I could hear raised voices behind me, and then the sound of a police siren in the distance. I hurried on, staying close to a hedge and ready to throw myself flat at the first glimmer of blue light.

None came and I reached the bottom of the hill in safety before pausing to listen once more. The siren came again, from behind and above, but the nearest town had to be Didcot, and if a car came from there it could hardly fail to pass me. I didn't want to be seen, and a lone girl on a bike at nearly midnight was sure to attract attention, while I had no real excuse for being there. I considered waiting, but it was getting cold and I decided to cycle west instead of north and hope for the best.

My bike was where I'd left it and I set off, my nerves feeling as if they'd been stretched on wires but the tension gradually reducing as I covered the ground. Eventually I stopped and looked back once more, but a spur of downland now hid The Barn from sight, while the sirens seemed to have stopped. A car passed me, briefly bringing my heart into my mouth, but it was not the police.

I wondered what to do, knowing that there would be a scandal and that as I knew three of those involved it was not a good idea to return to Boniface in the early hours of the morning. It was better to stay out, and pretend I'd been with James and Violet if I was questioned, accepting Dr Etheridge's disapproval as the lesser of two evils. Better still, I could make it the truth.

It was nearly three in the morning before I finally climbed off my bike outside James' house, sore and weary after riding for hours, as often as not with no idea where I was going. I was exhausted, but in the loneliness of the night my head had been flickering with images of what I'd seen; Lucy with her breasts bare as she stripped, the men with their cocks sticking up out of their dress trousers, but, most of all, Stephen down on his knees as he licked and sucked at Giles' erection.

19

I woke up cuddled onto James' chest; a moment of blissful calm closely followed by less pleasant emotions provoked by memories of the day before. Both James and Violet were asleep, but the clock by the bed showed twenty past ten so I hauled myself out of bed, worrying about everything from having broken my promise to stay away, through my Monday-morning economics exam to what might have happened to the Hawkubites. There was at least nothing to connect me with them, while there was every chance that my absence from Boniface had gone completely unnoticed.

The best thing to do was clearly to go back to college and behave as if nothing had happened, then perhaps go over to the Chamber in the evening and see who knew what, if anything, but without giving myself away. I knew from talking to Giles that the Hawkubites had a tradition of every man for himself and a rule about not incriminating each other no matter what, so there was a good chance that some or all of them had got away, especially if they'd had the sense to run as soon as they realised the police were being called.

I was worried for Stephen, despite the state of our relation-ship, and even for Giles, but most of all for Lucy, who was not only sure to be the slowest runner among them but had been stark naked at the time. Even if she'd managed to get dressed she'd have stood out from miles away in her blue gown, and it was a good fifteen miles back to Oxford from The Barn.

James woke up while I was making myself a hasty coffee and I explained to him what I was doing. He suggested coming back if I felt I should but made it clear the decision was mine and otherwise agreed that I was doing the best thing. I had told them what had happened the night before, over a hot whisky and honey before finally collapsing into bed.

Oxford seemed strangely quiet as I cycled in. Not many people seemed to be about, even for a Sunday morning, and Boniface was no different. There were two porters in the lodge but neither so much as glanced up as I came in, and to my immense relief my pigeonhole was empty. It looked as if I, at least, had got away with it. Not that I'd done anything, really, but I was sure I'd have got into trouble merely for watching, especially if I didn't report it to the authorities.

The day passed painfully slowly. I tried to revise but couldn't concentrate. At five o'clock I gave in and went to the Chamber, but while there were plenty of people about, Giles wasn't there, nor any other Hawkubites. I spoke to a few people but there weren't even any rumours circulating and in the end I decided to go to Mary's.

It was a perfectly reasonable thing for me to do, but as I walked along the High I felt as if I was walking into a trap and expected the lodge to be full of police, probably armed and with sniffer dogs trained to detect the scent of spit-roast. As at Boniface, the only people there were two porters and both looked bored. Giles wasn't there either and his window was shut, but as I left his stair I saw Lucy on the far side of the quad, dressed in jeans and T-shirt, with a pair of shades on but otherwise looking completely normal. I called out to her and she turned, then came quickly towards me, talking even before we were close.

'...has been arrested and...'

'Who has?'

'Giles! Stephen got away, I think, but they got Giles and they'd have got me if ...'

'Slow down, Lucy. Were you raided?'

I knew perfectly well, but listened in very real fascination as she told her story, leaving out only the rudest parts and carrying on beyond the point at which I'd run for it.

'Giles tried to talk them out of it, but they wouldn't listen and Nigel was supposed to drive the minibus but wouldn't do it and the rest of us were too drunk, and we tried to get away down the lane but the police came really quickly, and Giles stood up to them to let me get away ...'

'Giles attacked a policeman!'

'Two, two big coppers, on his own, just so I could get away!'

'And he got arrested?'

'He must have done, I think. I ran into the woods, and they didn't have dogs or anything so I got away and hitched a lift back.'

I could only shake my head, astonished both at her, and at Giles, who I'd have expected to abandon her and make good his own escape. Instead he'd tried to fight off two police officers, which was going to mean serious trouble.

'And Stephen?'

'He went off over the fields. I was just going to see if he's in.'

'I'll come with you. What a night!'

'Poor Giles. He's bound to get sent down!'

I nodded, unable to disagree and for once sympathetic. Whatever he'd done, however he'd behaved, when it really counted he'd stood up for his girlfriend and it was impossible not to admire that. As we walked to Emmanuel I was wondering if Stephen would have done the same for me, but couldn't decide.

He was in his room, looking slightly sorry for himself and very much the worse for wear, but he managed a grin when we came in, addressing me. 'Have you heard?'

'Yes.'

I sat down, waiting as he and Lucy swapped stories. He'd come down the slope no more than a few minutes after me, but struck out across country to Didcot, where he'd caught a night bus. Unlike me he hadn't slowed down for the hedges, and his face and hands were scratched, but he hadn't even seen a policeman. I could guess that Giles and he would have fled together had Lucy been there, which made Giles' act more noble still, but then Giles was quite clearly the alpha male of the group, as Stephen's behaviour towards him showed only too well. My man had to be in charge when it came to sex, which meant he didn't go down on other men, and he did spank me. That man was James, and I was in love with him. On that point I was absolutely certain.

It was not a good time, not after what he'd been through, but it never seemed to be a good time and something had to be said. Yet it was all so complicated, because I didn't mind him doing it, or even setting up a *ménage à trois* with Lucy, but if we couldn't fulfil each other's needs it was madness to stick together in what would ultimately become an empty relationship.

My fingers were on his ring, which felt wrong on my hand, but I could no more find it in myself to pull it off than to tell him the truth. I wondered at myself, because it had been easy enough with Ewan, and whether it was because I had made Stephen so much a part of my career plan. If so, then I was a cold, scheming bitch. I had to do it, and if there was no easy way, then there was a way to cause as little hurt as possible.

'Lucy, could I have a word, alone?'

'Er . . . yeah, sure.'

I took her outside, to where the tall window overlooked the magnolia.

'Lucy, you know that Stephen likes to go down for Giles, don't you? Please tell me the truth.'

She nodded, her eyes downcast and I went on.

'You don't mind, do you? Maybe you even like to watch, and that's OK, but . . . but it's not something I can get my head around. I think Stephen would be better off with another man, don't you?'

Again she nodded, then spoke. 'And you, you really prefer your friend Violet, don't you?'

It was my turn to nod, and if it wasn't the whole truth, it was enough. 'Yes. Could you support me please, Lucy, in what I'm about to say?'

She looked up, alarmed, but nodded her head a third time.

I pulled off the ring and we went back into Stephen's room, my face set in a forced smile as I spoke. 'I'm sorry, Stephen, but it isn't working between us, is it? I . . . I think we're both gay, deep down.'

I expected hurt, even anger, but what I got was a wan smile.

I had made my choice, admitting openly to Stephen that I was in love with Violet and that we slept together. He had guessed anyway, and tried to put a brave face on it for all his hurt. Yet I could still back away and take the cold choice by finding myself somebody to replace him, somebody who ticked all the right boxes for a politician's spouse. That meant giving up James, and Violet.

The rest of the day was spent busily trying to find out what had happened to Giles without giving Stephen and Lucy away to the police. Among the remaining Hawkubites most had escaped, but three had been arrested and released under caution, while the unfortunate Nigel was obviously in serious difficulty. Nobody knew what had happened to Giles, or even where he was, and nobody wanted the task of ringing round the police stations.

In the end we were forced to give up and I went back to Boniface in the hope of getting an early night. It didn't work, my head full of disturbing thoughts as I lay awake staring into the dark and yet more disturbing dreams once I'd finally got to sleep. When my alarm went I still felt exhausted, but forced myself to shower, down a large black coffee and eat a good breakfast before getting into my subfusc and making my way to hall.

My adrenaline took forever to kick in, even with a terrifying selection of economics and maths questions in front of me, but I gradually picked up the pace and managed to put my last full stop in place seconds before time was called. I knew I'd done well enough to pass, if no more, and I could feel the immense weight of my tension starting to drain away as we filed outside. A lot of people were there; friends with bottles of champagne, even relatives, but half of them seemed to be Chamber people, who converged on me. I hadn't expected anything of the sort, and was grinning and waving until I realised that they weren't there to congratulate me, each and every one looking serious, especially the Secretary.

'Poppy, we need you. Giles has done something incredibly stupid . . .'

I listened to the same story Lucy had told me, only from a different perspective and ending with the news that Giles had apparently been charged under the Sexual Offences Act and with assaulting a police officer, none of which surprised me and yet the news was still a shock. It was taken for granted that he could no longer stand for re-election as President, and who should stand in his place.

'. . . has to be you, Poppy, otherwise we're going to lose.'

'But Giles hasn't actually stood down?'

'How can he? He's in a police cell in Reading or somewhere.'

'Yes, but . . .'

'We've put your name forward, Poppy, and called an emergency meeting this afternoon. You need to speak.'

She was right, and I let myself be hustled across to the Chamber. It was packed and buzzing with rumours, Giles' name on everybody's lips and the opposition gloating over his downfall. I kept my opinions to myself and tried to work out what I should say and to ignore the unworthy sense of triumph welling up inside me. My speech was soon ready and I went down to the bar for a large gin and tonic, hoping to seem relaxed and confident while struggling to calm my nerves, then crossed to the debating chamber.

I'd never seen it so full, nor felt so much the centre of attention as I made my short walk to the podium. Everybody's eyes were on me, their whispered conversations suddenly stilled as I climbed up to face them, nearly two thousand people and every one of them intent on what I had to say.

'Ladies and gentlemen, as I stand here I find myself faced with a choice; a choice between on the one hand accepting your nomination as Presidential candidate for the Michaelmas term in place of Giles Lancaster and on the other declining that honour but retaining my own. All of you know by now, I am sure, that Giles was arrested on Saturday night following a Hawkubites Society dinner party. At this dinner party he encouraged a young lady who will remain nameless to perform various sexual acts. He also had sex with her and with at least one of his fellow diners. Unfortunately two members of the public witnessed this and the police were called, leading to his arrest on charges of indecency and assaulting a police officer.'

I waited for the shocked conversation to die down.

'Clearly the majority of you feel that in the circumstances he cannot stand for re-election as President, but if Giles Lancaster is to be condemned for his actions, then I too must be condemned for mine. I therefore decline the nomination.'

For a moment the rising buzz of conversation drowned out my voice, but quickly died once more and I carried on, now with my heart thumping in my chest.

'Instead, I propose to you that Giles' acts are more to be praised than censored. What he and his friends did was between freely consenting adults and was intended to remain private. Nobody was harmed, or need not have been had not the police seen fit to interrupt the evening. I cannot condone assault, but I will say this. Giles stood alone against two fully trained police officers in order to allow a female friend to escape arrest for what comes down to being accidentally seen while having sex. Call me old fashioned, but if any man did that for me he would deserve my devotion.

'So, let me ask you this: what did Giles do that any one of us has not done, in thought if not in deed? Think before you answer that, even if you answer it only to yourself. Giles may have stepped outside those moral boundaries to which we are expected to pay lip service, but has he done wrong? If you think he has not, then you should support his candidacy, while, if you think he has, then I cannot in good conscience ask you to support mine.'

I had hoped it would be enough, but they looked more puzzled than anything and as the whispering began again I caught Violet's name. A flick of my finger and the microphone was at max, my voice booming out around the Chamber as I spoke.

'Yes, if you want the juicy details I am involved in a flagellant *ménage à trois* with Violet Aubrey and Dr James McLean.'

The echoes of my voice died away to leave complete silence. I was choking back tears and I could feel the heat of my burning face, but I went on regardless.

'Yes, that's right. I sleep with Violet and I like to be spanked by James, and Violet too, yes, spanked, as in smacked on my bare bottom with my knickers pulled down. It makes me come and I heartily recommend it to you, but, if you don't like it, balls to the lot of you.'

I'd meant to flash my bottom, but my courage had given out and it was all I could manage to finish my speech.

'I therefore propose to you, for President of this Chamber in the coming Michaelmas term, Giles Lancaster.'

I stepped down, expecting yells of condemnation and outrage, if not actual tomatoes and eggs. For a moment there was only the sound of my heels on the floorboards, then somebody at the back had begun to clap, another and a third. A cheer went up and suddenly everybody had joined in. I turned to look, and found only a few glum, censorious faces among the hundreds clapping and cheering, yet it was definitely time to make an exit. A bow, a wave and I was gone, out through the lobby and into the deserted gardens.

My heart was hammering and I was having trouble controlling my breathing, but a glorious sense of elation had begun to well up inside me, and freedom too. I no longer cared what they said or what they did, who thought what about me and what the consequences might be. I was out, with a vengeance and it felt wonderful. Everybody was going to want to talk to me and I couldn't cope, so I hurried for the gates as the doors banged behind me, only to stop as an all-too-familiar voice called my name.

'Poppaea!'

It was Giles, hurrying towards me with a look of astonishment and gratitude on his face. As soon as he reached me he kissed me, laughing.

'I think you've sunk us both there, with a vengeance, but I'll tell you one thing: they'll still remember us long after any prime ministers that lot throw up are gone!'

I couldn't help but grin, but I was wondering what he was doing there. 'I thought you were in a cell in Reading or something awful like that?'

'What was good enough for dead Oscar would be good enough for me, my dear, but as it happens Uncle Randolph came and got me out. The scandal wouldn't do at all, you see.'

'You jammy sod!'

'My thoughts exactly, and I'm not going to be sent down either.'

'And Lucy?'

'Lucy got away, as you know. She's safe, but, as regards your speech, I do think that, perhaps, a comparison to Roland at Roncevalles might have been in order, or maybe...'

'Shut up, and come with me.'

I took his hand and led him from the Chamber grounds, walking as fast as I could. He followed, grinning.

In my room at Boniface I closed the oak and pushed him against it, taking the tag of his fly in my fingers.

'Just how discreet can you be, Lancaster?'

'Perfectly, I assure you.'

'Then this never happened.'

As I spoke I drew down his fly. His answer was a soft groan as I freed his cock into my hand and began to tug on it and to kiss him. He took my head in his hands, teasing the back of my neck as our mouths came open together and my intention of simply treating him to a suck had already begun to fade. I was breathless as we came apart, his cock now swelling fast in my hand as I went down on my knees.

'This is only going to happen once, Giles, but ... but do whatever you like.'

His answer was to pull up my top and bra, freeing my breasts as I took him in my mouth. I was stroking them as I sucked, deliberately showing off to him as well as pleasing myself and all the while hoping he'd take full advantage of my surrender. His hands found my head again, holding me in place on his cock and controlling the rhythm until he was fully erect, only to suddenly twist my hair hard and pull me back as he spoke. 'That's nice, but it's not really what you deserve, is it?'

I was pulled into my room, crawling on the floor with his hand still twisted tight into my hair, to the bed and over his knee. At the realisation that I was to be spanked I gave in completely, sobbing out my emotions as my skirt was lifted and my knickers tucked down around my thighs to leave me showing behind, with his cock a hard wet bar against my hip. His hand settled on my bottom.

'So you like to be spanked?'

'Yes. You know I do.'

'And you'd like to be spanked by me.'

'Yes. Yes, please, Giles, do it ... spank me hard.'

'That's Mr Lancaster to you, Poppy Miller.'

His hand lifted and came down again, a firm swat across both my cheeks, and then it had begun, a vigorous, no-nonsense spanking that had me kicking in my knickers and shaking my hair, and all the while with the same glorious thought held in my head, that I was over the knee of the most arrogant, self-satisfied bastard in the entire university, bare bottom and wriggling as I was smacked.

It took just moments to get me over the barrier before I was sticking my bottom up for more. He was laughing at my eagerness and began to amuse himself with my bottom, knowing he had me helpless, one strong arm around my waist. I was his anyway, far too aroused to want it to stop and enjoying every moment as he tormented me; opening my behind to inspect my anus, pulling my knickers tight up into the crease of my bottom and lifting me by them as he slapped at my cheeks, taking them right off and putting them on my head, laughing as he went back to spanking me.

'You should see yourself!'

I didn't need to, because I could imagine exactly how I looked, with my knickers on my head and my breasts jiggling as my red bottom bounced to the smacks, my legs wide open and my sex showing between, wet and ready for his cock. The thought of being fucked by him when he'd finished with me was too much, and I was unable to help myself as I cocked my legs open across his thigh, a trick James had taught me to make me come as I was punished.

'You dirty girl!'

The smacks got harder, every one pushing my open sex onto his leg and I was gasping out my pleasure into the coverlet, calling him a bastard and begging him to spank me harder, until at last it all came together in a long glorious climax that left me hanging limp over his knee. He chuckled, no longer spanking me but with his hand still on my blazing bottom, stroking my cheeks and tickling between them. It was his turn.

'Now make me say thank you.'

'What a nice way of putting it. I rather think I shall.'

I was completely spread to him, but I didn't care, abandoned to him as he slid a finger into me from behind. His cock was still pressed to my leg, as hard as ever, and I took it in hand, pulling on it as he explored my sex. I wanted him inside me, both for the simple physical pleasure and for the humiliation of being fucked by him after he'd spanked me, and quickly scrambled off his lap and onto the bed, lifting my rosy bottom for his enjoyment.

He shook his head and swallowed at the sight I was presenting to him. I gave him an encouraging wiggle as he climbed on the bed. His hands gripped my bottom, opening me. I felt his cock touch my sex, held in place as he savoured the moment before sliding it deep inside me and it was done. Giles Lancaster had fucked me, spanked me and fucked me.

I reached back for my sex, eager to come again while he was inside me. He was moving slowly, enjoying every moment he had me at his mercy, but as I began to play with myself and let the rude thoughts build up once more he spoke. 'Will this really be the only time?'

'Yes . . .'

'But I can do as I like?'

'Yes . . . anything.'

He pulled out. His cock slid up between my bottom cheeks, pressing to my anus.

'Oh God! Giles . . .'

My voice broke to a gasp as he pushed and I was panting out my ecstasy and clutching at my sex as he eased the full length of his erection slowly up my bottom. He got it all in, then began to push, with my muscles already starting to tighten in orgasm. Now I was well and truly done; spanked, fucked and now sodomised by Giles Lancaster, but it was my own choice and not done for advantage or to further my interests, but to give and to take pleasure with the freedom granted to me by my lovers, James and Violet.

Visit the Black Lace website at
www.black-lace-books.com

LOOK OUT FOR THE ALL-NEW BLACK LACE BOOKS – AVAILABLE NOW!

All books priced £7.99 in the UK. Please note publication dates apply to the UK only. For other territories, please contact your retailer.

To be published in April 2009

THE APPRENTICE
Carrie Williams
ISBN 978 0 352 34514 1

Genevieve Carter takes a job as a personal assistant, only to discover that the woman she will be working for is her literary heroine, Anne Tournier. Genevieve is soon drawn into a web of sexual intrigue and experimentation by Anne and unwittingly provides her with material for her new novel. But Genevieve has writing aspirations of her own. A competition ensues between mistress and apprentice – one that will push Genevieve to her artistic and erotic limits.

To be published in May 2009

LIAISONS
Various
ISBN 978 0 352 34512 7

Indulgent and sensual, outrageous and taboo, but always highly erotic, this new
collection of Black Lace short stories takes as its theme the illicit and daring
rendezvous with a lover (or lovers). Incorporating a breathtaking range of female
sexual experiences and fantasies, these red-hot tales of torrid trysts and passionate
assignations will arouse even the kinkiest of readers.

CASSANDRA'S CHATEAU
Fredrica Alleyn
ISBN 978 0 352 34523 3

Cassandra has been living with Baron Dieter von Ritter in his sumptuous Loire
Valley chateau for eighteen months when their already bizarre relationship takes an
unexpected turn. The arrival of a friend's daughter provides the Baron with ample
opportunity to indulge his fancy for playing darkly erotic games with strangers.
Cassandra knows that, if the newcomer learns how to satisfy his taste for pleasure
and perversity, her days at the chateau may well be numbered, something she can
hardly bear to contemplate. But help may be at hand from an unlikely source.

HIGHLAND FLING
Jane Justine
ISBN 978 0 352 34522 6

Writer Charlotte Harvey is researching the mysterious legend of the Highland
Ruby pendant for an antiques magazine. Her quest leads her to a remote Scottish
island where the pendant's owner, the dark and charismatic Andrew Alexander,
is keen to test its powers on his guest. Alexander has a reputation for wild and –
some say – decadent behaviour. In this rugged environment Charlotte discovers
the truth – the hard way.

ALSO LOOK OUT FOR

THE NEW BLACK LACE BOOK OF WOMEN'S SEXUAL FANTASIES
Edited and compiled by Mitzi Szereto
ISBN 978 0 352 34172 3

The second anthology of detailed sexual fantasies contributed by women from all over the world. The book is a result of a year's research by an expert on erotic writing and gives a fascinating insight into the rich diversity of the female sexual imagination.

Black Lace Booklist

Information is correct at time of printing. To avoid disappointment, check availability before ordering. Go to www.black-lace-books.com.
All books are priced £7.99 unless another price is given.

BLACK LACE BOOKS WITH A CONTEMPORARY SETTING

❏ AMANDA'S YOUNG MEN Madeline Moore	ISBN 978 0 352 34191 4
❏ THE ANGELS' SHARE Maya Hess	ISBN 978 0 352 34043 6
❏ ASKING FOR TROUBLE Kristina Lloyd	ISBN 978 0 352 33362 9
❏ BLACK ORCHID Roxanne Carr	ISBN 978 0 352 34188 4
❏ THE BLUE GUIDE Carrie Williams	ISBN 978 0 352 34132 7
❏ THE BOSS Monica Belle	ISBN 978 0 352 34088 7
❏ BOUND IN BLUE Monica Belle	ISBN 978 0 352 34012 2
❏ CAMPAIGN HEAT Gabrielle Marcola	ISBN 978 0 352 33941 6
❏ CASSANDRA'S CONFLICT Fredrica Alleyn	ISBN 978 0 352 34186 0
❏ CAT SCRATCH FEVER Sophie Mouette	ISBN 978 0 352 34021 4
❏ CHILLI HEAT Carrie Williams	ISBN 978 0 352 34178 5
❏ CIRCUS EXCITE Nikki Magennis	ISBN 978 0 352 34033 7
❏ CONFESSIONAL Judith Roycroft	ISBN 978 0 352 33421 3
❏ CONTINUUM Portia Da Costa	ISBN 978 0 352 33120 5
❏ DANGEROUS CONSEQUENCES Pamela Rochford	ISBN 978 0 352 33185 4
❏ DARK DESIGNS Madelynne Ellis	ISBN 978 0 352 34075 7
❏ THE DEVIL INSIDE Portia Da Costa	ISBN 978 0 352 32993 6
❏ EQUAL OPPORTUNITIES Mathilde Madden	ISBN 978 0 352 34070 2
❏ FIGHTING OVER YOU Laura Hamilton	ISBN 978 0 352 34174 7
❏ FIRE AND ICE Laura Hamilton	ISBN 978 0 352 33486 2
❏ FORBIDDEN FRUIT Susie Raymond	ISBN 978 0 352 34189 1
❏ GEMINI HEAT Portia Da Costa	ISBN 978 0 352 34187 7
❏ GONE WILD Maria Eppie	ISBN 978 0 352 33670 5
❏ HOTBED Portia Da Costa	ISBN 978 0 352 33614 9
❏ IN PURSUIT OF ANNA Natasha Rostova	ISBN 978 0 352 34060 3
❏ IN THE FLESH Emma Holly	ISBN 978 0 352 34117 4
❏ JULIET RISING Cleo Cordell	ISBN 978 0 352 34192 1
❏ LEARNING TO LOVE IT Alison Tyler	ISBN 978 0 352 33535 7

☐ DIVINE TORMENT Janine Ashbless	ISBN 978 0 352 33719 1	
☐ FRENCH MANNERS Olivia Christie	ISBN 978 0 352 33214 1	
☐ LORD WRAXALL'S FANCY Anna Lieff Saxby	ISBN 978 0 352 33080 2	
☐ NICOLE'S REVENGE Lisette Allen	ISBN 978 0 352 32984 4	
☐ THE SENSES BEJEWELLED Cleo Cordell	ISBN 978 0 352 32904 2	£6.99
☐ THE SOCIETY OF SIN Sian Lacey Taylder	ISBN 978 0 352 34080 1	
☐ TEMPLAR PRIZE Deanna Ashford	ISBN 978 0 352 34137 2	
☐ UNDRESSING THE DEVIL Angel Strand	ISBN 978 0 352 33938 6	

BLACK LACE BOOKS WITH A PARANORMAL THEME

☐ BRIGHT FIRE Maya Hess	ISBN 978 0 352 34104 4
☐ BURNING BRIGHT Janine Ashbless	ISBN 978 0 352 34085 6
☐ CRUEL ENCHANTMENT Janine Ashbless	ISBN 978 0 352 33483 1
☐ ENCHANTED Various	ISBN 978 0 352 34195 2
☐ FLOOD Anna Clare	ISBN 978 0 352 34094 8
☐ GOTHIC BLUE Portia Da Costa	ISBN 978 0 352 33075 8
☐ PHANTASMAGORIA Madelynne Ellis	ISBN 978 0 352 34168 6
☐ THE PRIDE Edie Bingham	ISBN 978 0 352 33997 3
☐ THE SILVER CAGE Mathilde Madden	ISBN 978 0 352 34164 8
☐ THE SILVER COLLAR Mathilde Madden	ISBN 978 0 352 34141 9
☐ THE SILVER CROWN Mathilde Madden	ISBN 978 0 352 34157 0
☐ SOUTHERN SPIRITS Edie Bingham	ISBN 978 0 352 34180 8
☐ THE TEN VISIONS Olivia Knight	ISBN 978 0 352 34119 8
☐ WILD KINGDOM Deana Ashford	ISBN 978 0 352 34152 5
☐ WILDWOOD Janine Ashbless	ISBN 978 0 352 34194 5

BLACK LACE ANTHOLOGIES

☐ BLACK LACE QUICKIES 1 Various	ISBN 978 0 352 34126 6	£2.99
☐ BLACK LACE QUICKIES 2 Various	ISBN 978 0 352 34127 3	£2.99
☐ BLACK LACE QUICKIES 3 Various	ISBN 978 0 352 34128 0	£2.99
☐ BLACK LACE QUICKIES 4 Various	ISBN 978 0 352 34129 7	£2.99
☐ BLACK LACE QUICKIES 5 Various	ISBN 978 0 352 34130 3	£2.99
☐ BLACK LACE QUICKIES 6 Various	ISBN 978 0 352 34133 4	£2.99
☐ BLACK LACE QUICKIES 7 Various	ISBN 978 0 352 34146 4	£2.99
☐ BLACK LACE QUICKIES 8 Various	ISBN 978 0 352 34147 1	£2.99
☐ BLACK LACE QUICKIES 9 Various	ISBN 978 0 352 34155 6	£2.99

To find out the latest information about Black Lace titles, check out the website: www.black-lace-books.com or send for a booklist with complete synopses by writing to:

Black Lace Booklist, Virgin Books Ltd
Virgin Books
Random House
20 Vauxhall Bridge Road
London SW1V 2SA

Please include an SAE of decent size. Please note only British stamps are valid.

Our privacy policy
We will not disclose information you supply us to any other parties. We will not disclose any information which identifies you personally to any person without your express consent.

From time to time we may send out information about Black Lace books and special offers. Please tick here if you do <u>not</u> wish to receive Black Lace information. ❏

Please send me the books I have ticked above.

Name ....

Address ....

....

....

....

Post Code ....

Send to: Virgin Books Cash Sales, Direct Mail Dept,
the Book Service Ltd, Colchester Road, Frating,
Colchester, CO7 7DW

US customers: for prices and details of how to order
books for delivery by mail, call 888-330-8477.

Please enclose a cheque or postal order, made payable
to Virgin Books Ltd, to the value of the books you have
ordered plus postage and packing costs as follows:

UK and BFPO – £1.00 for the first book, 50p for each
subsequent book.

Overseas (including Republic of Ireland) – £2.00 for
the first book, £1.00 for each subsequent book.

If you would prefer to pay by VISA, ACCESS/MASTERCARD,
DINERS CLUB, AMEX or MAESTRO, please write your card
number and expiry date here: ....

....

Signature ....

Please allow up to 28 days for delivery.